THE SEARCH FOR JOSEPH TULLY

The
Search
for
Joseph Tully

a novel by

William H. Hallahan

THE BOBBS-MERRILL COMPANY, INC.
Indianapolis/New York

Copyright © 1974 by William H. Hallahan

All rights reserved, including the right of reproduction
in whole or in part in any form
Published by the Bobbs-Merrill Company, Inc.
Indianapolis   New York

ISBN 0-672-51997-6
Library of Congress catalog card number: 74-1901

Designed by Jacques Chazaud
Manufactured in the United States of America

First printing

for
BARBARA NORVILLE

THE SEARCH FOR JOSEPH TULLY

The Armorer's Forge: Rome, 1498

The sweating arms of the apprentice began again to pump the asthmatic bellows.

All seven faces in the dark chamber glowed red, watching.

The sword maker used his gad tongs to tap the two molten blades a fraction of an inch deeper into the incandescent charcoals.

In a semicircle away from the rolling heat of the catalan forge, the three Italian gentlemen stood. Occasionally they flicked their eyes sidewise from the two blades to the two stripped captives who lay in shadow, bound and strapped to a stone slab. All waited.

The apprentice forced his aching arms to pump, flushing the charcoals to a brighter yellow. In the silence, the croupy bellows wheezed and panted. High on a wall, two torches in wall sockets fluttered like pennants against the permanent darkness of the chamber. The cloying odor of cat's urine was mixed with the acrid smell of charcoal.

The sword maker had patiently cold-hammered both blades from two bars of the finest Toledo steel. Under his celebrated hammer, they'd been formed and shaped, then heated and quenched and heated and quenched to be supple as whips and to hold an edge of legendary sharpness—a master's fencing set. One rapier blade for the right hand. One stiletto blade for the left hand. They were heated now for the final quenching. The sword maker's eyes turned whitely to the two bound captives. The eyes of the apprentice followed his in the light of the fire.

The men on the slab saw him glance at them. They lowered their heads in despair.

"Enough," said the sword maker. The bellows stopped. He used his gad tongs to draw the rapier from the bed of charcoals. He laid the glowing blade upon the anvil and tapped it tentatively several times with his cross-peen hammer. Sparks danced around his hairy forearms. He ran the blade back into the coals.

The tongs drew forth the stiletto. The sword maker studied the color for a moment, then laid the blade on the anvil and rapped it, too, with his cross-peen. Sparks rose again, and he rammed the blade back into the fire next to the rapier blade. He nodded to the apprentice.

Eye-stinging smoke rose in the air as the bellows slowly began again. The boy's arms were noticeably slower.

Patiently, with his arms crossed, the sword maker stood watching and waiting, intent upon his burgeoning blades. Finally he dropped his arms to his sides and stepped into the wall of heat around the forge. He fitted a wooden socket over the tang of the rapier blade and drew it out. He held it up and put his face as close as the heat would permit and peered carefully into the translucent metal, seeking for cracks or fractures. The blade glowed like a white torch in the darkness. Turning, he walked over to the stone slab.

The two bound men watched him with increasing terror. Naked and with their heads raised, they looked like figureheads from sailing ships. The captive on the left shook his head at the glowing blade. "No. No no. Ah. No!"

The sword maker stepped to the side of the man and, with accustomed skill, thrust the molten blade under his skin. The man screamed in a rising pitch at the incredible pain. The blade traveled across his back glowing yellow-red under the skin and emerged from the other side. He shrieked and shrieked again. The smith smartly withdrew the smoking blade and ran it under the skin in a lower part of the back, skin, muscle and cartilage. Then again. Across the muscle, across the back.

"No more!" screamed the captive. "God in Heaven. No more! Stop! Stop! Stop!"

The sword maker attentively studied his blade and frowned at it. He thrust the blade through a buttock, withdrew it and ran it through the other buttock. More clouds of acrid stinking smoke rose. The blade was a malevolent purple.

The man's screams rose in waves now, incoherent words screamed at the gentleman in the center of the trio, tugging a beard thoughtfully; screams of agony, screams of supplication. The sword maker raised the blade and with a swift cavalry chop drove it through the taut, screaming neck. The man's head tumbled to the floor.

The sword maker ran the blade through the scapular cavity of the left shoulder, down into the torso, through the lungs, heart and stomach. He left it there for final quenching. The sweet, sickening odor of scorched skin hung in the air of the chamber. He returned to the friendly glow of the forge fire and, using the same wooden socket, withdrew the shorter stiletto blade.

The other captive writhed and shouted at him as he approached. "No! No! Madness! Stop!"

The sword maker stabbed him deeply in the trapezius muscle, where the blade suffused an eerie red glow under the skin of his back and shoulder. The man's head rose slowly in horror as he inhaled deeply. Then he screamed. A long, exhausting, terrifying scream.

The sword maker withdrew the skinny blade. He glanced at it, and like a man sewing leather, he punched it under the skin and muscle of the other shoulder. Around the sebaceous wound, blood bubbled fiercely. At the third thrust, lower in the back, the captive fainted.

Indifferently, the smith buried the blade in the fatty tissue of first one buttock, then the other. When the blade had been quenched to an iridescent royal purple, he stepped to the man's limp head, which projected beyond the slab. With the ease of a chef slicing through roast meat, he severed the head. The head tumbled across the floor and stopped at the feet of the center gentleman of the trio.

The sword maker pushed the stiletto blade through the scapula into the left lung. Then he withdrew the rapier blade from the first body and bent it into a loop from tip to hilt.

He glanced at the apprentice. Hugging his pain-filled arms to his torso, the boy turned away from the bellows and vomited.

Reincarnated soul is bent on revenge against the individual responsible for his death in a past incarnation.

CHAPTER I

Friday, February Second
Apartment 4A

The sound woke him.

Someone was in his apartment.

Richardson lay in his bed listening, trying to hear over the rushing of the winter wind against his window, trying to keep his breath soft and audible, sensing that his pulse was racing, his ears throbbing.

He lay still, fighting an urgent need to hide like a child under the bed.

He listened in the darkness, waiting to hear that sound that had awakened him again. The wind rushed at his window.

It had been a single sound, a resonant sound, a sweeping sound: the sound of a supple, swinging golf club. *Whoosh!* In the middle of the night, in the pitch darkness of his living room, someone had swung a golf club. The echoes of it reverberated around the walls of his apartment, slowly dying in his ears: *whoosh.*

Richardson pulled back the covers and stood up. Softly, idiot, softly. He walked the carpeted floor to the bedroom doorway. His skin was coated with clammy sweat and his pulse was pounding in his ears. Death was near: the flash of a gun; the thud of an arcing knife hitting skin, bone, and organ. The clout of a golf club shattering skull bone. Terrible fear clutched his abdomen.

"Who's there?" he said to the vast darkness. His voice frightened him. "Who's there!" he shouted.

The living room remained dark and lumpish and still. Listen. The wind seethed once more.

Richardson reached into the darkness, probed along the wall and found a wall switch. He moved it: an overhead light illuminated the living room.

The room was familiar, unchanged, harmless. Empty.

He quickly walked to the front door. The chain was off. He turned the doorknob. Locked. He'd gone to bed with the chain off? He opened the front door and peered into the hallway. Silent. Empty.

Richardson resolutely yanked open the closet door. Clothing on hangers. Stuff and boxes on the shelf. Furled umbrella. Irish blackthorn cane. Dust-covered rubber boots.

He stepped into the kitchen and turned on the light. He opened the pantry door. He walked around the furniture in the living room. He checked the windows, walked into the bedroom, opened the closet door, went into the bathroom, prodded the shower curtain.

He sat down on the edge of the tub, spent.

Whoosh! That was the sound. The *whoosh* of a golf club swung at a ball. Didn't make any sense.

He roused himself, went and put the chain lock on the door. Someone could have entered with that chain off; someone with a key could have been there. Someone could have entered, swung a golf club in the dark and left, locking the door from the outside. The idea struck him as silly, and he almost laughed, picturing a man entering, swinging a club in the darkness, and hastily exiting, scurrying down the stairs.

Robbery? Richardson checked his wallet, then checked the drawers of the small desk in the living room. No. He put out the lights again, all but the bathroom light, and stood by the living room window to look out.

Cassiopeia was westering in the frozen February blackness, sliding below the horizon. The sky was blue-black, far from even a hint of dawn. A film of ice coated the lower panes. He touched the ice with his fingertips and felt the chill of bitter winter.

Richardson had never felt more alone in his life.

Below him, street lights made a geometric pattern around a great quadrangle of blackness. A quadrangle six blocks by nine blocks of flattened real estate.

What had been there, houses, apartments, stores, garages and other structural impedimenta, had all been battered to rubble by the flailing, smoking ball of the wrecker's tractor crane, conqueror of cities.

The crane squatted in darkness, holding its boom aloft like a menacing club. Faintly, very faintly, he could hear a wind-shook chain clanging on the frozen metal of the boom.

Beyond it, at the far corner of the quadrangle, the sign of a store hung whitely in the darkness at a crazy angle: Waite's Groceries. From the room of that empty building hung a great icicle.

Richardson listened again to the wan clanging of the chain on the tractor boom, then backed away from the window. The urge to flee was enormous—illogical, senseless. He fought it. Shave—he'd shave. Sleep was murdered; day, near; time to shave yet again.

He washed his face with care, then held a hot face cloth over it, feeling the restorative heat penetrate his eyes. He reached into his cabinet and pulled out a can of shaving cream. Then he put it back and crumpled down on the toilet seat. He wanted to hide in a closet, wanted to flee down the stairs and across the freezing quadrangle.

He felt the terrible loneliness of despair.

Something was come to kill him.

2

Apartment 3A

At precisely seven o'clock, and without the aid of a clock alarm, Albert Clabber opened his eyes. Dark eyes under thick hairy brows, alert eyes, piercing eyes. Humorless eyes.

He lay in the silence of that hour. He heard the ticking of his cheap wind-up clock. He heard the bitter cold wind that pressed against the walls and rocked the loose, open window. He watched a puff of his breath vaporize. *Bump bump* went the window. *Bump bump.* Cold air poured into his apartment and over his cocoon of blankets. *Bump bump.*

Clabber's apartment was military—monkish—in its furnishings. It pleased him to recall his freedom from possessions. He itemized: one cot (army surplus), four very warm dense-wool blankets (army surplus), pillow, some pillowcases and sheets, a table for writing, three wooden chairs, a wall filled neatly and meticulously with books, filed by subject and, within subject, by author, alphabetically. There were no rugs, no easy chairs, no decorations. His few clothes hung in the closet, his shirts and linens on a shelf above. In the kitchen, a few pots and pans, a few dishes, some cutlery and basic food staples. Freedom.

Albert Clabber peeled back the layer of four blankets and stood up. His vulnerable nakedness contracted and crawled against the frigid air that flowed through the open window. *Bump bump.* He shut the window.

By the numbers he went through his morning ritual that included, invariably, a tepid shower, a tooth scrubbing, a scarifying shave and finally, dressing—in baggy clothes purchased with an eye for warmth, comfort and long wear.

Clabber made a bowl of oatmeal and a cup of hot chocolate. A loose window rattled. The winter wind rushed the building in flurries while Clabber sat, eating and reading.

He read until eight A.M. precisely, washed the few utensils, folded all four blankets, set them squarely in the center of the cot, and returned the book to its slot in the bookcase.

He pulled a heavy bulk-knit cardigan over his flannel shirt, then began to put on his heavy pile-linen hooded parka. As he did so, he began the daily ritual of reading the two framed proclamations that hung on the wall next to the front door. Between them hung a crucifix.

He paused and shook his head angrily at the opening lines of the document on the left.

ALBERT CLABBER

My Dear Brother in Christ:

It is like a grievous wound to me that I fulfill this office. I am directed to inform you that by authority of a Decree from the Holy See under CIC c. 2258.2 of the Code of Canon Law, your name and person has been placed in a state of excommunication. Your soul is in the gravest peril and you are deemed a terrible heretic.

Because of your conscious, determined and obstinate error, you have been categorized an excommunicant *vitandi* and stand now *per sententiam* shut off from the fellowship and communion of your brothers and sisters in Christ.

I am further directed to inform you that as long as you remain stubbornly rebellious and contumacious, you are to be shunned by your fellows, cast out in a state of spiritual death and henceforth denied the following consolations of your faith:

1) you may not participate or assist at divine service
2) you are forbidden all sacraments
3) you may perform no legitimate ecclesiastical acts of the Holy Church
4) you are denied all indulgences, suffrages and public prayer of the Holy Church
5) you are denied Christian burial according to the Code of Canon Law, CIC 1240, 1m2

All of these—and their logical concomitants—are to be withheld until you repent of your willful stubborn heresy and petition the Holy See for readmission to your all-merciful Mother, the Holy Church.

Brother Albert, my soul trembles for you. The terrors of the damned loom before my eyes when I try to picture you wandering the earth in a state of gravest peril. If you should die in your present condition, eternal calamity may befall you. I beseech you with all the great love I feel for you to reconsider. Surely you realize in espousing the teachings of our erring brother, Bruno of Nolo, that you have raised up heresies and ecclesiastical matters deemed closed these last five long centuries. Brother Bruno was a willful stubborn man whose spiritual attitudes were based more on a stiff-necked pride than on religious principle and scriptural authority.

The Holy Church, under sterner hands, you will recall, burned Bruno at the stake.

I will continue to pray for you and your imperiled soul.

Yours in Christ,
Thomas

Next, he turned his eyes to the other, then pulled the parka over his head. As he worked his torso into the parka he looked at his words:

EXCOMMUNICATIO

Nomine patris et filii et spiritus sancti.

I, Albert Clabber, do by these articles, declare the Holy Roman Catholic and Apostolic Church to be in gravest error. I hereby separate the Church in Error, together with its accomplices and abettors, adherents and communicants, from the precious body and blood of the Lord Christ and from the society of all enlightened and true Christians. I exclude it from our Holy Mother, the True Church in Heaven and on Earth; I declare it excommunicate and anathema; I judge it damned, with the Devil and his angels and all the reprobate, to eternal fire until it shall recover itself from the toils of the Devil and return to amendment and to penitence.

So be it. By bell. And by Book. And by candle.

Ex auctoritate Dei omnipotentis, Patris, et Filii, et Spiritus Sancti, et sanctorum canonum, sanctaeque et intemertate Virginis Dei genetricis Mariae, atque omnium coelestium virtutum, angelorum, archangelorum, thronorum, dominationum, potestatum, cherubin ac seraphin, et sanctorum patriarcharum, prophetarum, et omnium apostolorum et evangelorum, et sanctorum innocentum, et sanctorum martyrum et sanctorum confesorum et sanctarum virginum, atque omnium simul sanctorum et electorum Dei—

EXCOMMUNICAMUS ET ANATHEMATIZAMUS

Albert Clabber

Albert Clabber straightened the crucifix between the two bulls and, holding a trouser-cuff bicycle clip in his hand, surveyed the barrack neatness of his apartment. He then left.

3

Apartment 3C

Oswaldo Goulart's cat sinuated lithely along the length of a long trestle table amidst a profusion of potted plants and stepped onto the windowsill. She sat down there by the warmth of the apartment radiator. Her feral golden eyes watched a sparrow that sat on a telephone wire in the freezing air just outside the windowpanes, deftly balancing itself as the wind turned its feathers.

Oswaldo Goulart sat at his taboret, washing his art brushes in a basin of brush cleaner and watching his cat.

The cat mewed at the unreachable bird.

Albert Clabber appeared in the street below, and Goulart leaned closely to the window to watch him. Bulky in his heavy, hooded parka, he sat on his bicycle and pulled on a pair of large leather mittens. Then he pedaled away, chased by a cloud of red brickdust.

"Where you going so early?" murmured Goulart. "Scurry, scurry, scurry."

Clabber rode along a side of the great quadrangle of leveled real estate. More clouds of dirt and dust were driven across the empty expanse by the bone-chilling wind. Clabber cycled past the tractor-mounted crawler that was being readied for another day of wall smashing.

Another day of destruction—of decapitated buildings, of smashed masonry, brickdust, showers of laths, plaster, splintered wood, shattered glass, the dull thunder of collapsed walls, and the ponderous parade of dump trucks carting off the rubble to fill in Jamaica Bay, which was slowly disappearing under garbage and trash at the other end of Brooklyn.

On the far side of the quadrangle, rows of vacant houses stood. Once stuffed with warmth, with the fury and cavalcade of the living, the buildings lay like abandoned honeycombs, broken into, emptied, the heat of life dissipated.

A sudden cloud of brickdust blew across the iron-frozen quadrangle. The bitter wind. A whining winter wind. A sentinel, it was posted out there to warn anything with the heat of life in it away from those frozen dead walls.

Man's insatiable appetite for land. Land.

The cat observed the stream of steam that jetted from the gurgling electric coffeepot on the windowsill. She observed how the steam was melting the skin of ice on the lower windowpane. Then she lost interest. She began to clean herself. With licking tongue and nodding, affirmative head. Lick lick lick. Yes yes yes.

Clabber rode past the corner store with its crazy sign, "Waite's Groceries," and was gone.

Goulart studied the sign. "Waite's. Wait. Waiting." He tried, again, yet again, to find that picture that skulked in the shadows of his mind. When he captured it clearly in his mind's eye, he would sketch it. But when? Waite, wait, waiting. Goulart meditated on the sign.

4

"Who's there?"

"Me."

"Come on in, me."

Richardson opened the door. "Hullo."

"Yeah. Yeah. Come on in." Goulart hastily put away his sketches.

Richardson sniffed the odor of fresh coffee. He crossed the room and looked down on the blank drawing board and at the brushes on the taboret. "Secret sketches of a new Russian missile site."

"You guessed it. You get a kiss on both cheeks. Take that crap off that chair and sit down."

Richardson hefted a large plant in its earthenware pot off the chair and set it carefully on the floor. He wiped the seat with his palm and sat down.

Goulart looked at him. "You need some sun."

"You mean I look pale, eh?"

"I mean you look pale. Here we are deep in February; it's cold enough to freeze hell over six feet deep, and we're a long long way from summer fun." Goulart shook his head. "Hiding from the cold under our pile of rocks while that tin demon out there goes *bash bash bash* on perfectly sound brick buildings. We are all gone mad. What can I do for you besides give you a cup of coffee? Aren't you going to go to work today?"

"What makes you think I'm not, nosy?"

Goulart shrugged eloquently. "You've got that look—

that I'm-not-going-to-go-to-the-goddamn-office look. You find an apartment yet?"

"No."

"You'd better, buddy. They're going to have this building down in jig time." Goulart poured a mug of coffee and handed it to Richardson.

"Yeah, yeah. How about you?"

"Don't ask me. What the hell am I going to do? Look at this stuff. Cartons piled to the ceiling. Filing cabinets. Ten thousand plants. But worst of all, where am I going to find a place with this light? I could look forever and not find a place with a light like that." He pointed at the skyline directly over his drawing board. He looked at Richardson. "Something bothering you?"

"What do you mean?"

"I mean, what's bothering you? Look at your hand. You cold?"

"Yeah. Cold."

"Come on, come on, Petey. You worried about something?"

"Nah."

"Well, what the hell is it?"

"How can you tell something's wrong?"

"I smell it. You've had bad news?"

"No no. I-ah-sheesh. If I told you, you'd have me locked up."

"Locked up? What do you mean—locked up?"

"Ah. Nothing. I had a bad dream."

"What are you talking about? A bad dream."

Richardson bowed his head and held it in the palm of his hand. He sighed. "I wouldn't tell this to anyone but you."

"Yeah, yeah. Get to it. I can't stand suspense."

"Maybe I'm going crackers."

"You said that. Talk."

"I woke up this morning around four."

"Yeah. And?"

"I was absolutely sure there was someone in my apartment. It sounded like someone was in my living room, standing there in the dark swinging a golf club."

"A golf club! In the middle of the night in your living room?"

"Yeah."

Goulart leaned back in his chair and crossed his huge arms. "So, in the name of sweet bleeding Jesus, go on."

"That's it. I prowled around, opening closets and cabinets and—nothing."

"Nothing?"

"Absolutely nothing. Zero. Zilch. But I couldn't calm down. Still can't. Look." Richardson held forth his trembling hands. "Now, I never shook like this before in my whole life. But I'm sure someone's going to kill me."

"What?" Goulart sat up. "What did you say?"

"I said someone is going to kill me!"

Goulart exhaled. He turned his head and gazed out at Waite's grocery store. "Is this the first time you've felt it?"

"Yes. And I hope to God I never feel it again."

"Do you still feel it?"

"Yeah. A little. It comes in waves. It's like—it's like panic. You just want to run." Richardson sighed deeply. "I've even begun to think my mind's going."

Goulart punched Richardson's shoulder lightly. "Easy does it, mate. Could be something you ate or just a bad nightmare."

Richardson hesitated. "I—ah. Well, hummmm. Tell

you what. The best way I can answer that is to say I don't know whether I know."

Goulart nodded.

"You understand that?" asked Richardson. "Really?"

Goulart nodded solemnly.

"Maybe you dreamed the whole thing, Pete."

"No. Nope. Not a bit of it. I was asleep. And the sound woke me. Wide awake. My eyes were open in an instant. I didn't dream that sound."

"Is a puzzlement."

"Yeah," said Richardson. "What's even more puzzling is—why would anyone want to kill me?"

Goulart's cat mewed at the bird, twitched her furry tail and reached for the plump featherball. The claws of her slow paw raked down the windowpane in vain.

5

Apartment 4B

He tapped on Abigail Withers's apartment door.

Mrs. Withers opened it promptly. "Right on time! Oh, it's a bitter bitter cold day out there. They're forecasting snow."

Richardson shut the door and patted Johnny the terrier on the head. "Great," he said unenthusiastically. He watched Mrs. Withers's portly figure waddle into the kitchen.

"We could get snowbound," said Mrs. Withers.

Richardson made a sour face. "Not me. The last thing I want is to be snowbound here."

"Oh?" Mrs. Withers whispered numbers to herself as she counted out scoops of coffee into the pot.

"Let them keep the snow in the mountains."

Mrs. Withers poured hot water into the coffeepot. "Do you hear that machine out there? Banging and whacking. They're in a terrible rush to get the rest of those buildings down. Oh, I do so hate to move—and this poor beautiful building. I think they ought to make the judge come over here and walk through it. It's a work of art. It makes my skin crawl to think of that monstrous ball smashing those beautiful slabs of Carrara marble—and that rose brick façade. One of the workmen told me that it's a lost art in this country, that kind of brickwork."

Richardson looked out at the cold morning. "It looks so cold out there I'm afraid to go to work."

"Have you found an apartment yet, Peter?"

"Oh." He brushed the subject away.

"I know. I know. But they'll have this poor beautiful building down in a matter of weeks. You'll have to find a new place, Peter. Very soon now."

"You talk like Goulart."

"Well, he's right." She touched her lips with her fingertips in sudden fear. "I'm going to miss him terribly. When everyone's gone to work, he's the only other person in the whole building." Her eyes began to fill. "I don't know what I'll do without the both of you."

"Ah ah ah. Enough enough enough, Abby. We'll all probably end up within three blocks of each other."

She shook her head. "It'll never be the same." She nodded knowingly at him. "I've got seventy-two years of experience to prove it. Nothing lasts long. Except death."

"Ah ah ah, Abby. Bright thoughts."

"Yes. Bright thoughts."

"Let's talk about our party."

"Party. Yes. We'll have a wonderful party. I told Griselda to wear her new pants suit and bring her deck of tarot cards."

"Does she really tell fortunes with those cards, Abby? Guy told me he saw her act in a Manhattan nightclub and everyone was so busy looking at her figure that she could have palmed the whole deck."

"Oh, it'll be very entertaining. She's very good at it." Mrs. Withers looked at him. "Well, you needn't be concerned. It's a very good act. She makes very good money at it."

"Okay, okay. As far as I'm concerned, she can do her act without the cards. I'd watch her even if all she did was stand in a corner and hiccup."

"She'd do it beautifully, if she did."

"Yes. The Carsons will be there, won't they?"

"Oh yes. They found an apartment. And Professor Abernathy and Ruth have signed a three-year lease on their apartment. And Mr. Clabber found a place near the library and Grand Army Plaza."

She abruptly took his hand. "Are you cold, Peter?"

"No." He withdrew his hand.

"You're right. Your hand's hot. Why is it trembling?"

Richardson paused. "Let's say I saw a ghost."

"Don't joke about such things."

"Maybe I'm not joking."

She searched his eyes for a moment, then turned away. "Oh, by the way, Mr. Clabber asked me if he could bring a friend of his. I hope you don't mind—I said yes."

"Sure."

"It's a woman."

"I'd like to see the kind of woman Clabber'd bring. Don't tell me. Let me guess. She's a witch."

"How did you know?"

"Know?"

"He's bringing Mrs. Quist."

"Who's Mrs. Quist?"

"But I thought you knew. Anna Quist is a clairvoyant. She calls herself a white witch."

"Oh. It was weird for me to guess that, wasn't it? Does she ride a broom?"

"No. Her specialty is scry."

"Scry."

"Crystal-ball gazing."

"Oh. Scry." He watched her narrowly with a faint smile. "Abby, do you believe that stuff?"

"Well—" She avoided his eyes. "I'm too old to laugh at anything."

"Have you ever been to a—whatchamacallit—séance?"

"Oh, yes. Several times."

"Ever see anyone do any scrying?"

"No." She smirked slyly at him. "Don't laugh at what you don't understand. We have a little mystery going on right across the way that may be supernatural."

"What? Where?"

Mrs. Withers looked out of the window across the quadrangle. The crane stood there, dauntless, a threatening gladiator in the arena, brandishing its clublike boom. The crane began to pivot. The boom with its pendulous ball swung in an arc. The ball struck the building. The whole upper corner of the building toppled, fell four stories, and burst open on the ground. Shattered bricks scattered across the barricaded roadway.

Mrs. Withers squinted, peering at it. "God. How—how —how remorseless that machine is. It's like—cancer! Yes, it's like cancer!" She pressed her soft white knuckles to her lips as her eyes filled. "You know, Peter, sometimes I feel like it's killing me, too."

Richardson put an arm around Mrs. Withers's shoulders. "Don't think about it, Abby. You'll move out soon and that will be the end of it. Tell me about your supernatural mystery."

"Oh yes. Of course. Here. Let's take the coffee to the table." Her hands fluttered about her face as she inventoried the table—cream, sugar, rolls, linen napkins, silver utensils, juice, butter. Abruptly she snatched open the refrigerator. She pulled out a squat jar of strawberry preserves. "I remembered," she said, smiling. "After breakfast take the jar with you. I'll never eat them."

They sat down to coffee. "I'm not being coy," continued Mrs. Withers. "After all this buildup, what I have to say will seem unimportant."

"Something new has turned up?" asked Richardson.

"Well. More lights."

"More?"

"Yes. The police were over there again last night."

Richardson nodded. "You called them?" He watched Mrs. Withers lean forward to the window and point.

"There. Right in the corner. Waite's grocery store. Lights going from room to room in that empty building. I sat up half the night with my opera glasses. The police came twice. But they're not very interested. Their only concern is to keep the bums out of there so they don't start fires."

"Why not? The buildings are going to come down anyway. Fire's quicker."

"Oh. Fires are very dangerous. Remember what happened in Chicago with the cow. Oh no. The police would never allow fires. But it isn't bums with those lights."

"Oh." Richardson leaned forward. "What is it?"

"Nobody knows."

"Oh."

"How long is it now? Two weeks. Three weeks. All kinds of people have seen lights there. All the police do is run through the buildings. If they don't find anyone, they leave, and that's the end of it." Mrs. Withers took a sip of coffee. "I'll tell you those lights mean something ominous."

Richardson tried to smile at her. He failed.

6

Peter Richardson descended the stairs of the condemned apartment house, crossed the vestibule and opened the front door. Freezing, sailing air wrapped around him. He put his head·down for the paralyzing walk to the subway three blocks away.

Abruptly, in the middle of the sidewalk, he stopped.

With the taste of Abby Withers's coffee in his mouth, the grip of the winter wind around his ankles, a luncheon appointment on his mind, an anticipation of seeing Griselda Vandermeer in her new pants suit, he was suddenly struck with an irrefutable fact; beyond argument: Someone was going to kill him.

7

At the top of the brownstone steps stood two gleaming old glass doors that rocked faintly in the wind. Inside, a tiled vestibule with a large fern in a huge ceramic crock.

A handsome middle-aged woman opened the inner door and studied him and his bags briefly. She opened the outer door. "Yes?"

"Good morning. My name's Willow. Matthew Willow. Is Mrs. Gundisun about?"

"Come in. I'm Mrs. Gundisun." She studied his face and clothes as he stepped past her into the vestibule. She followed him through the doorway to the hallway. It was wide and warm, paneled in handsome old walnut and thickly carpeted. Mrs. Gundisun shut the door and padded up to him on the heavy carpeting. A pendulum clock ticked slowly in the orderly silence. "I have your apartment all ready, Mr. Willow," she said. "Four to six weeks, you said."

"Yes. That's right." He met her eyes and found something merry lurking there.

"Follow me, then, Mr. Willow."

She mounted the stairs, and Willow followed. He realized that she had an excellent figure and walked with considerable grace.

"Did you fly in from England, Mr. Willow?"

"Yes. BOAC Flight 716 from London."

She stopped at an ornate walnut door on the second floor. She opened it with a key. The apartment beyond it was a comfortably furnished large room with an unobstructed view of New York Harbor. Willow put his bags down and walked over to the two large windows. Harbor traffic moved over the surface of the wind-driven bay waters. Smoke streamed westward from many chimneys and stacks. Directly below him and far down were the Brooklyn docks. Freighters were loading and unloading along all the piers in view.

She looked down. "I can often see my husband's ship from here."

"A seaman?"

"A captain, Mr. Willow, a captain."

"Oh."

"He is away," she said. "On a long voyage."

"Oh."

"I think you'll find everything you need, including linens. There are several delicatessens and food stores just up Montague Street."

"Banks?"

"Oh yes. Banks and other stores."

"A stationer?"

"Yes."

"I need to open an American checking account. I have several bank documents here that need processing." He tapped his breast pocket. "If you'll allow me a few hours to set things up, I can pay you the balance of the first four weeks as agreed."

"That will be quite all right, Mr. Willow." Mrs. Gundisun looked quite pleased, and she stood just a little too close to him as she smiled.

8

By midafternoon, flaws of snow blew through the air, and under a freshened breeze the temperature drifted slowly lower. Willow walked into the teeth of the breeze that, rising off the open harbor, rolled up Montague Street. He lumbered along with several bags of food and a large roll of construction paper.

Inside the warm hallway, he sensed again the pleasant and quiet atmosphere of the building. Mrs. Gundison was nowhere about and he mounted the stairs to the beat of the pendulum clock.

The wind was driving across the harbor and whined at his windows. The water's face was covered with whitecaps. A spray of sudden snow spun past the window. Willow had a front-row seat to a major storm. He dropped the packages onto the couch, pulled off his overcoat, and walked over to the wall next to the window. He estimated the height of the wall to be eight feet.

He walked back to his packages and prized out a box of push pins. Then he carried a chair and the large roll of construction paper across the room. He placed the chair between the two windows. He stepped up on the chair and unrolled the construction paper. With both hands he reached up and pinned it to the wall just under the seam of the ceiling. The unrolled paper dangled nearly to the floor. It was forty-eight inches wide.

Willow stepped down and studied the paper for a moment. Satisfied, he went back to his packages. From a small bag he removed a felt pen. He stepped back up on the chair and uncapped the pen. Reaching his left hand up, he positioned it at a point equidistant from the two edges. Just below the top edge of the paper he printed:

JOSEPH TULLY

He stepped down and looked at it.
"God help me," he said. "Let the game begin."

9
His hiking boots sank easily into the sand as he descended the wind-rippled side of the high dune.

At the bottom of the dune, he turned and looked back

up the sloping wall of sand, a series of craters marking his steps. Waves of transparent heat skimmed up the sides.

He sat down on the flinty floor of the desert and removed his hiking boots and socks, then flogged the woolen sock on a rock. Sand sprayed his sweat-wet face and neck. He banged his boots together. Finally, with great care, he rubbed all the grains of sand from his feet and toes and from the channels of skin at the edges of his toenails. Satisfied at last, he pulled the woolen socks on, slipped his socked feet into the boots, and laced them with attention, neither too tightly nor too loosely.

He stood up. The sun had westered. There were about two hours of daylight left, the best two hours of hiking in the desert's day. He hefted his forty-pound backpack, swung it easily up on his back and adjusted the shoulder straps and frame belt. He wiped his face, neck and head, mopping off the sweat and the sand grains. He took a large mouthful of water, delicious and cool, hearing his throat *quop,* feeling the water flood his gut.

He felt enormous. Complete, exhilarated, thoroughly animal and prime. He adjusted his broad-brimmed hat, hefted his bamboo walking pole, and set off at a steady gait across the scabrous floor of the desert, paralleling a long high finger of sand dunes. Once he was past that range of sand dunes, the walking was good again. The rhythmic movement of his body made the sweat run and the animal spirits rise. In the enormous silence of the desert, he heard his boots' shuffle and the faint rubbing sound of his pack. The binoculars, hanging from the tubular frame of the pack, went *tap tap, tap tap.* At longer intervals came the sound of his walking pole tapping on the flinty soil. Walking with such exhilaration became hypnotic.

At dusk in a sparse field of ocotillo clumps, he stopped to check his compass. Shimmering waves of heat rose around his bare legs, yet the coolness of the impending evening was already touching his wet face. He listened to the absolute silence of the desert. It was being dyed in a spreading stain of darkness. In a moment, myriads of stars would be flung across the night sky.

He turned his head. A noise. He listened. Heard it again. He turned and looked back to the undulating terrain he'd crossed, sinking in darkness. In one of the long dips in the desert floor, hidden from his view, the noise sounded again.

Whoosh!

When Richardson awoke, he was out of his bed and holding the door jamb to his bedroom.

And there, in the middle of the living room, precisely—that was where the sound had come from. He hadn't dreamed it.

Whoosh!

CHAPTER II

It was well after nine when Griselda Vandermeer rang
Richardson's bell. She was carrying a boxed deck of
tarot cards.

Richardson opened the door. He smiled at her. "Welcome, Griselda. Come in."

"Thank you." She stepped past him into his living
room, her eyes quickly conning the decorations. He led
her toward a group of people by the window. "Have
you met the Abernathys and the Carsons?"

"No. Not really." Richardson watched her eyes as
they glanced from painting to painting, sketch to sketch.
She looked down at the rug and at the Scandinavian
furniture. Then she shied another glance at Richardson.

"Abernathy is professor of history at Brevoort College,"
said Richardson, pausing. Griselda studied his eyes, nodding to them as he spoke.

"And Carson is an industrial psychologist with his own consulting business."

"The parallels," Professor Abernathy was saying, "are frightening. America has lost its way just as Rome did. In the latter days of the Roman Empire, rational people who should have known better consulted soothsayers—" He paused and looked patiently at Griselda and at Richardson.

"This is Gordon Abernathy," said Richardson to Griselda. "And Ruth Abernathy, Carol Carson and Christopher Carson. This is Griselda Vandermeer. She's a soothsayer."

They chuckled and nodded at her. Richardson smiled as he watched the eyes of the two women. They studied Griselda's hair, her knotted pearls, her lapelled jacket, her pants, rings and petite black shoes. Christopher Carson's eyes were frank: he looked at the swelling expanse of soft pink skin that lay under the knotted pearls, then at her face.

"What's the matter with soothsayers?" Griselda asked Gordon Abernathy, smiling.

"Don't show him your tarot deck, Griselda," said Peter Richardson. "Gordon foams at the mouth."

"What's wrong with soothsayers?" echoed Professor Abernathy. "Why—everything. When an emperor takes advice from a soothsayer, you've got an empire in deep trouble. And that's what happened in Rome. And that's what's happening here. Rome lost its way. Everyone consulted fortunetellers. Auguries were made from the flights of birds. Prognostications from the entrails of animals. Charlatans, frauds, diviners, haruspices abounded. Rumors of graves bursting open and spirits stalking the land were on everyone's lips."

"Why?" asked Griselda patiently.

"Why? Because Rome lost its self-confidence. It stopped believing that it could solve its problems. In fact, it lost the will to solve its problems. And the future was no longer a vista of promise. Instead, the future became a forbidding land of gathering shadows. Rome was bankrupt spiritually. And so are we. Overwhelmed. Frightened. No longer able to cope with our problems, consulting horoscopes in the daily newspaper. America is a dead duck. The most dangerous aspect of it all," Professor Abernathy added, "is this the-heck-with-you-I've-got-mine attitude in our country. It spells doom."

"In both cases, American and Roman," said Christopher Carson in his rich voice, still conning Griselda Vandermeer's figure, "a major breakdown in morality preceded disaster."

2

Richardson walked toward the small bar. He was weary of the tyranny of his fear. *Whoosh,* endlessly reverberating. Like the clock in the croc endlessly pursuing the captain in Peter Pan. *Whoosh.*

He saw Goulart by the window talking to Clabber. Clabber gripped his arm, said something intensely. Goulart frowned and leaned his head closer. Clabber said it again, intensely again. He drew his head back, studied Goulart's eyes. Goulart jabbed himself on the chest with a forefinger several times and frowned. Clabber shook his head and walked over to Mrs. Withers and Mrs. Quist.

"Oh yes," Abigail Withers was saying to Mrs. Quist.

"This building has had a tremendous history. Filled with ghosts."

"Ghosts!" exclaimed Anna Quist.

"Oh, I don't mean ghosts. I mean—" Mrs. Withers gazed doubtfully at Albert Clabber.

"Memories," put in Clabber.

"Well. Yes. Memories, if you will." Mrs. Withers noted how Clabber's thin neck protruded from his ill-fitting turtleneck jersey. "Dead actors, writers, poets, statesmen, foreign dignitaries of all sorts. Simon Brevoort was descended from one of New York's first families—Dutch, you know. He helped put together some of the first traction companies in the city."

"Traction?" asked Mrs. Quist.

"Trolley lines and, later, elevated trains. Oh yes, he inherited a good deal of money and made even more with his own finances. When he built this building, this section of Brooklyn was out in the green countryside. But he soon turned it into a center of the arts. It was originally built with eighteen bedrooms."

"Eighteen! Good heavens."

"Yes. It was a wonder in its day. Mrs. Brevoort grew wildflowers in the steam-heated greenhouse on the roof all winter and sent them to her friends. It's a national tragedy to tear it down. It took five years to build. It has materials and statuary and walls and beams and carved doors from all over the world. Dreadful. Perfectly dreadful."

Mrs. Quist clucked her tongue. Her pale eyes looked out from a gaunt white face. "I read about the court decision in the paper. And I gather that's the end of it."

"Yes," said Mrs. Withers. "That thing out there will

do its work." She solemnly and Mrs. Quist gauntly and Albert Clabber smolderingly turned and looked out at the silhouette of the wrecker's boom in the dark night. Beyond it were the lights of the bridge to Manhattan and, beyond, the island itself.

"The prognosis for it was never really good," said Mrs. Quist. "I foretold five years ago that it would be torn down."

3

Ruth Abernathy touched the cameo pin at her throat. "Right down on the street," she said.

Carol Carson's mouth was slightly parted in wonder. "What did it say about him?"

"The article was very short. It just said that police had arrested a young man suspected of being a dope pusher. They arrested him right as he got out of his car. They found quantities of LSD. Apparently he was going to make a delivery to some house on this street."

"Oh, I can't believe that," said Carol Carson.

"Oh, it's true!" insisted Abby Withers. "This neighborhood has declined terribly in the last few years."

"He's a graduate student from Columbia," said Ruth Abernathy.

"Who?" asked Mrs. Withers.

"The pusher. You know what he was majoring in?" Ruth Abernathy looked at Mrs. Carson and Mrs. Withers. "Philosophy and ethics. Ethics."

"Wouldn't it be fantastic," mused Mrs. Withers, "if someone in this room were his customer?" The three women looked curiously about the room.

"Oh," said Ruth Abernathy, "I don't think so. Nobody here is the dope type."

"You never know," said Mrs. Withers. "I was just reading in the *Daily News* the other day about a model husband who was caught feeding microscopic amounts of LSD to his wife."

"Oh my heavens," said Ruth Abernathy. "What did it do to her?"

"Oh, she had hallucinations. She began hiding from people. Hearing things. Mortally terrified. She had all the symptoms of a psychosis. He was trying to get control of her money by locking her away in a mental institution."

"When was this?" asked Carol Carson.

"Just the other day in the *Daily News*."

"Oh. How terrible. What happened?"

"Well, when the wife learned what he was doing to her, she went insane and they locked her away."

Ozzie Goulart strolled past Richardson carrying several drinks. "We give weird parties, buddy."

"Yeah. Weird. Fortunetellers and white witches and unfrocked priests and history professors and psychologists and illiterate Portuguese artists and handsome, charming, urbane, nutty editors. All we have to do is keep pouring out the booze and we'll have a swell coeducational fist fight on our hands."

Goulart paused. "If it starts, I get to square off with that Griselda. She can beat me up anytime and I won't raise a finger. I turned the heat up. Maybe we can get her to take her jacket off." He frowned at Richardson. "You ain't smiling."

"Yeah. I notice you ain't smiling either."

Goulart tossed his head slightly. "Good day, bad day."

"Let's match notes sometime."

Whoosh.

4

"I tell you that man tampers with things beyond his ken," crooned Mrs. Withers, clasping her hands under her chin. She gazed from Clabber's face to Mrs. Quist's. "And those buildings resent being torn down, I'm sure. Like killing sacrificial lambs. You see where the sign is —'Waite's Groceries'? Well, for several weeks now, I've been seeing lights in the windows of that building. And so have many other people. The police have been there— oh, so many times, but they never find anyone there. Yet the lights always return."

"Ohhhh?" Mrs. Quist's pale moist eyes looked significantly at Albert Clabber, then squinted prudently at Mrs. Withers. "Lights, you say. Have you ever walked over there to examine the premises?"

"Me? No, thank you!" Abby Withers shook her hands at the ceiling.

"It would be most interesting, I would think." Mrs. Quist studied the grocer's sign, then looked at Clabber's nodding face for endorsement. "Lights are a very interesting phenomenon. I recall a famous story of lights in an abandoned stone house in the Fort Hamilton section. A building that was built long before the Revolution. A witch-killing. But I must tell you a few things you can do about those lights of yours over there."

5

Richardson refilled the ice bucket and watched Clabber. He crossed the room, gripped Goulart's arm and led him away from Mrs. Withers. They stood again by the window. Clabber spoke emphatically and shook a finger at Goulart. Goulart shook his head, pointed at himself and spoke several short words. He returned to Mrs. Withers.

Carol Carson arrested Richardson with a smile. "This is the first time I've gotten a view of the wrecking from this side of the building. I can't believe it. It's like a bombed-out city. Brevoort House looks ridiculous without all the other buildings around it. Christopher says it looks like a plucked chicken." She gave a short laugh.

Richardson smiled. "I guess it does."

"Abby Withers says there are ghosts here."

Richardson shrugged and smiled. "You've lived here for three years, Carol. Have you seen any?"

"No." She watched her husband stroll up to the bar and stand next to Griselda Vandermeer.

6

"I heard what you said," said Albert Clabber, "about spiritually bankrupt countries."

"Oh?" said Professor Abernathy.

"However, I think you should understand that when people turn to spiritualism, they're admitting that their formal religion is a flop. Empty ritual. The spirit world always seems most active when nations are in crisis, not because people have become superstitious but because the spirit world is trying to help with messages."

Professor Abernathy's mouth opened. Slowly he shook his open mouth. "You mean—are you telling me—do I understand you to mean that you believe people can talk to the spirit world?"

"Why, of course, Professor. Of course."

Professor Abernathy's eyes went from Clabber's face to Mrs. Quist's pale eyes and wan face. "I can't believe it."

"Of course," said Clabber fiercely. "That's the trouble. You're so deeply imbued with that scientific methodism that you can't believe anything beyond the scope of science's very puny measuring tools."

Professor Abernathy pursed his lips. He studied Clabber's black hair and sallow face and the deep black smoldering eyes. "You mean you really believe that a haruspex can read the future in the intestines of a freshly killed animal? You must be soft in the head, Clabber."

"There's none so blind as those who will not see."

"Well, I will not see the future in a bunch of bloody guts, Clabber, and neither will you. A terrible waste of good meat."

"Have you ever examined the spirit world, Professor Abernathy?" asked Mrs. Quist.

"Examined it? How do you mean, Mrs. Quist?"

"Well, some of your colleagues, especially in psychology, have been nibbling on the fringes of the subject with their studies in ESP, mental telepathy, random chance and mind over matter—and the more deeply they explore, the more questions they unearth that current scientific knowledge cannot explain."

Christopher Carson loomed over Professor Abernathy's shoulder blowing cigar smoke. "Come on," said Carson. "That's not spiritualism. That's a study of the power of the human mind. There is not one single shred of scientific data to indicate that there's a spirit world."

"That depends, Mr. Carson, on what you mean by spirit world."

"I'm talking about transmigration of souls. Reincarnation. Spiritual limbo. Metapsychosis. I can tell you as a professional psychologist—"

"Mr. Clabber is making an extensive study of that subject," said Mrs. Quist. "And I have had many occasions to delve into it myself."

Christopher Carson frowned at her. "You mean you're telling us you've contacted the spirit world?"

"Many times, Mr. Carson. Many times."

"Now that's just a plain crock of sheep dip."

"Indeed, Mr. Carson. Indeed."

"Are you going to tell me that you can prove reincarnation? That Bridey Murphy crap?"

"Bridey Murphy was thoroughly documented—"

"Ah, bull. Can you give me one scientifically documented case of reincarnation?"

"Jess Stearn's *Search for the Girl With the Blue Eyes.*"

"Ah, bull. I read it. Very equivocal. Inconclusive. Name another."

"Mr. Carson," said Mrs. Quist sweetly, "I could go on all night and you could go 'Ah, bull' all night."

Carson addressed himself to Professor Abernathy. "See. These people are all big words and no proof. There's not a shred—not a jot or tittle of proof."

"How do you know?" demanded Clabber.

"I've made a study of it. Let me get you told, Clabber. Let me tell you something about that world of spooks you live in. When I was in college, I got involved in the study of hypnosis. We used a lot of subjects, many of whom could be hypnotized by the snap of a finger. One day, somebody brought in a little girl and they hypnotized her. When she was under she identified herself as a little girl who lived in Savannah, Georgia, just before the Civil War."

"What kind of controls did you use? How do you program feedbacks to prevent spillovers from current consciousness to the unconscious?"

"Hold on to your drawers, Clabber. I'll get to that." Christopher Carson puffed on his cigar, cocked an eye at Mrs. Quist and continued. "This girl became the eighth wonder of the universe. Everytime they put her under, they unearthed more stuff. Detailed stuff like you wouldn't believe. She described vases and frames on paintings—oil portraits—and the porticos of long-gone plantation houses, costumes, dresses. And it was authentic right down to the nails and pegs. Why, for Pete's sake, we had sketches made based on her descriptions and taken to antique dealers for verification. It was incredible. One day, she really outdid herself. She described an entire room of furnishings, piece by piece. Now, my roommate at the time was studying cinematography. And I came in one afternoon just agog with this stuff about this little girl. My roommate listened, fascinated. Finally he began to scratch his head thoughtfully. 'Hell, Chris,' he said, 'this whole thing sounds very familiar,' and just sat there scratching his head. All of a sudden, he snaps his fingers. '*Gone With the Wind*,' he said. And that was it. This little kid had seen *Gone With the Wind* eight or ten times until it was part of her unconscious mind. And that's exactly what's going on with most of these amazing reincarnation stories. We have an incredible passion for exact reproductions in our movies, novels, plays and magazines. All of us have our heads stuffed with movie sets from every period in history. Most reincarnations are nothing but remembered movie sets. Say what you want about the scientific spirit. It has a very healthy skepticism. And I never yet met one of your spook nuts who had even a trace of skepticism. You believe anything that you want."

"Have you ever attended a séance, Mr. Carson?" asked Mrs. Quist.

"What's that got to do with it? You people are as elusive as a puff of smoke."

"Why, everything. You're evading an answer. You've never been to one, and yet you claim to have made a study."

Abigail Withers steered Griselda Vandermeer into the group. "Now. Griselda is going to do her club act. Let's see. Who'll be first?"

"Abby," said Christopher Carson, "are you changing the subject?"

"Ah. Yes. Griselda is going to tell your fortunes with her cards."

"Oh sure," said Carson. "Griselda honey, what are your credentials?"

"Hmmmmm?" She smiled sweetly at him.

"Credentials. Do you really think you can tell fortunes?"

"Oh—well."

"Well—what? Do you or don't you? Are you with them or with us?"

"Well. I don't really tell fortunes—"

"See?"

"Wait," said Mrs. Quist. "Let her finish."

Griselda looked at Mrs. Quist. "I just normally read the good cards and skip the rest . . ."

Mrs. Quist pursed her lips. "Tell me, Griselda. What do you do if you see real danger in the cards? Do you warn your subject?"

"Oh. Most of the time, to tell the truth, Mrs. Quist, I leave the bad cards right out of the deck."

"What? But you can't. You can't get a true reading."

"Mrs. Quist, I do this for a living to entertain people. That's all it is."

Christopher Carson snorted.

"Do you have a full deck with you tonight?" asked Mrs. Quist.

"Almost. I've left out just the thirty-six numeral cards."

Mrs. Quist shrugged. "Well, at least you didn't leave out the *bad* cards."

"Well, let's do a reading for Mr. Carson," said Abby Withers.

"Oh, come on," Carson protested.

Griselda took the oversize cards out of a wooden box. "This is a very good deck. Are you familiar with the four suits of the tarot deck?"

"Oh, I suppose," said Carson.

"Suppose?" exclaimed Mrs. Quist. "Name the four suits."

"Oh. Come on."

"Name the suits," demanded Mrs. Quist. She waited. "As I thought. The vaunted scientist doesn't even know what he's condemned out of hand. I submit, Mr. Carson, that if there's a fraud in this room, it is you."

"Oh, bull."

"You already said that. You seem to have a very limited vocabulary."

"Lay out the cards, Griselda," said Mrs. Withers with her elfish smile.

"Let's see. Who'll be first?"

"Oh, me," said Ruth Abernathy. "I volunteer."

Mrs. Quist exchanged a glance with Albert Clabber and shrugged again.

Peter Richardson arrived with a card table. He opened the legs and set it down.

Griselda Vandermeer looked around the array of faces. "There are forty-two cards in my deck. These are the four suits: Pence, Swords, Wands, and Cups. Now I'll shuffle the deck." They stood in a group around the table watching her beautiful hands skillfully, with fluttering motions, blend, merge and collate the cards. The cards stuttered and snapped briskly. "Now," she said. "Would you like to cut the deck, Mr. Carson?"

Sourly, Carson stuck his cigar in his mouth, then reached out a fist and rapped once on the deck.

"Done," said Griselda Vandermeer. She picked up the deck and counted thirteen cards off the top. She laid down the rest of the deck.

"This is called a thirteen-card oracle." She placed the first card face down at the center of the table and looked at Ruth Abernathy. "This is the Card of You, Mrs. Abernathy. We'll come back to it. Meantime, do you have any question you'd like to ask the cards? Or is there a wish you'd like to make?"

Christopher Carson brushed a hand at her and blew cigar smoke at the ceiling.

"Oh, come on, Chris," said Ruth Abernathy. "Yes, I'll make a wish."

"This is silly," said Carson.

Griselda counted off four cards face down. "This is the oracle of the tarot. We'll come back to them at the end. It will tell you about your wish."

She placed a card face down just to the left of the You Card. "This is the Card of the Recent Past." She laid another above the You card. "This is the Card of Now." She placed the third card to the right of the You Card. "This is the Card of the Trimester Hence." She laid the fourth card below the You Card. "And this is the Card of the Year to Come." She repeated the process with the four remaining cards. "Now. You can see there are two cards in each position. Two to the left, two to the right, two above and two below the Card of You. We'll start with the center card." She turned it up. "This is the Card of You. Hmmm. It is the Card of Temperance. It says that you are a gentle person, moderate in your habits and outlook, a good money manager and home economist. It also indicates a competing interest outside your marriage. A career, perhaps?"

Ruth Abernathy looked thoughtfully at Griselda Vandermeer.

"It also indicates firmness of purpose," continued Griselda. "And this card—"

Christopher Carson snorted.

"Mr. Carson," said Griselda, "I don't make this up as I go along. I read the symbolic meaning of the cards as they lie. Now, this is a Card of the Recent Past, Mrs. Abernathy."

"Call me Ruth."

"It's the King of Wands. A good card. It signifies honesty. It means a good marriage. And it often indicates an inheritance."

"Oh, that's true. I inherited three thousand dollars from an aunt two years ago."

"It may also mean good advice that you didn't take."

"Oh, come on," exclaimed Christopher Carson. "Everyone's life is filled with good advice they didn't take."

Griselda Vandermeer smiled winningly at him. "Yes," she said. She turned up the next card. "The King of Pence is your second Card of the Recent Past. It symbolizes a brown-haired man with blue eyes."

"Oh, I've got one of those," said Ruth Abernathy, and she turned to smile at her husband.

"It is the card of a highly placed business executive or a professor."

"Come on," cried Christopher Carson. "You've just made that up."

Griselda smiled at him and turned to look at Mrs. Quist.

"Griselda is quite right, Mr. Carson. The King of Pence points quite clearly to a brown-haired, blue-eyed college professor. In fact, with the King of Wands, it indicates that the querent has *married* a brown-haired, blue-eyed professor and can expect an unusually happy marriage."

Carson shook his head and turned partly away from the crowded table. "Ah, bull."

Griselda Vandermeer reached out and turned up a card above the Center Card of the You. "This is the first Card of Now. It tells you about your current state of affairs. This is the Ace of Cups. It's a card of fertility —babies. Contentment, the warmth of the hearth."

Ruth Abernathy touched her mouth with her fingertips. "I'm pregnant?"

45

Griselda Vandermeer spread her hands in mild helplessness. "I can't say. It may simply mean a warm and happy home." She reached for the second Card of Now. "This is the Knight of Wands. It means movement, change. It symbolizes an alteration in residence—"

"Well, that's true," said Ruth Abernathy. "We're all of us moving out of here." She nodded her head emphatically at Christopher Carson. He saluted her with his scoffer's smile.

"It can also mean a confusion about your future plans—"

"Now that's true," said Ruth Abernathy. "If I don't get pregnant pretty soon, I'm going back to teaching."

Carol Carson gave Professor Abernathy a poke with her finger. "Get to work."

He looked at her. "Take your own advice."

Carol Carson flushed, lowered her eyes and then glanced sullenly at her husband. "Oh, sure."

"There's also a possibility of a gift from a relative— a rich relative."

"Well," Ruth Abernathy reflected. "My Aunt Alice just gave me a bowl from her cut-glass collection. But she's not very rich."

"Oh, come on, Ruth," said Carson. "Stop trying so hard. This is all make-believe and innuendo and guess. Not one hard fact."

Griselda reached for a card to the right of the center card. "This is the first Card of the Trimester Hence. It tells about the next three months or so. Let's see. This is the Card of the World. A good sign. It indicates a change in residence, too, and that backs up the Knight of Wands Card of Now. It points to a voyage of some

kind. But most of all it points to success in some undertaking. Maybe the next card will tell us."

"Pregnancy?" asked Ruth Abernathy. Everyone
laughed.

Griselda turned up the next Card of the Trimester
Hence. "Oh. The King of Swords. This is the card of
authority and judgment. If you undertake a lawsuit,
you will be successful. You may get involved with a lawyer
or a person who has been elected to office or even a
doctor."

"A Ph.D.? Well, that's Gordon. He's a doctor of
philosophy. That's got to mean I'm going to have a successful undertaking with Gordon—"

"Don't say it," said Carol Carson. Laughter was general
around the table again.

"Now," said Griselda Vandermeer. "Here are the two
Cards of the Year-to-Come. Let's see. The first one is the
Knight of Cups. A messenger. It means you will get a
good business opportunity or an invitation of some kind,
a job offer, maybe a visit from a friend with a gift of
money. Let's see—" She turned up the second Card of
the Year-to-Come. "Oh, very good. This card is the
Wheel of Fortune. It governs your fate and fortune. It
predicts success in your chosen career. It means luck and
happiness in your work. You've had marvelous cards."

"What about my wish?"

"Now, Ruth," said Christopher Carson. "Everyone
knows what you wished for—even Gordon." He led the
laughter with his face beaming ceilingward.

Griselda Vandermeer picked up the four Cards of the
Oracle of the tarot. "The first card is—the Judgment.
This is a good card if the others in the Oracle are good.

It signifies rebirth, change of position or renewal. Let's see the next card—oh my! The Ace of Pence. This is the very best card in the entire tarot deck. Happiness, complete contentment, ecstasy. Great wealth. And this card—the Queen of Cups. Success in marriage. Motherhood!"

Everyone around the table applauded.

"Forget that job, Ruth," said Carol Carson.

Griselda turned up the last card. "The Star. You can't get better cards than these. This is the card of hope and a bright future."

Everyone applauded as a finale.

Christopher Carson walked over to the bar and put his glass down. He nodded at Peter Richardson and watched him refill the glass.

Gordon Abernathy followed him.

"What a bunch of hocus pocus," said Carson. "This occult stuff is the haven of sick minds. It relies on hallucinations, the whole phony business, and hallucination is the hallmark of the psychotic. And the psychotic just loves public condemnation anyway to shore up his persecution complex. Ninety-nine percent of all these people are paranoids who find plots against them everywhere. Most of them are absolutely convinced that someone is trying to kill them."

Peter Richardson's pouring hand paused. "Kill them?" he asked.

"Sure. That's the world's commonest complaint of the paranoids. 'Someone is trying to poison me. Someone is trying to get into my home and murder me in my sleep. Steal my job, get my girl, steal my invention.'"

Richardson studied Carson's face thoughtfully.

7

Richardson brought clean glasses from the kitchen. He saw Ozzie Goulart flanked by Clabber and Mrs. Quist. Goulart leaned forward to lower his head. He listened attentively to her low voice, then straightened up. He held up two palms to her, spoke briefly and walked away from them.

They exchanged glances.

8

Griselda came over to the bar and plucked Richardson's sleeve. "Come on. I'm dying to do you. If you're going to inherit a million dollars, I want to be the first to know."

She strolled back to the table towing Richardson by the hand. Carson turned and watched her figure as she walked, then found his wife's eyes on him. He shrugged and puffed on his cigar.

"Observe," said Griselda to Richardson, "my fingers never leave my hand." As she shuffled the cards, Mrs. Quist strolled back to the table.

Deftly, Griselda shuffled the deck. She smartly put the deck before Richardson. He cut them. She picked up the deck and counted off thirteen into a pile, putting the remainder of the deck aside. "Okay. The thirteen-card Oracle again." Her hand put down the Card of You in the center of the table. She laid aside the four cards of the Oracle and then positioned the four piles of temporal cards. "Now." She turned up the Card of You and paused. Hesitantly she put it back, still face down. She glanced at Mrs. Quist. In one scoop, she gathered up the cards again. Quickly she shuffled them.

49

"What happened?" asked Richardson.

"Nothing. Wrong card. We'll do it again." She put the shuffled deck before Richardson to cut. He knocked it with a knuckle and she picked it up, dealt the thirteen cards and quickly positioned them. She reached for the Card of You and paused again. Before Richardson could make a move, she skimmed up the thirteen cards and placed them back on the deck and quickly shuffled them. "I think I'd like a drink first," she said.

"Now?" asked Richardson.

"I'm very thirsty." Griselda Vandermeer's eyes avoided Anna Quist's.

"Finish the story you started to tell about the witch killing," said Abby Withers.

"Oh, well," said Mrs. Quist. "That was a celebrated story in its time about an old woman. She lived in a pre-Revolutionary stone house out in the Gravesend section of Brooklyn. You know that section?"

"Oh, it was lovely there when I was a girl."

"Yes. Well, this old lady I'm discussing was given to making predictions on crops and the weather, on children and such. Oh—some fifty years ago."

"Scry?"

"Oh, I think not. I don't think she had any training at all. A natural clairvoyant, perhaps. She was a recluse mostly, although friendly enough to her neighbors. Anyway, there was another woman in the neighborhood—a Mrs. Dimmity. Very religious she was, and she condemned the old woman's prognostications out of hand. Bad-mouthed her as a fake, don't you see? Well, in the spring of the year, Mrs. Dimmity's roses were all blighted, and she accused the old woman of putting a curse on them—a very strange ability for a woman who wasn't supposed to have such an ability, if you read me."

Abby Withers nodded eagerly, her mouth partly open in rapt attention.

"The old woman said nothing. But soon after, Mrs. Dimmity took to having hallucinations. She claimed that the old woman had become an incubus."

"Incubus?"

"A spirit that sits on your chest when you sleep and kills you."

"Oh. Say it again."

"Incubus."

"Oh."

"Mrs. Dimmity took to having terrible nightmares. She feared for her life."

"Oh, dear."

"Yes. Well, Mr. Dimmity took a poor view of all this. He watched his wife visibly failing before his eyes. And of course the poor creature in her mental state kept him awake all night with her shrieks. Neither one of them could get any rest."

"Oh my heavens."

"Yes. Well. In the full of the moon in October, the Hunter's Moon, you know, Mr. Dimmity went over to the old woman's house and he murdered her with an ax."

"Oh my God in heaven!"

"Oh yes. Well, Mrs. Dimmity's hallucinations disappeared immediately. She was completely cured."

"Oh I see. What happened to Mr. Dimmity?"

"Oh yes. Well, he was put in jail and became very despondent and he committed suicide."

"Oh my God in heaven."

"And right about that time the lights appeared in the

old woman's house. Many people saw them—lights going from room to room, restless, never still. Skeptics slept in that empty old house, trying to see the ghost. No one would buy the place. It was finally pulled down to make way for the Belt Parkway system. It was quite a tale in its day. It used to be one of the first stories off people's lips when they talked about witches casting spells."

"Has anyone looked out of the window lately?" called Ruth Abernathy. "It's snowing."

They crowded about the two living room windows.

"Put the lights out so we can see," said Carol Carson.

Pete Richardson went about the living room turning off the lights.

"Oh, beautiful," said Ruth Abernathy. "Snow in the city."

High over the apartment house, high over the city, a line of snow squalls passed, moving northeastward across Long Island and out to the turbulent, tumbling black North Atlantic, passing over the small group who watched from Richardson's window. They stood in the darkness, absorbed by the furious, blowing snow that seemed as remote and harmless as a child's snow scene shaken inside a crystal ball.

9

Mrs. Quist was the first to go. She shook hands with Richardson. "I have a cab waiting, so I'll be short," she said. "It was a delight to meet you. I'd like to see you again. You strike me as a young man—there's something in your eyes that I see that I might help you with. Call me when you get settled. Come over with Albert." She nodded her head at Clabber.

Richardson took her small thin hand. It made him think of a mouse's paw. "Nice of you to come, Mrs. Quist. Maybe what you see in my eyes is scotch."

She smiled palely at him. "No. Not scotch, young man. Not scotch."

"Sorry about the cards," said Griselda Vandermeer. "Next time, okay?"

"Thank God," said Richardson, shaking her hand.

"For what?"

"There's going to be a next time."

10

The Carsons and the Abernathys left together, the men sidewise stepping, talking earnestly, the two women strolling behind, murmuring scandal-eyed. After them, left Abby Withers and Ozzie Goulart.

In the quiet, crystals of snow tapped on the window-pane.

Richardson hated to see the party end. He didn't want to go to bed.

He stood in his darkened living room watching the snow blow and swirl.

CHAPTER III

Before first light, a bird cried.

A small bird and a shrill cry. Outside his window, near, far, the bird screeled as it fluttered and fled in darkness, its cries failing, fainter, fainter.

Richardson, wearily awake, turned back his blankets and walked into the living room to the window. He looked out at the still winter night. The winds were calm, the skies were clear, the cold had bitten deep. Spring was many miles away but death was near. He considered his own death: the searching blade of knife thrust upward past his blocking hands. A hand's push in front of a subway car. A raised club behind a fence. Fingers closing around an empurpled windpipe. In his bed. At the dark turning of a stair. A shadowed doorway. Where? When?

He leaned on the windowsill. To have come this far for nothing? Nothing? To have been born with the right genes, to have inherited the right brain, the right talents, to have gone to the right school, to have chosen the right career, to have such a prized chance to live a fabled life. In the whole race of man in his billions upon billions, to be among the pampered few who were elevated enough to live the ideal life. And just as he's to nibble the cheese, the trap snaps. Farewell, destiny's tot.

Other lives—slow lives, dull lives, safe, timid, clinging lives—would grind on day after day to no purpose, with no joy, no direction, no meaning. Absurd.

Maybe he was mad. Or under a spell. Or victimized by minuscule doses of LSD. A brain tumor. A message from the spirit world. What? Richardson looked out and down. Goulart's light was on. Richardson put on his robe and slippers. He went down the dark stairs and tapped on Goulart's door. There was no answer. Richardson stood in the darkness, frowning.

At eight, he knuckled Goulart's door lightly. He listened and sensed the emptiness within. He knocked again. At last he turned and descended the stairs.

The day surprised him on the front stoop. Clear, dry, bright, the light layer of snow already begrimed. Footsteps of others who had preceded him descended and turned to the right. All except one: one set of tracks turned left and led away across the quadrangle into the white emptiness.

Richardson frowned at the solitary tracks. He buttoned his overcoat and walked to the right to the subway.

With a squat pot of rubber cement, paper shears, a jar of pencils, a roll of cellophane tape, and a large unabridged dictionary, Bobby Pew plied the editor's trade.

His pencil tracked across lines of typewritten copy, leaving a trail of deletion marks, transposition symbols, excised words, added connectives, changes in verb tense and number, corrections in grammar.

Pew paused and sipped his coffee. He dropped his pencil and looked at Richardson, who was reading his corrections.

"The guy can write well enough," said Pew, pointing at the page of copy. "But he's kind of dee-yew-em and can't ess-pee-ee-el so hot."

"It's a good story," said Richardson. "Let's use him again."

"Okay. How about the profile on the German preacher from the concentration camp?"

"Okay."

"Existential man was born in Dachau," said Pew. "You read any philosophy these days?"

"No," said Richardson.

"Existential man is the first man in history to renounce the consolations of religion," prated Pew. "He has to look at death as final, with no provable life beyond it. For that reason, existential man is inconsolable."

"So am I," said Richardson disinterestedly.

"You ever read Buber?"

"No."

"Heidegger?"

"No."

"Oh, you've got to. Here." Pew peeled a sheet from a pad. "Get these books." He picked up his pencil and wrote quickly. "Change your life." He thrust the paper at Richardson.

Richardson read the names. "Martin Buber, Heidegger, Kierkegaard, Sartre, Camus and Nietzsche. Nietzsche?"

"Especially Nietzsche. He's the apostle of madness."

"Great. Just what I need." Richardson walked back to his office. "See if you can raise Goulart," he said to the secretary.

She nodded at him. "I've been trying all morning." She reached for the telephone.

Richardson looked down on Court Street at the figures walking the street.

He unfolded and brought out the terrible idea to look at once again, yet again, forever again: Someone was trying to kill him. It was true in spite of all the rational equipment in his head that denied it. It said: I am an absurd idea. Nonetheless, I am true. Someone is going to kill you.

He looked at his secretary. She shook her head and put down the phone.

Ominous. Goulart wasn't home, and that, strangely, was ominous.

Richardson crumpled up the list of names in his hand. "Read existential philosophy? I'm living it. Dying it."

2

Squeak. Squeak.

Mr. Ian McMurray of the Boston Society of Professional Genealogists wrote in precise square letters and numbers on the smooth expanse of white paper: 7 August 1832. Carefully, his squealing felt pen decorated the letter A with serifs. *Squeak. Squeak.*

"Really," he said in his broad accent, "I think you might have saved the trip up to Boston, Mr. Willow. The whole Henry Tully genealogy was published years ago by Mrs. Adora Hammett of New York City." Mr. McMurray scuttled a tough dry old man's hand across his bald skull.

"Mrs. Adora Hammett?" Willow asked in his low voice.

"Hammett. Hammett. Don't you know her?"

"No."

"Ummm. Mr. Willow, you have a lot of homework to do." The light caught the old man's hand, caught red hair on the fingers and wrist, thick like bits of rusted wire, on a crinkled terrain of freckles and liver spots. "Mrs. Adora Hammett is the most fervent genealogist in the world, and the richest. She also happens to be a lineal descendant of Joseph Tully. She's a leading light of the Federalist Dames of Colonial America and she published the genealogy of the Henry Tully branch of the family exactly as she presented it to the Federalist Dames as credentials for admission." He scratched his head again. "You just don't get any more genealogical than Mrs. Hammett."

"I see. Who did the genealogy?"

Mr. McMurray drew another 7 August 1832. Then he raised his eyes to Matthew Willow. "I did."

"Oh." Willow watched him write the date a third time. "Do you have a chart of all the descendants?"

"Descendants? There are descendants, Mr. Willow, from here to hell and back again. Hundreds of them."

"And the most vocal one is Mrs.—er—Hammett."

"Yes. Are you English, Mr. Willow?"

"Yes."

"I see. Well, if you're doing a study on the American branch of the Tullys, you've got a big job ahead of you.

There were four brothers who came over prior to the American Revolution."

"Yes. That much I know. Four sons of Joseph Tully. A London wine merchant, Henry, came first on the British sailing vessel *Bristol Home.* Arrived in Boston February 19, 1745."

"Ah, you know that. All right. Then you've got one of the few pieces of hard information that exists about Henry Tully. We know he married a Hannah Gorges, but we don't know when. We know they had three children. We know he renounced allegiance to his king, his country and his own father back in London. We know he was at Concord and fired on British troops. We know from the muster rolls that he served in the American army, and after the war he settled in New Haven, Connecticut, where his wife had moved during the Revolution. He and his wife apparently died there and left an army of descendants. Tullys all over the place. In fact, Mrs. Hammett has them organized into some kind of a family association. I understand now there are descendants of Henry Tully all over the world."

"*Apparently* died, you said."

"Yes. No will. No grave."

"No will? Very interesting."

"Yes. That bothers a lot of people. No will. No probate records."

"Did Mrs. Hammett have you do a genealogy on Hannah Gorges Tully?"

"No record. Not one reference prior to her marriage. She's a mystery woman who dropped out of the sky."

"Hmmmmm. Weren't there any death records in their church? A gravesite?"

"The Church of New Haven burned to the ground in

1850 or so. Burned all the church records with it. They're in that graveyard, both Henry and Hannah. I'm sure of it, but the tombstones are hopelessly weathered. You'll never identify the gravesites. Frankly, all Mrs. Hammett wanted was proof of lineage. When she got it, she stopped me from further research. She's very tight with money, you know."

Matthew Willow watched the precise hand of Mr. McMurray block-letter the date again, 7 August 1832.

Mr. McMurray raised his eyes. "Well," he said thoughtfully. "Mr. Willow, I was paid by Mrs. Hammett to turn up an unequivocal Ahnetafel Chart connecting her to Henry Tully. I did. There's more work that can be done on that Tully genealogy, I suppose, but the essential facts and proofs have been turned up. If you'd like to search the probate records for yourself, they're kept in Hartford. The land records, deeds, *lis pendens* and other records are in the town clerk's office in New Haven. I'd suggest that you go to New Haven or see Mrs. Hammett for a current list of living descendants of Tully."

Willow studied the blunt stiff neck and tufts of red nape hair. Lean old fox, he'd scrambled through many an overgrown cemetery on a Vermont mountainside or a Berkshire meadow to scrape away the sod and lichens on a table-slab tombstone.

Hepzibah, wife of Jedediah Winsloe
Died 3 May 1803. Mother of 14

Ah, here you are, Mrs. Winsloe. Your great-great-grandson has been hunting all over New England for you.

How many hundred hours had he spent at the courthouse, searching, searching? Find an uncle whose middle name was Claustrick. Locate all the heirs of . . . Probably known to every lawyer in town, a detective, a genealogical detective, plucking ancestors from wills and Bibles and antique lawsuits, from church records and diaries and ships' passenger lists, yellowed newspaper obituaries, name-change petitions.

The life of the genealogist: a fresh trail every day and a new puzzle to solve.

And something to haunt him all his days: 7 August 1832. *Squeak. Squeak.*

Matthew Willow stood up. "Which way is New Haven?"

"South."

Squeak. Squeak.

3

The two moving men carried the couch onto the moving van, set it down, positioned it and lashed it.

"She said there were some boxes in the cellar," said the tall man.

The other nodded and finished knotting the line. "Let's go," he said.

They entered the main hall of Brevoort House and paused, looking for the cellar stairs. Somewhere a telephone was ringing, faintly.

Their heavy work shoes crackled on the brick cellar steps and they walked along a length of corridor partly lit by angled sunlight. "Carson. Goulart. Here— Abernathy."

They paused at the door to the bin and opened it. They paused, looking down the corridor at the cat.

Goulart's cat stood there, frozen, staring at them, poised.

"Black cat," said the tall man. "Wild-looking, ain't he?"

"Ah. Just a cat. Let's get this stuff."

They carried up the trunks and suitcases, the boxes and bundles, and trussed them in the van. Then they shut the van doors, then returned to the main hallway.

As they closed the doors of the building, the steam pipes banged loudly to overcome the chill.

Up in Goulart's apartment, the telephone rang and rang.

It was two-thirty.

4

Down Route 91, at the estuary of the Connecticut River, New Haven lay like a blighted junk yard sprinkled with dirty snow under a cauldron of filthy clouds. New Haven: a dreary February landscape, with sewer-stained Long Island Sound at the shoreline.

Matthew Willow felt weary. Hundreds of descendants. Each to be examined singly. He remembered McMurray's sympathetic handshake. A genealogist's nightmare come true: hundreds. So be it. The game had begun.

The young woman in the New Haven town clerk's office was helpful. She showed him the index to the Register of Deeds. "These," she said, "are the Grantor's Indexes and these are the Grantee's. Buyer and seller. The indexes are for a span of years. This one covers the years 1780–1799. See? And within each, there's a chart in front for alphabetizing each name to the third letter. See? Here's the T and the U and the L. Turn to the page indicated in the chart, and there— If Mr. Tully bought land or a house in New Haven between 1780 and 1799, he'll be in these pages. And if he sold real estate it'll be in those Grantor's Indexes. Okay?"

Willow leaned both elbows on the counter and started down the list of names written in flowing script. He found the Tully names with ease. Henry and Hannah Tully. Deed recorded 21 September 1785. He noted the liber and page number and continued. Another Tully. Edwin and Susannah Tully purchased from Henry and Hannah Tully. Same property. Date: 3 July 1795. Willow noted the liber number and page. He continued. Nothing else.

Out of curiosity, he obtained the Grantor's Index. And there he found cross-referenced the sale Henry and Hannah Tully, grantors, to Edwin and Susannah Tully, grantees. Date: 3 July 1795. And then, curiously, 17 February 1798, Edwin, the son, and his wife sold the property. Why?

Why had Henry and Hannah sold the property to their son and daughter-in-law? There was no record of their having bought themselves another home. Where did they go? And why a few years later had Edwin sold it? Willow decided to examine the deeds. He noted the liber and page shown in the index and went into the archives.

The first deed identified the property that Henry *et ux.*, Hannah, had purchased. "All that certain lot of prime meadow situate lying and being in said town limits bounded and described as follows to wit: Beginning at the northwesterly corner of T. Timmon's land in the line of the land of J. W. Rankin and runs north 46° west eight chains and forty links south 71° west four chains south 82° west five chains fifty-three links south 45½° east eleven chains seventy-five links north 57½° east eight chains to the place of beginning containing seven and 116/160 acres of land to be the same more or less." Price paid: $1100.

The second deed indicated that Henry *et ux.*, Hannah, had sold the land and the house thereon to son Edwin *et ux.*, Susannah. Price: $1100.

Willow considered looking at the third title transfer —from Edwin and Susannah to whoever bought it. But that would tell him nothing about Henry and Hannah. It was a time-wasting byway.

So he skipped the third deed and went instead to the Index of Mortgages. From there, he examined the *lis pendens* for civil lawsuits, for quitclaims, leases, liens, petitions and quiet title. Nothing there.

He felt futility. This was all ground that McMurray had gone over, must have gone over many years ago.

Willow started to leave. Then paused. Neatness counts. He didn't like nagging voices at three A.M. disturbing his rest. So he got the third deed out—Edwin's title transfer, dated 17 February 1798.

And there he found a clue to the whereabouts of Henry and Hannah.

Edwin declared in the transfer of deed that he had had the property from his parents, Henry *et ux.*, Hannah, now residents of Goshen, New York.

Goshen, New York.

Willow sat down and stared at it. One of those common pieces of luck born of instinct and persistence that genealogists detail to each other over drinks. Goshen.

He stood up and opened his attaché case. He withdrew a New York State road map and unfolded it. Goshen. It lay in Orange County. County seat, in fact. Sixty miles from New York City. Three, four hours from New Haven.

He sat down again to consider. Did he want to go to Goshen? After all, he was through with Henry *et ux.,* Hannah. He was into the next generation, Edwin and his two brothers, Thomas and George—and then hundreds of offspring.

He considered: Should he bother going to Goshen?

And the hunch player's voice said: Yes.

5

It was dusk when Richardson emerged from the subway. An old man with a winter-white face looked at him solemnly through a steam-stained window. An old face at the gray end of another winter day, locked in until spring.

As he walked in the relentless cold of the evening, Richardson thought of his wife. For the first time since the divorce, he felt lonely. Vulnerable. The thought of seeing her almost overwhelmed him.

In the bleak light, he turned a corner and saw Brevoort House, looking like a beached gunboat, besieged and isolated. Beyond it, the frozen metal of the wrecker's boom loomed in the twilight.

He knocked on Goulart's door. No answer. He knocked again. In vain. He mounted to his apartment, pawed through a desk drawer, found a key and returned to Goulart's door. He knocked again, loudly. He waited. Finally, he pushed the key in the lock and opened the door.

The lights were on, had been on all night and all day.

The bed was made—a neat rectangle amidst piles of magazines and art supplies and plants.

He descended the stairs and found the tracks in the frozen snow that led across the quadrangle. His feet crunched as he followed them in the darkness. They led him to the middle of the vast quadrangle, then disappeared. The wind had scoured the snow down to the brick rubble and packed dirt. Around the empty windy fields lay blocks of empty buildings.

Richardson returned to the apartment building.

6

Abby Withers's eyes searched every bit of his face. "Where can he be?" she asked. "It's not like him at all. Oh, I tell you I'm worried to death. I saw those lights again last night and I tapped on his door and he didn't answer and I tried again every few minutes and he never turned up. All day long I've been trying his door. I thought sure he'd show up when the Abernathys moved. Ruth and Gordon waited awhile for him. And his cat's down in the cellar and nobody can catch it. Where can he be?"

Richardson absently patted the dog's head. "I don't know, Abby, but I think I know who does. I'll be right back."

7

He knocked on Clabber's door. "Have you seen Goulart?"

Clabber frowned and shook his head. "Last night. Not since then."

"Then he's missing."

"Missing? What are you talking about?"

"I mean missing. He hasn't been in his apartment since last night . . . at least since around five this morning."

Clabber shrugged. "He'll turn up. He's a big boy."

"Come on, Clabber. You know Goulart, and I do too. If he was planning to be away for a day or more, one of us would have known it. Are those his tracks that lead out across those empty lots?"

Clabber took a long, insolent look at Richardson. Then he gazed with slow disgust at Richardson's suit and shoes. "I'm a librarian, Richardson, not a detective."

"You've also been having some close conversations with Goulart lately. It doesn't take much brains to see that he had something on his mind."

"I could say the same about you. In fact, you look worried to death."

"This is no help."

"Okay, okay." Clabber spread his hands in surrender. "Come on in."

Richardson stepped, for the first time, into Clabber's apartment. The barracklike starkness surprised him. He followed Clabber into the kitchen. A book was propped against a table lamp, surrounded by soiled dishes.

"Here," said Clabber. "Sit down and have a coffee."

Richardson sank down slowly.

"I'll make a deal with you, Richardson."

"What kind of a deal?"

"You tell me what you know. I'll tell you what I know."

Richardson shrugged. "What I know you could put in a gnat's eye."

"Okay. I'll put it another way. I'll tell you what I know if you'll answer some questions in return."

Richardson nodded. "Okay."

Clabber poured coffee into two cups. "Here's the straight of it, then. I have a lot of books out there," he pointed toward the living room.

"That's all you *do* have out there," said Richardson.

"Okay. A number of those books deal with the occult and the spirit world."

"Oh." Richardson snorted. "Well, that fits. That's what you and Mrs.—ah . . ."

"Quist."

"Yes, Quist. That's what you were full of last night. Are you some kind of a medium?"

Clabber studied Richardson's face again. "Go over to the wall by the door and read the two documents hanging there."

Richardson was slumped in his overcoat, and he sighed. Then he gathered himself and stood. Slowly, wearily, he walked across the uncarpeted floor to the door. He stood reading while Clabber watched.

Richardson returned with a quizzical smile on his face. "You excommunicated the Catholic Church—the whole Catholic Church—and all the Catholics in the world?"

"Sure. They did it to me."

Richardson sat down again, half-smiling. "Are you for real?"

"I'm for real, Richardson. I'm an orthodox Catholic and I believe devoutly in life after death."

"Who's Bruno?"

"A fourteenth-century Italian prelate. He was burned for heresy—especially for his views on the transmigration of souls."

"Oh."

"You asked me if I was a medium. I just gave you an answer. Okay?"

"What's this got to do with Goulart?"

"Goulart is one of the few men I've met with a mind free of chains. Recently, he's been having some authentic religious experiences."

"What do you mean?"

"He may be developing psychic powers."

"I don't understand, Clabber."

"He and I have been talking about some of his experiences. And he's reading my books. So you're right: we have been having some close conversations lately."

"What experiences has he been having?"

"If you want me to answer that, you'll have to read a couple of my books first."

"Oh."

"How about answering a few questions of mine, Richardson?"

Richardson shrugged. "Shoot."

"Goulart has been having a number of 'religious' experiences. What do you know about them?"

"What religious experiences?"

"Suppose you tell me, Richardson."

"I don't know anything about religious experiences, Goulart's or otherwise."

"Oh, goody," said Clabber.

"You asked me. I told you."

"You're holding out on me."

"No I'm not, Clabber. If I knew something, I'd probably refuse to tell you on the grounds that it's Goulart's personal business. But I don't."

Clabber's intense dark eyes searched Richardson's. "You heard a noise the other night. Right?"

Richardson was startled. It took him a moment to catch himself. And in that moment, Clabber read him. And Clabber knew that Richardson knew that he'd been read. Richardson straightened up and reached for the sugar. "How'd you get that piece of information?"

"Mostly a guess. What kind of a noise was it?"

"Now come on, Clabber. You're intruding on private territory."

Clabber studied him again with those black eyes. Then he shrugged. "Look, Richardson, I haven't tried to fake you out. I'm a student of the occult. It's a very serious matter to me—I destroyed my whole life inside the Catholic Church because of my convictions. Whenever I hear of anything that might relate to my interests, I get very curious. Something has been going on in Goulart's life, but lately he's been shutting me out."

"Oh yeah? Why?"

Clabber's eyes were furious. And, again, he shrugged. "Nothing. Methodology."

"What's that mean? Methodology?"

"We disagreed on the techniques he was using to—ah —study his manifestations."

"Maybe it's about time you told me something concrete about this, Clabber. I can't make head or tail out of anything you're saying."

"And I told you I can't explain it unless you read a few books on the subject."

"Fencing."

"No, Richardson. Not fencing. Esoteric. Unless you're familiar with certain basic concepts, it'll all be gibberish to you. And I'll tell you something else. If you're having religious or occult experiences, I'm sure I can help you."

"Religious and occult? Me?"

"A phenomenon that defies rational explanation—at least on the surface. Maybe that noise you've been hearing—"

"It's nothing."

"Okay. It's nothing." Clabber reached out for the coffeepot and poured more coffee into Richardson's cup. "It's a long cold evening out there. We've got a full pot of coffee and a night to talk it away in and two highly intelligent minds. Conversation is one of the few meaningful acts open to intelligent men. I'm very interested in strange noises. So tell me about it."

It was Richardson's turn to take a long hard look. Clabber's gaze was steady, patient. "It's very simple, Clabber. The other night a noise that came from my living room woke me up. It could have been caused by a million things. Old buildings are filled with odd noises."

"What did this noise sound like?"

"A kind of whistling noise. Like—" Richardson shrugged inadequately. "Like a golf club when you swing it."

Clabber frowned at him, composing a question. Richardson already regretted the confidence. Clabber was inside the circle now, inside Richardson's private world, and in an instant a relationship was formed: superior-inferior; doctor-patient; officer-enlisted man; master-slave.

"Look, Clabber, before you ask any more questions, I don't want this to be a subject of lengthy discussions."

"Oh, it won't, it won't. Tell me about the sound again."

Richardson blew through compressed lips. "Like that. Okay? Let's drop it."

"In a moment. You were asleep when you heard it?"

"Yes."

"Hmmm."

"No, I didn't dream it, Clabber."

"Okay. Have you heard it again?"

Richardson hesitated and exhaled. "Can we drop it?"

"Just a couple more questions."

"Okay. Yes, I heard it again. Same thing. I was asleep and it woke me up. *Whoosh*. That was it."

"Can I see your apartment?"

"Stow it, Clabber. I don't want to pursue it any further."

Clabber studied him. "Okay. For the time being, we'll stow it. Just do me a favor."

"What?"

"Notice I'm not smiling."

"Okay."

"I mean this with deadly seriousness."

"Okay, okay. What's the favor?"

"Any time you hear that noise again—day or night— come directly down here and pound on my door."

8

The sun was nearly gone, down behind the foothills of the Catskills, when Willow found the church. It was a block away from the famous Trotters' Race Track.

He stepped out of his car and felt the sundown breeze freeze his ankles as he crossed the roadway. There was a warm light in the front window of the parsonage. Willow stumped hollowly across the wooden porch, rang the bell hunched against the wind, feeling the cold pain in his ears. He turned and saw the railing and spindles of the famous Trotters' Race Track. It looked forlorn in the bitter darkness.

A young man in a woolen sweater opened the door.

"Good evening," said Willow. "Is the rector about?"

"Ah—come in. Come in," said the young man. He eagerly shut the door behind Willow. "He's gone over to Campbell Hall to visit the sick. Might I help? I'm the curate."

"Oh. Fine. I'm trying to locate the death records of a man named Tully and his wife, Hannah."

"Hmmmmm. Interesting. Tully."

"Yes."

"When did they die?"

"In 1800—1810, possibly. I've been to the Goshen town clerk's office, but his records go back only to 1881."

"You obviously believe they were attached to this church."

"Yes."

"Hmmm. Tully. Yes. Well. Let's see. Let's go in here." He led Willow through a large living room, through a dining room and into a small study. A safe stood in the corner, and the curate knelt before it. "Actually," he said, "you're very fortunate. These records shouldn't be here. We ought to have turned them over to the County Historical Society long ago. But let's see." He opened the safe and peered into it carefully. "Ah yes, here we are."

He stood up with a ledger in his hands and carried it to a desk. "This is the original church register. Goes back to 1740. Let's see. Tully." Small red alphabetical tabs extended from the side edge of the volume. T,T,T. Here. T." He opened the tabbed page to the T's. "Oh. Bad luck," he said. "Badly foxed." He pointed to the freckles that marred the page. "Dampness over the years. Yet other pages are perfectly preserved." He squinted at the list of names, set off in a sinuous Spencerian script done with a split-tip quill. The ink was faint, faded to a beige that blended with the foxing. "I'm afraid—practically illegible. Is that Tull there?"

"Tull?"

"Yes. It might be Tully." He reached into a desk drawer and pulled out a magnifying glass. "It might be Ann Tull or Hannah Tully." He examined the rest of the page with the magnifying glass. "Here's another. That could be Tully. What do you think?"

Willow examined the page with the magnifying glass. "Can't be sure. May be, may not be. How about the tombstone?"

The curate's mouth opened. "Tombstone?" His eyes slowly slid to the window and to the waiting winter night outside. "I suppose you mean now."

"Yes."

"And I suppose that means that I should go with you to find the plots."

"Is that an offer?"

"I was hoping it sounded more like a lament."

"Strange," said Willow with a smile. "Sounded just like a firm offer."

9

A cold flow of bitter air poured down the hill and moved through the acres of headstones, obelisks and tablets, a conclave of hooded shapes. A wind was stored up in the east and the temperature was dropping rapidly.

Willow followed the bundled curate, who led the way with a flashlight. "Amazing," said the curate, shivering.

"The sun goes down so quickly and night falls like a thrown blanket."

A slow freight eased through Goshen somewhere over the hill and slowly picked up momentum. Briefly, on a curve, its headlight backlit the hill. There was a low rumble of train wheels and a slight vibration of earth. The train emitted a long shriek from its whistle—a lonely homeless cry.

The curate turned off the graveled path and walked quickly up an incline. The thick turf was matted with ice crystals and streaks of old snow. The beam of light picked up the names on the stones and tablets. A flotilla of dead.

Our Jim. Mother. Jeremiah Cornwall. Boone. Margaret, beloved daughter of . . . Annie, wife of . . . Scoll. Pierce. Birdwhistle. Throne.

"Here," said the curate. "This must be it." He knelt beside a table-slab stone and brushed away the ice crystals and the winter's debris. He squinted, squatting, trying to read. "Hmmm." He struggled a hand into his pocket and withdrew a small box. He handed the flashlight to Willow. "If you'll do the honors—" He opened the box and lifted out a large lump of chalk. Quickly he rubbed it across the stone's facing. The surface was badly weathered in spots, and spalled. His hand was trembling with cold. The name came up *Hannah*. And *Tull* came up. "No Y?" asked the curate of the stone. "Come now, a Y." But the chalk failed to reveal it. "Oh, well. It is undoubtedly Mrs. Tully." The chalk exposed the dates: 1740–1808.

He stepped over to the other stone and set to rubbing it. Willow watched attentively and the freight rain rolled faster through the valley.

The chalk revealed the name, Henry Tully, and the dates, 1728–1811. No further legend on either stone.

Willow looked at the chalked areas of the two stones, then at the shivering, patient curate.

He'd found the graves that had eluded Ian McMurray. He wondered if he'd find the will.

10

The night sky was framed in a hinged square eave window. From his bed in the inn, Willow watched the black clouds rolling in from the northeast, gradually covering the stars. The wind had picked up noticeably and the temperature was below zero.

Willow lay awake, staring, waiting for sleep. He considered going back downstairs to the tavern to have another scotch by the fire, to watch away the embers crumbling through the grate.

He sighed and looked at his watch. It would be so easy to get up and drive directly to Kennedy. To fly home. Fly home to England. Six hours' flight time home. Instead he'd be up in the morning and out on the frozen roadway to search for Tully's will. Then on and on beyond that until he'd found his man, a living, breathing contemporary human who lay somewhere right now in a bed, sleeping.

Willow hoped deeply that his quest would fail.

CHAPTER IV

On the windy steps of the Surrogate's Court for Orange County, a man stood shivering in a heavy overcoat. His breath came in pale puffs of vapor; his hair turned and twisted as he moved his freezing head in the wind. He looked at his wristwatch; then, cupping his hands over his ears, he scowled up the street.

Willow stepped briskly past him and entered the courthouse lobby. Behind a counter, the information clerk sat at her desk with a sweater over her shoulders watching a maintenance man work on a long radiator.

"May I help you?"

"Yes. I'm tracing a man named Henry Tully who died here in Goshen in 1811. I'd like to see his probate packet if it exists."

She stood up. "Yes. Come through this gate, please.

77

Probate records that old are down in the archives." She smiled. "Anything to get out of the draft. Do you think spring will ever come?"

"Yes," said Willow, smiling. "I'll give you a guarantee in writing."

He followed her down the steps and into a room shelved to the ceiling with heavy, case-bound dockets of wills and intestate records. On a table were the Surrogate Clerk's Indexes to Administration and Estates.

"What was the man's name?"

"Tully. Henry Tully."

"In 1811, you say?"

"Yes."

The woman opened an index, consulted the alphabetic table in the front and picked off the page number and opened to it. "Tully. Tully. Hannah Tully?"

"Yes. His wife. Here. Here's Henry."

The clerk glanced at the liber number, then turned, reading the numbers on the spines along the shelves. "Liber 28. There it is. Both of them are in the same liber."

She reached up and lifted it down—a heavily bound thick volume. "Why don't you sit right there in that chair? If you want to make any photographic copies, I have a machine upstairs. It's twenty-five cents per copy."

Willow nodded at her and eagerly thrust his coat from him in a ball and sat.

"She's on page 214 and he's on page 235," said the clerk. "The entire packet is there."

He only half-heard her steps going up the stairs. He went to Hannah's packet first. Quickly he leafed through the petition for probate of the will dated November 29, 1808, bond of administration, the will itself, notice to creditors, the list of inventory and appraisement, and the

78

decree of distribution. Then he turned back and read the will, scanning the customary legal phrasing, the verbal catchalls and protestations, then the list of species. Here his reading began to slow: Hannah Kirk Gorges Tully left a set of pewterware to a sister in Boston (Mrs. George Bestwick). She singled out her own three children for specific bequests from the goods and chattels of her home. She selected her husband, "the most loving, gentle man ever to tread the earth," as her executor and prayed God to be merciful with her peccant soul. Hannah Kirk Gorges. Kirk her maiden name and Gorges a previous marriage? And a sister? Ian McMurray had indicated that Mrs. Tully had seemingly dropped from the skies historyless.

Willow turned his attention to Henry's probate packet. He riffled the pages to identify the customary documents, noted the letters of administration *cum testamento annexo*, noted that Henry's son, Edwin, from New Haven was appointed the executor, noted the inventory and decree of distribution, then returned to the will.

As with Hannah's will, the clerk had laboriously copied the original document by hand. In the flowing script of the professional copyist, Henry's final wishes unfolded themselves.

It began in standard nomenclature:

"In the name of God the Father in Heaven be it known that this is the last will and testament of Henry Tully of Goshen, Orange County, New York, husband of the late Hannah Kirk Gorges Tully and son of the late Joseph Tully, wine merchant of London, England."

Henry protests his heart's anguish at the separation of his country from its motherland and at the separation of his life and family from "my father, who died with his heart hardened against me and mine for my participation in the late Revolution of the Colonies." He laments, too, the loss of the friendship of his three brothers.

He praises God for the gift of Hannah as his cherished wife. Here, a word caught Willow's eye. A shocking word. Another. Willow stopped, astonished, and reread the sentence.

"But—" he said aloud to the will. He leaned back in the chair and looked around the vault. His eyes returned to the will and finished reading it. He stood up and stared down at the page.

It must be so. Willow reached into his briefcase and pulled out a road map. He needed to get to Boston as quickly as possible.

2

Mrs. Abigail Withers stood in the middle of her empty living room. She had on her heaviest wool hat and her imported tweed coat with the fur collar. Johnny, the terrier, in his plaid cover prowled around her ankles, trailing his leash, whining and sitting, then whining and walking by turns. The canary cage stood on the floor beside her. Inside, the bird moved restlessly, cheeping and trilling. His calls rang hollowly in the empty apartment. The wrecker's bashing ball distantly cannonaded another hole in another brick wall.

Mrs. Withers looked down at the whining dog and the shrilling bird. Abruptly, softly, she wept. Her fingers probed limply into her handbag and withdrew a handkerchief. She balled it and pushed it up under her eyeglasses, dabbed at her nose and sighed.

"Enough of that, you two babies. I told you we'll have

a nice new home soon—just a cab ride away. Now, let's go."

Stooping, she caught the end of the leash, pulled the straps of her dangling handbag up on her forearm, then rose erect with cage and leash. As she stepped toward the doorway, she heard a footfall in the hallway.

"Ah-ha," said Peter Richardson. "Made it! I thought sure I was going to miss you. Couldn't get away from that office phone. So—" He strode around the empty living room. "It's done. I see they've loaded the truck down there. Is that your cab waiting?"

Mrs. Withers looked at him with great solemnity. She wept again.

"Aah ah ah ah ah, Abby." He gripped her arm. "It'll all be as good as new when you get set up." He watched her slowly shaking her head.

"It can never be the same, Peter. I'm too old to take myself in with fables. Once it's broken and done, that's it; broken and done. I feel like this old building. Useless and unneeded, something to be torn down and thrown away."

"Come on, Abby. Bright thoughts."

"It's true," she sighed. "But I'm not crying about that. It's Ozzie. Oh, dear God in heaven, I haven't slept a wink. Where can he be? I'm sure he'd be here to see me off if he were able. I can't help but believe that something's happened to him." She walked about the room, touching the light switches with her fingers, smoothing the fold in an abandoned curtain, softly shutting a closet door. "Something has happened to him."

Richardson listened unhappily. "Ahhh, Abby. He'll turn up."

"Saying doesn't make it so."

She stood in the pale winter light and touched her fingers doubtfully to her lips. "I just can't leave like this."

"Yes, you can. I told you—the minute I have any news I'll call you. And I'll be there for dinner tomorrow night."

She crooked a finger at him. "My phone is already installed. Same number. Don't fail to call."

"I won't. I'll call. I'll call."

The dog whined and the bird fluttered in the swinging cage and Abby Withers seemed disoriented. She looked out at the quadrangle of red-tinged snow roiled across the field. "It's all ending badly. You have no apartment to move to, Ozzie is missing, and his cat—listen, Peter, his cat. I must tell you. She's down in the basement, crying. I tried to get her—oh, any number of times. I brought food down to her. And I think one of the Abernathys' moving men kicked her or something. Listen, Peter, you get that cat and bring her to me. She's alone and confused. Peter, I tell you Ozzie would never leave his cat like that."

"I'll get the cat, Abby. And I'll bring it in a cab. You can keep it until Ozzie turns up . . ."

"And his plants. You'll have to water them. I did them all today. But they need water every five to seven days."

"Yes, yes. Abby. It'll be all right. I'll take care of everything. Come on, now. Pull yourself together. In a few days, you'll be all settled again."

Abby Withers walked slackly to the doorway with her dog and her birdcage and wended her way down the hall, down the stairs, across the lobby to the front door. The dog walked hesitantly by her side, looking upward for directions as he went. She stopped in the lobby. "My God," she exclaimed. "I forgot the cover for the cage. He'll freeze out there." She groped a hand into her bag and pulled out a quilted lump.

Richardson took it from her and draped it around the cage, then knotted the tie strings. "There. He's all set to travel."

Abby Withers reached up and touched his face. "You're a good friend, Peter."

"You ain't seen nothing yet, Abby."

He opened the door for her. "Call me when you get there."

"Yes." Carefully, sideways, she descended the outside steps and entered the cab. The driver shut the door after her, then drove off.

Now, two apartments were empty.

3

Richardson descended the outside steps in the perpetual dusk of the sullen winter day.

Heavily dressed against the weather, he followed the frozen snow prints, followed them again to the middle of the quadrangle where the wind-scoured earth was bald of snow. No tracks. Directly ahead of him the crane stood in the distance. The ball swung on the boom and struck yet again, sending another clatter of building materials to the ground. Plaster dust rose above it and the earth vibrated.

Richardson walked slowly toward the crane. He felt menaced by it, yet fascinated. The ball had eaten halfway through a brick house and store. As he drew closer, he could see the old tin-sheeted ceiling of the store hanging down in broad metal strips. In the rooms above, exposed like underdrawers, were the papered walls of someone's former home. He could see scuff marks from furniture on the wallpaper and square outlines where pictures had hung. A green pull shade still hung halfway down just as it was left, blocking winter's pallid light from an empty and half-gone bedroom.

The cold and loneliness and the architectural slaughter and the never-gone fear in his stomach depressed him. He turned away from the ruins to walk slowly back to the Brevoort House. Soon it too would show the frozen outdoor world of winter the colors and hues and mute marks of life on its papered walls.

Soon the whizzing, chained cannonball would arc down and through Abby's window, carrying all before it, window frame, glass fragments, bricks—and Abby's ghostlike, abandoned curtain, rising high, fluttering softly around the implacable ball.

Richardson saw again the tracks left by Ozzie's feet. He paused to stand staring down at them. Presently he turned to look at the ranks of empty buildings behind him. Where had Ozzie been going?

Richardson turned and watched as the wrecker's ball dropped an entire side of the building into the street in a thunder of noise.

The green shade and its window were gone.

4

Pew had slicked it out. It read as smooth as butter. But there were still flaws in the structure. Richardson sat on his backless stool in the middle of his living room looking down at the thirty-odd pages of manuscript, seeking, groping for a shape.

He shook his head, remembering Pew's words. "Existential man was wombed in a German oven and, born, walked into the world from a concentration camp."

Heeesh. He looked down again at the sheets on the floor, mentally shifting the sequence of elements.

Inappropriately, without preparation, the memory of *Tom Jones* intruded on his thoughts. He sat up, recalling Tom Jones, and was filled with gratitude. Like an old friend, a college days' friend, Tom Jones was there, patient, benevolent, enduring. Not seen or heard from since college days. Squire Allworthy presented himself along with the earthy Squire Western—and Sophia. Sophia and the sunshine and green rain of the eighteenth-century English countryside. How green was his memory of it. He felt a strong desire to read the book.

Richardson left the stool, left the strewn papers and crouched before a bookcase. He found it and pulled it out. He looked for a place to sit. Wine. A glass of wine. Wine? Port. Why port? He went to his liquor cabinet and poked among the bottles. Sherry. Riesling. Burgundy. Port. Never opened. Port? Come on. Yes, port.

Richardson pulled the cork and poured a glass of port. Then he sat down with the wine at his elbow and opened the pages of *Tom Jones*.

He took a gratifying sip of wine.

"My God," he said aloud. "I'm pregnant."

5

It was astonishing. He found he could quote with near accuracy a number of passages of the novel. He recalled with great vividness Blifil's episode with the bird, Squire Allworthy's great sickness and Tom's drunken screed. And Fielding's salty, sane disquisitions on Tom and London and life. A man who didn't squint at human nature and didn't lament. Balance.

Richardson wondered how he had acquired such a vivid memory of the book. He read passages with great enjoyment, skipping from section to section. When he looked up, he found that he'd nearly finished the wine. He recalled Goulart's cat and decided to go down and get it from the basement.

He rose, puzzled. It seemed as though there was a third element missing—the book and the port and something else. What was it he couldn't quite remember? He felt as though he could reach his arm into a dark tunnel and touch it—the thing forgotten. But he didn't—didn't reach, didn't remember. He didn't remember because . . .

He didn't remember because he was afraid to.

6

Abby's front door was shadowed. He felt the emptiness behind it. As he descended, he passed Clabber's silent door and Goulart's; next, Griselda's. On the first floor he heard a radio in the Carsons' apartment, then stepped past the Abernathys' vacant apartment. He opened the door to the basement and snapped on the lights. He stood at the head of the stairs and listened. Hearing no sound, he descended and looked at the wooden bins.

"Here, puss," he called. No sound. Under pale rafter lights he walked slowly down the corridor between the bins. "Here, puss." At the end of the corridor was a door and he opened it. A large room, empty, with an exit door at the side wall. No cat. He pushed the door to and turned. "Here, puss."

Goulart's cat appeared. She stood at the other end of the corridor, at the foot of the stairs. She mewed softly.

"Here, puss." Richardson walked slowly toward her. He got closer. "Okay, puss, just hold still."

But she didn't. She sprang up four or five steps, then leaped through the boards of a tenant bin. Richardson opened the bin door. "Come on, puss." He saw her eyes that glowed yellow for a moment before she stepped off the back of a couch and ghosted away.

Richardson tried for fifteen minutes to get the cat. Then he mounted the gritty stairs to the top and turned. "When you get good and hungry, I'll be back," he said. He put out the light and shut the door behind him.

The silence and the darkness stole back up the cellar stairs and waited.

7

Whoosh!

Richardson opened his eyes.

He was in the wingback chair. *Tom Jones* had slipped to his lap. Arrayed around the chair on the floor were the sheets of manuscript.

The sound had occurred right in front of him, right in front of his face, right in the middle of the living room. He stood up urgently and the novel tumbled to the floor. Lights were on throughout his apartment. He quickly strode through the rooms. It was two-thirty.

He was alone.

Richardson felt beset, tormented. It was an hallucination. Had to be. Someone was doing this to him. Minute doses of an hallucinatory drug in his food. Seizing the bottle of port, he carried it to the kitchen. He poured the remaining liquid down the drain. He opened the door to his refrigerator and studied the interior. He threw away a jar of mustard. A jar of ketchup. Mayonnaise. Jam. Salad oil. Pickles. He filled his kitchen wastebasket. A box of salt. All his sugar. Pepper. Flour. Coffee. Tea. Several paper sacks were filled. He went to the bathroom cabinet and got his toothpaste. Then he sat down on the wing-back chair and stared at the frozen darkness outside his window, expectantly, patiently, like a man waiting for someone.

8

At nine A.M., Richardson called a medical center and made an appointment for a thorough physical examination, including his ears.

"I particularly want tests to determine the presence of any drugs in my body."

9

He found her legs lovely.

They were long and slim. Symmetrical. And her personality was altogether "right." Her face proclaimed it, the sly mirth in her eyes flashed it. Willow could easily place her in the cockpit of his sailboat beating into port under a squall, her face and hair rain-rilled. She had merriness lurking about her eyes and a sense of—of humor, and more, of absurdity. Willow wanted to try to make her laugh, wanted to hear her laugh. If her laughter tinkled, if it trilled and rippled, if it struck no false notes, no artificial construction—ah then, if it rang, he was had. Set. Taken. She'd own him.

She stood pondering a file folder, stood in front of the

very large arched window of the Hammett townhouse, stood with a halo of hair lit by the pale winter light. Light through the mullioned branches of the bare trees.

She glanced doubtfully at him and returned to the desk where he sat. "This is the genealogical chart of the Tully family in New Haven and the collateral lines."

"I'm familiar with that, Miss Polsley. I'm more interested in what you have on Joseph Tully's son, Roger."

Miss Polsley studied his face doubtfully. "Mrs. Hammett would be more cooperative, Mr. Willow, I'm sure, if you'd be more explicit about your reasons for studying her family tree. To be quite honest, Mr. Willow, I think you may have more information than she does."

"Oh? Well. You mean you have nothing on Roger."

"Very little, I'm afraid."

"Strange. He's a collateral line to Henry. His brother, in fact."

"Well, it seems he wandered off into Connecticut and wasn't heard from again. There was a falling-out among the brothers over the Revolution."

"And the other two brothers . . ."

"Ah, yes, well. Mr. Willow, what did you say was the reason you—"

"Miss Polsley. In this business of genealogy, information is the currency. It's the medium of exchange, the barter material. Now it's swaps-time. You tell me something and I tell you something. You see? But Mrs. Hammett has no stock to trade with. No information. She's not in the game. Shall I hint darkly at family secrets she doesn't know about? What will I get in return?"

Alice Polsley studied his eyes and suppressed a grin. "You're a very clever fellow, Mr. Willow."

"No, Miss Polsley. I'm not. I'm a simple-headed man

and I look at your legs and do you know the only word that occurs to me?"

Miss Polsley was shocked. Embarrassed. She stepped behind the table. "Legs?"

"Yes. Legs. I look at your legs and all I can think of is one word."

She frowned fearfully at him.

"Seaworthy."

"Seaworthy!" She put two hands over a child's grin.

Don't laugh. If she laughs, I'm done for.

10

"Culper, Jr.," he echoed politely, looking at her eyes. They looked back at him over the large menu card.

"Yes. An American spy. That was his code name: Culper, Jr. He was a member of the Townsend family in Oyster Bay and he was a spy for George Washington. The British officers lived right in his home. Any information he got was rowed across Long Island Sound to Connecticut, then carried to General Washington."

"Hmmmm. And he was an ancestor of yours?"

"Yes. It'll make a wonderful biography. I've been working on it for five years."

Willow shook his head. "I know this story from somewhere."

"James Fenimore Cooper."

"Right! Of course! *The Spy.*"

"You read it."

"Absolutely. And now I remember it clearly. I was fourteen, I think. And I read it in a bunkhouse in Wyoming."

"Wyoming!"

"Yes. You wanted me to say I'd read it in an ivy-covered castle overlooking a British moor?"

"Wyoming?"

"Sorry. But I spent my summers in Wyoming right through college."

"In a bunkhouse? A British cowboy." She smiled at him in disbelief.

"It's true." He held up a pledging hand. "Relatives on my mother's side. They own a vast ranch in Wyoming. Have you ever been to Wyoming, Alice Polsley?"

"Yes. But it's hard to believe that you—"

"I did. I did. In fact, for one whole summer, I was an apprentice blacksmith. Jeans, boots, ten-gallon hat and a leather apron. I must have shod half the horses in the state. Before the end of the summer, I was graduated to ranch tools and implements. I could take a piece of cold steel, heat it and make nails, files, harrowing blades, metal fence straps, barndoor latches, horseshoes—you name it. I'll make you a three-penny nail sometime."

She put down the menu, put her arms on the table-cloth and leaned forward. She watched him solemnly. "What's it like—a ranch in Wyoming?"

"Well, the first time I saw the ranch, I wanted to hide somewhere."

"Oh? Why?"

"Well, the ranch was in a basin between three mountains—a vast bowl of grass. And the sky overhead has no end. And the clouds are like whipped cream and enormous. The whole feeling is one of incredible immensity, of limitless height and breadth. I felt two inches high and terribly exposed."

"Now I believe you. That's Wyoming. Are you a genealogist by profession?"

Willow clasped his hands in front of him on the table. "Okay, back to business."

"No. Please don't answer if—"

"I'm a lawyer."

"Oh." She looked at him for a moment. "I see. You're settling an estate?" She tilted her head at him quizzically. She did that with each question and he liked it.

"Something like that. You know, Mrs. Hammett has a lot of people impressed with her dedication to genealogy."

"Oh, yes. Very active woman, Mrs. Hammett. And very conscious of her background and social position."

"Yes, I gathered that in my telephone conversation with her."

"She would have loved to meet you."

"Oh?"

"She loves the English. She—ahh"—Alice Polsley paused, weighing the expression on Willow's face—"well, she thinks all well-spoken Englishmen are lords. But you—well, you were evasive, and Mrs. Hammett doesn't approve of that."

"The evasiveness, you mean?"

"No. The threat."

"What threat is that?"

"Well, you see, as a member of the Federalist Dames of the Revolution, she is obliged to open her historical and genealogical archives to any bona fide research effort. But if the researcher refuses to divulge the purpose, then she gets doubtful and aloof. She is always concerned that her credentials will be challenged."

"Why? Is she doubtful about their authenticity?"

"Oh no. She believed in her genealogical credentials even before they were proven. No, that's not her problem.

You see, Mrs. Hammett has a very high opinion of herself. She works very diligently to create her superiority in the minds of other people. If someone found a defect in her pedigree, she'd lose face among inferior people."

"My God. How did you ever manage to get a position with her?"

"Oh. Genealogy, to be sure. The Townsends are very 'American Revolution.' *The Spy,* Richard Townsend, and then there was the chain that was forged and stretched across the river to block the British fleet. Another Townsend family opus."

"Okay. You qualified."

"Yes. At least at the personal-secretary level. I think that the best example of her patrician attitude occurred last spring. I arrived for work one morning and had a number of papers that required her husband's signature. And Mrs. Hammett told me"—Alice Polsley elevated her face and crooned in a fruity voice—" 'Mr. Hammett shan't be in today. He's on jury duty.' " She paused. " 'Grand Jury, to be sure.' "

Willow chuckled. "Oh marvelous. You've taken her off in three sentences." He studied her face for a moment. "Alice Polsley, you and I are going to have a private little laugh at Mrs. Hammett's expense."

Her smile dropped and she frowned. She looked at him dubiously. "Mr. Willow. I may have gone a little too far in my comments about Mrs. Hammett. I didn't mean to maliciously ridicule her."

"Ridicule is not what I'm suggesting, Miss Polsley. I live in a country where genealogy is a disease—where utterly worthless people, the shabbiest creatures that God ever made, walk about swollen with self-praise because of their potty little genealogies. No, I wasn't suggesting a back-ripping episode. But I would like to tell you an amusing tale about Mrs. Hammett's family tree. I have to share it with someone discreet, someone with an appreciation for the ridiculous."

Alice Polsley frowned. "Ridiculous?"

"Yes. Did you ever hear of Alexander Gorges?"

"Oh, of course. He published a Loyalist newspaper in New York during the Revolution."

"Yes. That's the one. Well, he originally came from Boston, a printer's devil. This is fresh information. None of his biographies give any inkling of it. As was the custom of the day, he lived with a printer and worked in the print shop in return for room and board. When he was sixteen, he found himself betrothed to the printer's daughter, a very pretty girl of fifteen. In fact, there's good reason to suppose that he had to marry her. It was the custom of the time for parents of a marriageable daughter to look the other way at appropriate moments. The need for haste eliminated arguments about dowries. In any case, Gorges found himself the father of three sons before he was twenty."

"Oh, my heavens."

"That must be what Gorges said, because he fled. Left his wife, his apprenticeship, his employer and his three wee ones. He disappeared for two years, then appeared in New York City and soon had his own printing business. Shortly thereafter, he began a newspaper. I suppose you know the rest."

"He was bitterly hated by the Revolutionists. He was the most ardent Loyalist in the colonies."

"A noble patriot, loyal to his king," said Willow.

"Patriot!" She looked at him with surprise, then comprehension. "Oh. English patriot." She considered for a moment. "If what you're saying is true, then you've opened up a new area of biography on Gorges. It's a major development."

"Miss Polsley, as they say west of the Pecos, you ain't heard nothing yet. *Attendez:* After Gorges debouched, his wife waited the prescribed seven years and filed a petition with the court to have him declared legally dead, which was done."

"You mean the people in Boston never connected the New York Loyalist with—"

"Later, Mrs. Gorges did, but then . . . well. You see, Mrs. Gorges, now legally a widow, married again. Then she discovered that her first husband was alive and, in her eyes, notorious. By this time the Revolution was on, and she protected herself and her family in two ways: she gave the boys the name of her second husband, and she moved out of Boston. Now, are you ready for the big news?"

"Yes. I'm ready."

"Mrs. Gorges's second husband was—"

"Tully! Henry Tully!"

"Yes. Those three boys are not his sons. They're Gorges's sons." Willow pulled a packet of papers from his inside coat pocket. He unfolded the topmost sheet. "This is Henry Tully's will—certified copy." He pointed to a sentence in it. She read . . .

"—having been denied the natural issue of my body, I rejoice in the sons of my wife who were like true sons to me and to whom with great pride I lent my father's name—Tully."

Alice Polsley sat back and studied Willow's face, astonished. "That means that Mrs. Hammett is not a descendant of an American patriot. She's the descendant of an anti-Revolutionary Loyalist fanatic."

"Yes."

Alice Polsley laughed.

Across the table, thence throughout the dining room, merrily her laughter tinkled.

11

TO: Matthew Willow

Mr. Willow. I have taken the liberty of excerpting a rather longish piece from the private and hitherto unpublished papers of Peter Pounell, who, as you are well aware, was a King's Magistrate at the time of Joseph Tully's death. I have excised only those passages that are clearly digressions. The whole matter would have passed unnoticed, as your reading will discover to you, had not Pounell conceived a strange interest in Mad Tom, an itinerant and harmless thread seller—and probably a thoroughly unreliable witness. Mad Tom was the only witness to Tully's death, and only a curio collector like Pounell would have bothered to note down his incoherent testimony. Mad Tom merited his name—but read for yourself.

J.H.

Notes excerpted from the unpublished papers of Peter Pounell, King's Magistrate, pertaining to the sudden death of Joseph Tully, London, England, February 19, 1799:

I feel obliged to discourse at length on a peculiar set of occurrences that took place this evening a short walk from my very door.

Joseph Tully, a wine merchant of this city and a gentleman who has held public office on occasion, who has been honored from time to time by his fellow citizens and merchants for his many acts of public weal and goodwill, fell dead this night in his doorway.

Mr. Tully being a very aged person, some averring him to be in excess of seventy-five years on this earth, to be stricken so suddenly would merit no great notice. Indeed, his commodious home lying above his warehouse wherein he was wont to store his spirits and vintages, the descent of the stairs alone might engender that extreme splenetic condition that would induce stroke and, concomitantly, death.

Yet due to the lateness of the hour and the vileness of the weather—fog with freezing needles of ice and very uncertain footing—no one was abroad to bear witness to the event except the indigent thread seller and ward of the church, Mad Tom.

I summarize his testimony for the virtue of brevity, admonishing he who reads these private journals to keep in mind that Mad Tom is blind in one eye, senile, mentally incompetent, being able to neither read nor write. All these attributes would render his words utterly worthless except for the vigor with which he delivers them. Indeed, he repeats the tale without variation to any who will listen. I suggest that something happened in the doorway of Joseph Tully that may never be explained to us.

This evening, Mad Tom was afoot and with the aid of his staff, finding his way to his bed. He heard whilst still a distance from Tully's residence and out of sight around a corner—heard a sharp pounding on Tully's door. As he approached, he heard Tully's door open, then a great gagging sound. A moment later he haled into view of the doorway and he perceived Mr. Tully prone upon the doorsill, his arms hanging out into the cobbled street.

Mad Tom further states that he saw an angel in a long cloak bearing a flaming sword round a corner, slowly rising heavenward.

No amount of interrogation will sway Mad Tom from his description of this picture of an angel, wearing an English gentleman's boot cloak and bearing before him the flaming sword of the Lord.

Matthew Willow stared thoughtfully at the excerpt, then laid it aside. He looked up at the large area of construction paper fixed to the wall between the two windows. There were still five names at the top:

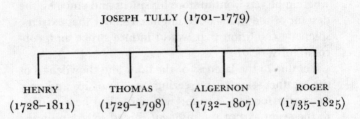

JOSEPH TULLY (1701–1779)

HENRY (1728–1811)   THOMAS (1729–1798)   ALGERNON (1732–1807)   ROGER (1735–1825)

He stared at the name Roger for a moment, then extracted a file from the desk drawer. The tab read: "Roger Tully 1735–1825." He riffled the pages in the folder thoughtfully, then climbed the stepladder to the top of the wall poster.

He drew a line through Henry's name, with the initials: N.I.

No issue.

He turned his attention now to the youngest son.

Roger.

CHAPTER V

Richardson waited.

He sat slumped on the examining table in an unironed lumpish surgical gown, his dignity crumpled, his confidence shattered, feeling his heart throbbing rapidly, feeling the never-gone cold spot of fear in his gut. He rubbed wet palms together. Seeing a vein beating in his arm, he watched it with foreboding. Time. Life. Going. He raised his eyes.

Doctor Edward Eddy, brain surgeon, sat reading reports. He sat amidst his medical paraphernalia, a latter-day alchemist, shaman, soothsayer, a transistorized warlock, surrounded by the impedimenta of the physician's trade, a collection of shiny junk calculated to lull the patient and to conceal medicine's bottomless ignorance.

Deft surgical fingers lifted thin sheets of medical information on a clipboard. Once, he glanced significantly at Richardson.

Traffic sounds from the street were far away. Richardson turned his head and looked out through a cleft in the fluted white curtains. He saw cars moving in the street, saw streams of pedestrians crossing at the light. Immortal, remote, filled with other concerns, the immemorial people of the world, bundled snugly against the winter and hurrying to places of warmth and sanctuary.

A woman crossed. She was striking, well dressed; she guided a little girl in quilted garments. From a small child's cap, a wisp of hair protruded and undulated like a merry banner. The child half-skipped, half-hopped eagerly, holding her mother's hand. At the corner, she hurried to a man who picked her up and hugged her. The three moved quickly, happily down the street, impelled by the cold, the little pennant of hair fluttering in the wind. He felt overwhelming pity for the little girl. Richardson looked again down at his arms, reading eternity in his pulse beat.

He wiped wet hands on his surgical gown. So far, it had been altogether like a scavenger hunt, traipsing along shining corridors from medical station to medical station, in disposable slippers and ugly gown, an ambulating problem in medical chemistry. He had followed that menacing and slowly fattening clipboard and was followed by growing apprehension. Like a piece in a game board controlled by the roll of dice. Advance three squares to urology, proctology, cardiology, hematology, specialty after specialty.

If I survive, yea, if I survive this, if I'm granted a stay of execution, I'm going to change the way I strut my stuff. Hear me, stupid: I'm going to take my dragging little butt down to Absegami Camper's Supply and outfit myself for a walk across Death Valley. Yes. I'm going to outfit myself right and do it right. I want the best hiking boots. Pivettas from Italy, you bet your blue booties. Wool socks with ten percent nylon, and with heels and toes forty percent nylon. A new Trailwise packframe. Yes. That new number, 502, with single nylon mesh instead of the double bands, with the three-inch-wide yoke and padding plus the wide waist belt. For a stove, I want a new Svea number 123. And that Wilderness Tent from Sierra Designs with the nylon fly sheet. I'll make a new Colin Fletcher hiking staff. Bamboo, fifty-four inches long. Diameter just right for the hand, an inch and three eighths. Yes. Exactly. Banded with rip-stop tape, top and bottom. Bamboo for lightness. Find one in a carpet store when they unroll new shipments of rugs. A new hat, leather, Anzac style. Lightweight, loose-fitting, oversize cotton shirts, three-quarter-length sleeves, porous. Water caches placed strategically across the desert floor beforehand. Yes. Sealed and concealed. And for food, ah, let's see . . .

A long, patrician finger beckoned to him. "Please have a seat, Mr. Richardson."

Richardson shuffled across the floor, feeling like a sick patient. He was definitely dying. Dr. Eddy's eyes told him that. He was filled with despair. Medical center: a place where the well are made sick. This man could save him. He was not alone: here was a friend. He was eager to trust Dr. Edward Eddy implicitly, grateful for such a champion during his battle with death.

He sat. That he was to die was clear; what he was to die from would now be related. Medicine: a primitive art of identifying the cause of death.

"I see from your questionnaire, Mr. Richardson, that you indicate a concern over the possible presence of a brain tumor." A washed white finger tapped the paper. "We have done a number of tests on you today which will tell me a great deal about the conditions inside your skull. They're not completed yet, so I cannot make any kind of judgment. Now, there is a series of other tests I can give you if any of the preliminary tests show up positive. If they return negative, further testing should be superfluous. This auditory hallucination you report I find interesting. Its locus, you say, is internal. Are you sure it isn't supported by visual hallucinating? A tumor can place considerable pressure on the brain. It can cause severe headaches, blacking out; can press eyes out of focus, cause loss of balance, create ringing in the ears as well as create symptoms in all other parts of the body. If you have any symptoms, I want to know them immediately. Now, you left a question mark in this box. You don't know whether there's a history of brain tumors in your family? No. How about mental aberrations, psychosis, mental incompetence?"

"I don't know. Should I find out?"

"Yes. Find out." Dr. Eddy sat back. "You can get dressed now."

2

His name was Abel Navarre and he was a detective, Police Department, City of New York. He sat in a car at the curb in front of the Brevoort House and watched the crane smash its way through a block of buildings.

When Richardson came up the street, Navarre stepped from his car and nodded at him.

"Mr. Richardson?"

Richardson nodded back.

"Sorry I had to pull you out of your office." Navarre slammed his car door and opened a small leather folder to show his police identity card. "I'm Abel Navarre."

Richardson nodded at him.

"Now, you understand that I have no search warrant with me. I'm being admitted to his apartment at your invitation and in your presence. I'm just going to take a look around to see if I can find an indication of his whereabouts."

"I understand."

"Chances are I won't find a thing that'll tell us anything. If he follows the pattern, he'll turn up in a day or two himself."

"I'll get the key."

Navarre nodded. "Looks like snow," he said.

3

Navarre sat down heavily in Goulart's chair and smoothed a sheet of layout paper. He looked up at the skylight over his head. "Light," he said. "Lots of light on a cloudy day." He glanced through the window at the crane. "Front-row seat." He opened a few drawers in the taboret, glancing at the felt pens, brushes, and art supplies. He looked around the room at the throngs of plants. He rubbed a hand over his beard-dark muzzle, thinking, ingesting a sense of place, trying to get the feel of the absent owner.

He got up at last and walked about the apartment. "A plant nut," he murmured. "Where did he get them all?"

Richardson sat down on a bench next to one of the

plants. "Well, a couple of years ago he was commissioned to do a series of illustrations for a botany textbook. So he went out and bought these plants. When the job was finished, the plants just stayed on and multiplied."

Navarre opened a closet door slowly and peered in. His hand brushed back a few garments hanging inside. Then he scanned the shelf and the closet floor. He strolled next into the kitchen. More plants. He snorted. "If we were in a joking mood, I'd say the plants drove him out of here." He turned back to Richardson. "But we're not in a joking mood." He walked his massive bulk back to Goulart's chair and sat in it. "I would guess this man was big and bulky—like me."

"Was?"

"Is, was. He must have been over six-four and ran maybe two thirty, two fifty."

"How can you tell that?"

"The clothes in the closet. Neck size. Jackets. Shoes. The bed, the height of this chair off the ground, the height of his drawing board. An exceptionally large man." He raised his eyes to Richardson. "I have very little to go on. There's a tenant in the building—Clabber's his name. I talked to him and he's filled with some strange ideas. He says that Goulart was messing around with the spirit world. What is it? Occult?"

Richardson sighed irritably. "I got my ear filled with that the other night from Clabber."

Navarre had unwavering eyes. They rested, staring, on Richardson's face. "What do you know about it?"

"Nothing. Not a thing."

"This Goulart never mentioned anything to you about it?"

"Not a boo."

"You two guys were buddies."

"Yeah."

"Goulart never married?"

"No."

"Are you?"

"Was."

"Oh. Divorced?"

"Yes."

"Your wife—she grew up over there, too?"

"Yes."

"Well, if Goulart was involved with ghosts or spirits or whatever, it figures that he would have mentioned something to you. Wouldn't you say?"

Richardson shrugged. "I think we managed to stay good friends because we never crowded each other."

"Meaning—"

"Meaning he had a private life of his own that I didn't nose too much into."

Navarre stared at him at length. "You notice any moodiness lately?"

"Yes. He was moody at times lately. Sometimes I would find him just sitting and looking at me. I got the feeling on a number of occasions that he wanted to say something."

"But he didn't."

"No."

"You have any idea where he might be?"

"No. The snow is pretty well gone, but I followed some tracks the day after he disappeared. I was sure they were his."

"Tracks?"

"Yes. I followed them out into the middle of those empty lots and they disappeared. The snow was all blown away out there."

Navarre looked out. "Could he have gone back to his old house?"

"It's down. And it was over this way, anyway."

"Oh. Are you sick?"

"Huh?"

"Sick. When I called, you were out to the doctor's."

"No. I was getting a physical."

"Oh. Why?"

Richardson looked at the unwavering eyes. "Navarre. I'm not missing or lost. I'm sitting right here looking at you."

"Uh-huh. Okay. You want to take a guess why Goulart was moody lately?"

"No. But he was and that was unusual."

"That's what his sister said."

"Patty? You talked to her?"

Navarre looked at him. "She was the one who reported him missing."

4

The wind was raw and wet. It blew in from the south off the Sound up through the trees and across the bald brow of the hill. The old snow lay decaying in streaks along the gullied shoulders of the road and amongst the thicket of dead stalks under the trees. The lowering sky and the biting wind promised more snow—a driving, wind-borne, fine-grained snow.

The local Connecticut historian, Mr. Morrow, read the familiar weather signs and pressed his thin bones further into his overcoat. He bowed his behatted head into the wind and walked away from the car with Matthew Willow.

Their leather-soled shoes crunched on the gravel and snow-ice of the old country lane.

"The church was built in 1731. It was damaged by lightning in 1758 and restored. That's when they added the extra benches. There's good evidence to indicate that the cemetery was established first, probably as early as 1728."

Willow walked at Mr. Morrow's slow pace, smelling the impending snow in the wind. They turned at the break in the wall of forsythia and entered the cemetery.

"Few people come here now. Rarely used. One burial six years ago."

At the top of the rising, beyond the cemetery, stood the church. Gaunt, narrow, with an elongated steeple and narrow windows, it bespoke an austerity of mind.

"Termites," said Mr. Morrow, pointing at the church. "Abandoned now. There was a movement to restore it and use it, but when the estimates came in, the preservation committee quietly disappeared." Mr. Morrow smiled with perfect dentures. "Seen it happen many times. The price of preserving the past puts too much of a burden on the present."

"Tell me about Roger Tully's family," said Willow.

"Hmmmm. Yes. Tully. You know, sometimes it's difficult to identify with the past. I have read many old court records where the amount at issue is so trifling that the litigation seems silly. These old colonists bickered over small things which it turns out aren't so small. A barrel of nails, for example. Someday you and I will sit down in front of a couple of hot toddies and I'll tell you a story about a barrel of English nails that nearly tore this county apart. But now, back to Tully. You can identify with this. I've stood here in this cemetery and pondered those graves many a time. I wonder how he kept from going mad." Mr. Morrow gripped Willow's arm and led him to the left at a deliberate pace while drawing breath through a round O of a mouth. He stopped without warning and Willow found a row of graves before him.

"Eight of them. Mother and seven children. The stones are somewhat weathered, but I know the names by heart anyway."

With his eyes, Willow counted the graves. A table stone and seven small markers with first names.

"The mother, Elspeth," murmured Mr. Willow. "Her father was a farmer and a lawyer. Few miles from here. Tully married her in 1763 and built her a house on the next hill beyond the church. In February of 1779, Tully was in a bad way financially. The war was on and trade with Europe was nonexistent. Must have been rough on him. This Englishman and mercantilist was forced to farm with his bare hands, practically, waiting for the war to end so that he could get back into trade and prosperity. That February of 1779, he went up to Providence on some kind of business, and while he was gone his oldest"—Mr. Morrow shook a foot at the grave next to Elspeth's—"Roger, Jr.—he was fifteen and in charge of the family. They had a windstorm one night—I've seen so many of them roll off that Sound out there—and that was the night the Tully fireplace decided to have a fire in the chimney above the flue. Flames came out of the chimney and set fire to the cedar shake roof, and the high wind did the rest. Before the family was even aware, the wind had blown the flames down the roof and down the side of the building and—*poof!*—there it was, a raging fire and no way out of the building. The fire was so ferocious that the bodies were practically char. I'll bet you that there was some doubt as to identities among these seven kids."

Willow looked at the last headstone and did some mental arithmetic.

"Three," said Mr. Morrow, watching him. "She was three. After naming her children after every relative in the country, Elspeth gave her own name to this one. And they say she was the spit of her mother. A lively blue-eyed little girl."

Willow looked away unhappily at the church on the brow of the hill.

"Imagine how he felt," said Mr. Morrow. "Riding over that knob of land there and looking for his house on the spine and not seeing it. Then the second look and seeing only the chimney. And nothing else."

And nothing else.

"The minister of the church had been watching for days for Tully, and when he saw him, he went running down the hill to him. How Tully ever survived what the minister told him I'll never know."

Willow saw the minister running. Saw the minister gripping the horse's mane and gasping for breath, struggling to give the man the information.

"All dead?"

"Yes, Mr. Tully."

"All?"

"Yes, Mr. Tully. All."

"But—"

But. Willow looked down at the grave of the very least one. Spit of her mother. Elspeth. 1776–1779.

Surely, the fire could have spared one. She was barely a morsel worthy of the flame's attention. Her hair would have made a mere spark. The small bones—still a baby. And the merry eyes of her mother. Eyes that Roger Tully recalled later in a rare letter—eyes that echoed her mother as a young woman, newly married, pregnant with her first child. Dancing blue eyes. Never to dance again. No more. No more. No more.

Willow stared at Long Island Sound, looked back along the road where Roger Tully's feet had shambled down to the pier, back to England—shuffled out of history to a room in London, there to gnaw a knuckle and stare his days away. The fire's ninth casualty.

How did he survive that conversation with the minister?

Willow turned away from the graves and walked slowly back toward the cemetery gate. Genealogy: an instructive and fun-filled pastime for the whole family.

At the car he said, "Could there have been any offspring of the children?"

"Oh, I hardly—ah, no. No no. All the children were at home. Roger, Jr., as I say, was just fifteen. The second, Joseph, barely fourteen. No no."

"I understand that families with marriageable daughters were not averse to having young men climb into bedroom windows."

"Oh yes, young men capable of supporting a family. But no farmer in his right mind would let a fifteen-year-old boy—no. No. I hardly think so, Mr. Willow. Hardly think so.'"

Willow saw the first grains of snowfall fly across the field of the cemetery. He looked down the road that led to town, to a pier, to merchantman windship, to London and lonely last years for Roger Tully.

The road was empty and filling with snow.

5

The windshield wipers flogged back and forth, back and forth, wiping away the grains of snow. The snow morseled a white covering across the land.

Willow drove onto a shoulder and stopped to read his map. Crystals of snow chattered lightly on the steel shell of the car. He could see clouds of it blowing languidly before him. The least one—a frozen grave. Another winter of snow tapping on the gravestones, filling the cemetery under a freezing moaning wind.

Cut and go home. Yes. Now. Forget death. Remember, oh remember the booming wind in the Channel, the tumbling seas, sea rime and banging, flying spume, the resonant humming of the rigging, the canted mast and deck and the swollen sails and the seething wind. Remember, oh eejit, remember, in your ears the roar of it all, the rhythmical banging and creaking of the sailboat, the seething sizzle of the surf, rolling under the Freeboard line. The hand on the wheel, the eyes going from the compass to the luff of sail, to the compass. Hold her, hold her steady just at the luff point. Sailing on a tilted sea. Just you and the swollen circle of horizon on a limitless sea.

Look at the water, the black-green water, look—see? and where it's swollen and stretched and humpbacked. Aqua and paler green where the great shafts of sunlight falling through the tumbling masses of incredibly high clouds light the crests of the swells. And everywhere like albino vines, the trails of sea foam. Smell the salt and fish rot in the air, enough to intoxicate you for life.

Exultant. Alive. In the wild world of the Channel. Remember life. Remember and go home. Now. Away from here.

Willow raised his head and looked through the rilling windshield of snow-melt. No. I'll find him. I'll see the game out.

And sail no more?   •

6

At five o'clock, Dr. Martin of the Medical Center called Richardson's office.

"This is unofficial, of course. I'll go over your report in detail with you later. But I know you were concerned and I thought you'd like to know that with almost all of yesterday's tests completed, you're as healthy as a horse. No evidence of any drugs in your system. No reason to suspect a brain tumor. Nothing wrong with your ears. Nothing. The only comment I find is from Dr. Asher himself. He notes that you catch cold easily and may need a vitamin supplement."

Richardson capered, a broken-ankle vaudeville routine, then rooted through his desk files and pulled out a folder on a new bright-orange backpack. A six-weeker this time. Pew could run things. A week—say two—to plan everything. Find an apartment to dump his furniture into. Death Valley in February or early March at the latest. Great, great. He'd do it. Do it.

Then he stopped. Ozzie was still missing.

And the sound was still unexplained.

7

"Deductive reasoning, Richardson." said Christopher Carson, shaking snow from his coat. He tapped his newspaper lightly on the jamb, spraying the floor with grains of snow. "You can have deductive reasoning, inductive reasoning, or a combination of both. There are no other valid scientific ways of thinking. And deductive is your method, the technique of the scientific detective."

He stood in the vestibule of the Brevoort House, watching two men lug a couch down the main stairs. It was broadly banded in black and white.

"Zebra stripes," said Carson absently. He looked again at Richardson. "Deductive reasoning is also called the process of elimination. You find out what it is by finding out what it isn't. What's left is the culprit."

"Tell that to Clabber," said Richardson.

"Clabber! Listen, Pete, that guy is something that lives under a rock. I'm not sure he's human—and I know he's not rational. Look, you know your problem isn't physical, from the medical report. So now look for an outside agency—hidden microphones, tape recorders . . . something tangible and real—"

"—like spirits or hypnosis."

"Pete, stay away from that Grand Inquisitor. He's a loser, something chased out of the Catholic Church with a stick. He's an unfrocked priest—did you know that? A dim-witted crackpot heretic. Look." Carson turned to him. "Your emotional house has to be showing some kind of strain. You just had a divorce. The house you were born in is torn down, the neighborhood you grew up in is a pile of bricks somewhere. And Goulart's missing. In a few steps, you've lost your childhood, your history, your wife and your best friend. And you're living alone and hearing things. No, God damn. You've got to show the strain of all that somewhere even if it's only a tic in one eye. Anybody would wake up screaming." He gripped Richardson's arm. "You take a plane to Florida and lie on a beach. Bring a girlfriend. And I'll guarantee you all your symptoms will disappear. Provided—"

"Provided what?"

"Provided you stay away from that Clabber and all those ghost stories that he lifted from Boy Scout council fires."

Richardson shrugged.

"Pete. You're a victim of modern life. Period."

Richardson nodded and smiled wearily.

"So help me God, if I thought there was the slightest chance that the Clabbers and the Quists were right, I'd be on my knees right now—twenty-four hours a day."

The two moving men got the couch past the turning in the stairs and descended with deliberateness like two mechanical men synchronized to the same rhythm. They rested the couch on the tiled floor of the lobby, and one of the men opened the door. An avalanche of freezing air filled the lobby. Crisp crystals of snow hissed as they hit the outside step.

"Well, me for a warm tuxedo," said Carson. "I've got a banquet to go to tonight. Think we'll be snowbound? When are you moving?"

"I don't know yet."

"Hmm. You'd better hump yourself, buddy. That's Griselda's stuff leaving. We're moving in a couple of days. Even Clabber's got a place. You'd better be out of here before that wrecker's crane goes to work or it'll slam you right over the Brooklyn Bridge, bed and all."

Richardson, following him upward, sighed. Carson paused and looked back at him. "Nothing on him yet? No clues?"

Richardson shrugged. "They sent a detective around today to ask questions."

Carson resumed climbing. "We'll see." At the landing he looked into Griselda Vandermeer's apartment. She stood near the door shoving a box with her foot.

"Nearly done? You deserve a medal, a special award. Follow me to the trophy room." He paused. "Free drinks. No? Sympathetic ear. No? How about a strong shoulder to cry on?" He walked closer. "The quality of men has deteriorated sadly in the last few years. If I were your boyfriend I wouldn't have let you handle this alone. As a matter of fact, I'd handcuff you to me and never let you out of my sight."

Griselda smiled at him wordlessly. Her eyes went back and forth between his face and Richardson's. Behind her, an overnight bag sat on the empty floor. From a door, an evening dress hung on a hanger.

Carson kissed his fingertips and wiggled them at her, then banged his evening newspaper on the railing and mounted the next flight of stairs. "I've got to talk to Abby for a moment."

Griselda's amused eyes followed him. Then she looked again at Richardson. "Found a place yet?"

"No."

"Oh? And no news of—"

"No. No news." Richardson glanced around her nearly empty apartment, then clucked his tongue. "Sorry to see you go."

"Well. Come day. Go day. New Yorkers spend their lives moving.'"

Richardson nodded. "Ah—" He flipped a helpless hand at her. "You mind if I ask you a question?"

Griselda stepped back a pace. "What question?"

Richardson put a hand on an upended trunk. Then he smiled. "You look like you're braced for the worst."

"Oh. No. I can't imagine what you're going to ask me."

"Maybe I'm going to ask you for a date." He smiled at her.

"Oh . . ."

"Maybe I'm going to ask you for a date for tonight—"

"Oh, I can't. I have—"

"Yes. I know what you have. But that's not my question. I wanted to ask you about the cards the other night."

"Ummm. I was afraid that's what it was."

"What did you see?"

"Oh. It wasn't anything. Look, I do those cards for entertainment. I should have left all the dark cards out of the deck, but—well, Albert Clabber told me that Mrs. Quist collects old tarot decks and—well, that's how it was."

"I understand. What did you see in the cards?"

"Oh, do I have to tell you? As I said—"

"I know. But I'd like to know what you saw. Mrs. Quist's face went white. What was it?"

"You don't want to know. It isn't a valid reading."

"Yes, Griselda. I want to know. What did you see?"

She lowered her eyes. "Assassination."

"Oh." He paused. "Whose?"

"Yours."

8
He found the phone number in the book and dialed it.

A police telephone operator answered it on the first ring.

"Detective Navarre, please."

There was a pause. "What name?"

"Navarre."

"Navarre?"

"Yes. Navarre. Abel Navarre."

"Abel Navarre?"

"Yes, operator. Abel Navarre."

"Just one moment, please." The operator clicked off.

Richardson sat, holding the phone, waiting and telling himself he wasn't thinking about the tarot deck. What difference did it make that he had no brain tumor if he was slated for assassination?

The telephone clicked. "This is Detective Tomey."

"Oh, I want Detective Navarre."

"Abel Navarre?"

"Yes."

"Who's calling, please?"

"My name's Richardson. I'm calling in reference to the Goulart case."

"What's your first name?"

"Pete. Peter. Why? Isn't he there?"

"Ahhhhhh, ummmmm. Mr. Richardson. Would you describe Detective Navarre for me?"

"Describe? Sure. Why?"

"I'll tell you in just a moment."

"Well, he's big. Massive. Over six feet. Maybe six-three or -four. Runs maybe two twenty-five, two thirty. A touch of gray at the temples. Broad flat face. Deep brown eyes. Very thick neck. Flat nose."

"That fits. Light-colored hair?"

"Yes."

"Noticeably large hands and very heavy legs?"

"Yes."

"I see. When did you see him last?"

"This morning. Right here."

"Oh."

"Can I talk to him now?"

"Mr.—ah—Richardson. Are you pulling my leg?"

"No. What's going on?"

Detective Tomey sighed audibly over the phone. "Mr. Richardson. Detective Abel Navarre was killed by a bank bandit in lower Manhattan with one shot through the heart. I know. I was there. And it happened twenty-two years ago."

9

A few minutes later the rear door on the moving van slammed, and Griselda Vandermeer's goods and chattels rolled away in the van in darkness. The road was empty and filling with snow.

Now four apartments were empty.

CHAPTER VI

H e dreaded the thought of bed.

He knew he'd lie in the darkness, wide-eyed, listening for the slightest sound. Sleep would come in short spans, never deep. Wakefulness would return with the familiar knot of fear.

Richardson stood by his bedroom window in darkness watching the snow falling into the zones of light of the street lamps.

The falling snow had a lulling effect on him. He put a lamp on in the living room, then went to bed and lay there listening to the crystals of snow tapping on his window.

Somewhere between sleep and consciousness he found himself on a high iron picket fence, holding onto the bars and standing on a metal crosspiece. It was many stories high, ten—twelve, or more. Below him were the rows of other fences, with menacing lines of spikes.

He sat up in bed. The image was as compelling, as convincing as the soaring dizziness of fever. He walked to the window and looked out. The wind had shifted more to the west and was blowing the snow in puffs across the quadrangle.

Richardson returned to his bed and lay down. He was awake, yet he was on the fence again. He was afraid of the fence, afraid of the waiting spikes below him, afraid of the height. The fence could fall and cast him down to the spikes. His body would be torn to pulp, bouncing off one row of spikes, tumbling to another, impaled and bouncing and tumbling down down down. He felt gouts of meat torn from his limbs.

He decided to pretend to climb to the bottom. He reached one foot down to a crosspiece. Then the other. Now, he slipped his hands down the square rods of the descenders. Another step down to another crosspiece. Foot after foot, hand after hand, he descended. Eventually, his feet touched the roadway—a roadway with deeply worn stones. Ancient worn black stones. Same as before.

He awoke a half hour later. Wide-eyed. Alert. Listening. No. No sound. He hadn't heard a sound. He got up and looked out at the snow. It was swirling now. The flakes were thicker. The white ground cover obliterated topographic detail. The wrecker wore a thin coating of white on its cabin and on its caterpillar tracks.

Richardson walked into the living room. The lone light was still burning. He returned to his bed.

The fence appeared again. He was on it again. It was

toweringly high again. He could not shake the illusion. He must climb down again, down to sleep. A weary business: he put down a foot to the next lowest crosspiece. Then another. Hands slipped carefully down the square from descenders. Another step down. More hand sliding. Down. Down. Down. A step at a time until he touched the ground—the same worn and rutted roadway. Where?

He slept.

He awoke. It was after three A.M. He stood up and walked into the living room. In the single light, the room remained unchanged. He looked out at the snowstorm.

The fall had nearly ended. The wind was stronger, rolling directly out of the northwest. The front had passed through, and soon the clouds would be blown out to sea, and the stars would appear.

Richardson was exhausted. Tormented. He felt leaden in every limb. Sleep. Unbroken sleep. Sleep without fear. He returned to his bed.

He lay back on the bed and pressed his face into the crook of his arm.

In the name of God, be he Beelzebub or a butterfly, set my adversary in plain view before me.

The fence appeared again. Yet again. He lay awake, face in arm crook, and began the descent for the third time. The height seemed lower this time and he made good progress, sensing the growing closeness of the roadway. He looked down finally and saw the road twenty feet below him.

On it stood a man.

Richardson got up quickly and walked into the living room.

A monk. He'd seen him clearly. He stood, arms folded, head canted back, staring at Richardson, watching him climb. His face was a dark shadow in a peaked cowl.

He was a large man. Was it Goulart? Navarre, twenty-two years dead? A stranger? Who?

Richardson got a blanket off the bed and, his body wrapped in it, sat in a living room chair and stared out at the white world and the massive black shadows of broken clouds moving rapidly across the sky.

Between them he could see bright stars.

2

Willow left the New Jersey Turnpike at Interchange 4 and followed Route 38 to Camden.

The snowplow and salt had reduced the snow in the roadway to puddles. Car tires churned up a mist of dirty brown water and Willow drove with his windshield wipers going.

He parked in downtown Camden and looked around with dismay. The major hotel, the Walt Whitman, was boarded up. Whole blocks of old tenements had been torn down, and snow covered the empty lots. Abandoned cars, dead weed stalks and empty stores and offices were everywhere apparent.

Old weathered campaign posters proclaimed: "If Major Coxon Was Mayor, These Boards Would Be Down." Willow wondered if Coxon won.

The county courthouse was a high granite-block building, with wide granite steps leading to the entrance. He went through the revolving door and followed the trail of water and snow-melt to the banks of elevators. Men stood about in groups. Their roles were obvious: politicians, county civil servants, lawyers, jurors, defendants, witnesses, policemen, detectives, and clutches of poor people strolling doubtfully down long corridors with limp pieces of official paper in their hands, seeking various bureaus.

"Probate Records," he said to the elevator starter.

"Room 100, right around the corner there."

Willow walked around the corner and found the door to Room 100: Passports, Identity Cards, County Records.

"Good morning," he said to the middle-aged woman behind the counter. "I'm interested in a probate package for the years 1800 to 1810 or thereabouts."

The woman shook her head slowly.

"You mean those records don't exist?"

She nodded her head. "They exist, so far as I know, but not here."

"Oh. Isn't this the county records office?

"Yes. But not for those years."

"I don't understand."

"Well, Camden County wasn't formed until 1844. You see, originally Camden was part of Gloucester County, and Gloucester City was the county seat."

"Oh, I see; records for 1810 are in Gloucester City."

The woman shook her head again. "Wrong. You see, Gloucester City had a bunch of ramshackle old buildings that burned down one night. They moved the county activities to Woodbury. Then in the 1830s they chopped Gloucester County in half again and created Camden County."

Willow listened attentively, patiently. At last he nodded. "The probate records, such as they are, are located in Woodbury, which is now the county seat for Gloucester County."

"Such as they are," she said, nodding.

"How far is Woodbury?"

"Straight out Route 70 to Route 295 and head south. You can't miss it. Maybe fifteen miles."

3

Woodbury had the glow of health about it. The main street, Kings Highway, was crowded with stores. There were no vacancies, no boarded windows, no litter, no sense of despair or burned-out terrain.

The woman in the county records office was very helpful. The index of administrations and estates was alphabetical, cross-referenced by year to the ledgers.

"Would this be your man?" she asked.

Willow looked at the entry. Algernon Tully. Died August 3, 1807.

"Hmmm. Yes. That could be him. Did he leave a will?"

The woman looked at the entry and nodded. "Let's see." She turned, her eyes searching the shelved volumes. She pulled one out and lifted it to a desk. She opened it, leafed through several pages, then turned it to him. "Call me if you need me."

"Thank you." Willow glanced quickly through the familiar papers. Executor was a lawyer. Heir was one Eric Lermonx. Willow glanced at the letters testamentary, the bond, the inventory and appraisement, notice to creditors (there apparently were none) and decree of distribution. Eric Lermonx had gotten it all.

Willow settled back and read the will slowly. Algernon Tully declares himself to be the husband of the late

Annie Coffee Tully, the son of Joseph Tully, London wine merchant, and avers he is of sound mind at the time of drafting the will and testament.

Tully was a plainspoken man, apparently. In the second paragraph he listed his property—several houses, a warehouse for wines and spirits, several parcels of land, some household furnishings, some books, and a fluctuating supply of dollars.

The third paragraph states flatly that he wants his daughter, Margaret, to have everything. If she predeceases him, Tully wants everything to go to Eric Lermonx.

Willow frowned, then returned to the index. He found no probate record for Mrs. Tully or for daughter Margaret. Suppose Margaret had married—her probate record wouldn't be under her maiden name. She must have died before her father did, because Lermonx, the alternate name, received the estate.

Willow sat down. How would he find Margaret's death records and marriage—if there was one? And who was Lermonx?

He got up and walked into the clerk's office. "Vital records?" he asked.

"They're in the custody of each community on a local basis."

"So the death or marriage records for someone born in Camden—"

"—would be in Camden."

Willow nodded and exited. Back up Route 295 to Route 130 to Route 70 to Camden.

Willow had a feeling he was going to have to get some help.

4

The city clerk was patient and helpful. There was no birth or death or marriage record for Margaret Tully.

"Church registers may help," she said. "Do you know what religion she was?"

"Oh my," sighed Willow.

"Look," said the clerk. "Why don't you consult Judge Cooper?"

"Who's he?"

"He's a retired judge of the state court of appeals. He's a genealogist and a local historian and—what's the word? —antiquarian book collector. I know a few years ago he gathered all the early church records in two or three counties and made copies of them. And he indexed them too. I think he got a grant from the New Jersey Historical Society and hired some law students to do the work. Anyway, he knows more about early Jersey history than anyone else around here."

"Where can I find him?"

"In Haddonfield. You know where that is?"

"Uh—give me a push."

"Okay. You go out Route 70. Know where that is?"

"I'm getting to know it very well."

"Follow it to the Garden State Race Track Circle. Take the righthand road and follow it a couple of miles and you're there."

5

The two hemlock trees were filled with snow. A late-afternoon breeze spilled across the horizon under a darkening sky. It skimmed crystals of snow from the branches and spun them across the cleared driveway.

Between the two trees, a wooden sign hung from a wooden post and crosspiece. "The Old Book Shop. T. E. Cooper, Prop."

The shop was an old carriage house down a lane. The upper floor was apparently the judge's residence.

Through the small-pane window of the shop, Willow saw a man sitting by a fireplace with a book in his lap. When he stepped through the shop doorway, the man stood up.

He held a book in his hand, using a forefinger for a bookmark. "Mr. Willow?"

"Yes." Willow held out his hand. The pleasant bookstore odor of old books pervaded the room.

"I'm Thomas Cooper. Come sit down." He led Willow by the fireplace to a large wooden table surrounded by captain's chairs.

"Just the day for a good book," said Willow.

"Yes. And that's just what I've got here. A history of some of the Indians of New Jersey. Absegami Indians who lived here. Do you know this book? By Frederick Josephson. Astonishing writer. After my forty years of miserably written legal briefs, I can tell you this fellow's a positive delight. You know that lawyers can't write worth a hoot. What business are you in?"

"I'm a lawyer."

"Hmmm." Judge Cooper considered that. "English?"

"Uh. I gave myself away, eh?"

"A little. I bet you can't write any better than the rest of the tribe of lawyers here. If this Josephson had entered law, he'd have conquered the field just on his skill of writing briefs. He writes like Addison. You know Addison? Neat parallelisms. Balanced sentences with that same concessive construction of Dr. Johnson. He concedes something, then takes it back. Concedes. Takes back. Quiet authority. And precise use of words. Oh, I tell you, he's well worth reading."

"Good," said Willow, smiling. "I'll buy it."

"Get out," said the judge. "This is the only Josephson I've got. And there are six people waiting to buy it." He nodded at a small escritoire. "In the spring, after I've dined a whole winter on this volume, I may sell it to one of them. It's out of print, you know. Trouble with that Josephson is he doesn't do nearly enough writing. There are at least fifty basic subjects right here in southern Jersey that need his attention and—" Judge Cooper stopped. "And you have miles to go on a snowy day. You mentioned the name Tully when you called."

"Yes. I'm trying to get some hard facts on a Margaret Tully who lived here with her parents late in the eighteenth century."

Judge Cooper nodded. "Yes, that's what you said on the phone. Well. Let's see. I have a large quantity of primary source material for genealogists centering on what is now Camden County. While I was waiting for you I examined my records, and I find no Margaret Tully— and that's no surprise. Very few church records have survived since the eighteenth century. Confidentially, it wasn't a very literate age, and many records aren't really lost. They never existed. But having said that, I do find an Algernon Tully whose death was recorded in a Camden City church. Does that help?"

"I don't know. Her father was named Algernon."

"I have a date of death of August 3, 1807."

"That should be the same man. I have already found his will."

"I see. Now you want to find the daughter, Margaret. Hmmmm. Well."

"This is his will," said Willow, holding forth a photostat.

Judge Cooper took it and read it, tilting the page to the light from the window. "Hmmm. Uh-huh. Mmmmmm. Well. Yes. She must have predeceased him. A tart kind of a writer, wasn't he? Blunt. Maybe laconic is a better word. No explanation given for his actions. And that's an interesting name—Eric Lermonx. And Annie Coffee, Algernon's wife. I may have something on those names. But let's get back to Margaret. Aside from this reference to her in Algernon's will, there's no record of her ever having been here. Now, I'm going to make a couple of educated guesses. He doesn't refer to her by a married name, and I'll bet at the time of writing of this will, Margaret was no longer a young girl. Tully himself was an old man and somewhat crabby, judging from the tone of his writing style. Now, spinster ladies stayed home. If my guesses are right, then Margaret never married, died before her father and died a spinster under his roof. Now let's see if we can prove that. Can we use your car?"

"Yes, of course."

"I hate to leave my snug little fire here, but—tell you what, Willow. You and I can come back here in a little while and stir up the ashes and have a toddy. They say it's going to get cold enough tonight to freeze the heart of an Episcopal minister. And a toddy will keep the chill off things for a bit. Let's see—" He touched his chin with his fingers. "I want some warm clothes. Boots. Rubber boots! And a broom." He eyed the weather through the window. "A shovel too, I suppose. Are you good at digging up bodies, Willow?"

6

The judge directed the car into the heart of Camden's ghetto. The wheels shuddered on old cobblestones, frozen snow and the traces of an old trolley track exposed through a worn tar surface.

"Here, here," said Judge Cooper. "Ahead there. Pull over at the curb there."

Willow stopped the car and looked to his right. It was an old cemetery fenced in ornate black wrought iron. The fencing, broken in many places, was clotted with old newspaper sheets. Brown weed stalks stuck up through the snow.

The cemetery gate was hinged with an old length of clothesline. Judge Cooper, carrying his broom like a halberd, opened the gate and stepped into the cemetery. His eyes gazed at a row of jagged whiskey-bottle bases that stood on a tombstone. Inside each was a measure of snow.

"Watch now," he said to Willow. "There's all kinds of broken glass, rusty cans and trash under the snow." He gazed around at the stones. "Let's see how good a guesser I am." He set off down the main lane of the cemetery, walking carefully in his boots, his eyes searching the names on the stones. He turned to the left and followed a narrow lane almost to the wall of brick tenement building.

He reached out his broom and swept a tablet stone. "Cowan. Hmmm. Old family. Came from Salem originally." He looked at an upright stone, noting the name, and sauntered among the stones, scuffing snow as he went. "Hmmm. Bailey. Starr. Culpepper. Shipbuilders, originally. Hmmmm. Douglas." He paused and swept snow from another stone. "Hmmmm. Weathered. I make it Aston or maybe Maston. What do you think?" He walked on and paused again. He squinted at a stone, bent and squinted more closely, then prodded filaments of the broom into the lettering. "Tully," he said simply.

Willow stepped abreast of him and looked at the stone. Algernon Tully 1732–1807.

Judge Cooper broomed away the snow from the lower part of the headstone. "And Mrs. Tully," he said. Annie Coffee Tully 1738–1799.

Judge Cooper swept at the snow around the perimeter of the headstone. "Maybe I should have brought that shovel from the car."

"I'll get it," said Willow.

"Don't bother. I think I've found what we want." His broom cleared away snow from the low stone. He stepped close and, bending, squinted at it. He straightened up and looked at Willow. "Daughter Margaret."

The legend was as simple and unadorned as the ones on the parents' stone. "Margaret Tully 1761–1801."

"Family plot," said Judge Cooper. "My guess was right."

"But why wasn't there a probate packet on the two women?"

"Quite common. There was no need for a will. Household furnishings went from mother to daughter. Property and things of value were in the man's name, except the house, which was quite often in both names."

Willow looked at the two stones exposed from the shielding snow in the midst of a decayed ghetto.

Another Tully line ended with the barren womb of Margaret Tully, spinster.

7

There was a crosswind on the New Jersey Turnpike. It picked up granules from the snowbanks and blew them in clouds across the roadway.

Willow drove with his windshield wipers slowly wiping away the tire spray.

He reviewed again the facts of the day. He'd found Algernon, found Algernon's will. Algernon identified himself as Joseph Tully's son and identified Margaret as his daughter.

Margaret: Judge Cooper had found her buried beside her parents. She was still Tully, still unwed when she died. A spinster.

Case closed.

But who was Eric Lermonx?

Willow dismissed Lermonx. Clearly, he was of no consequence to Willow's search for Tullys.

The sun was westering and New York was only eighty more miles away. Maybe dinner with Alice Polsley and her lovely legs. Willow touched up his speed a bit. One more son to go.

Maybe, if he was really lucky, his search would be fruitless.

8

The sun had set behind the handsome old Victorian clapboard house across the path. The wind prowled through the dusk with increasing strength. It curled around Judge Cooper's house and chased the thin thread of wood smoke from his chimney. A link of metal chain tapped forlornly against the frozen flagpole above it. A homeless evening star appeared in the frosty black sky.

When the shop door opened, Judge Cooper looked up and smiled.

"I thought you'd be back, Willow. I bet you haven't eaten any dinner yet, have you?"

9

The wind blew up a gale that rushed across the eastern part of the continent, bringing with it the coldest temperatures in thirty-five years.

Judge Thomas Eakins Cooper sat at the table by the restaurant window, stirring his after-dinner coffee and watching the stiff tufts of sedge shudder in the howling wind. The lake in floodlight was under a deep layer of ice and snow. Spinning devils of snow crystals ran across the lake's white surface into darkness.

"That Molasses Act of 1735 was a stupid piece of business for Parliament to get involved in, Willow. British or not, you must be able to see that it was strangling the baby in the cradle."

"But it was never enforced."

"It was unenforceable."

"It was a joke," persisted Willow. "But Joseph Tully smelled profit. The Molasses Act would have increased the price of rum and increased the consumption of wine in the colonies. And he had good wines—from the Azores and the Canaries and Madeira. That's when he hatched his plan. It was a good idea, only—"

"—only it destroyed him and his family."

"Well, it was circumstance that destroyed his family. Maybe it was the seeds of dissension among the sons that destroyed it. Anyway, Tully began exporting sons to the New World. His grand design was to have a son with a warehouse and a proper importing license in Boston, New York, Philadelphia, and Williamsburg, Virginia."

Judge Cooper nodded, listening.

"The eldest son, Henry, arrived first. In the 1740s. He set up shop in Boston, and things went so well that father Joseph sent over his second son, Thomas, in 1747. For some reason, Joseph waited five years before sending Algernon over."

"That's"—Judge Cooper squinted his eyes—"1752?"

"Yes. Algernon had just turned twenty."

"And the fourth one?"

"Roger. He arrived in 1759. On his twentieth birthday. By then trade had heated up a bit, and Joseph, back in London, was ready to expand. Roger was too young to set up by himself. But Henry was a seasoned merchant now and Thomas had been a good understudy. So, Joseph ordered Thomas to New York City to set up a wine-importing activity there.

"Then came the real bonanza. The Sugar Act of 1764 was passed, and it carried a heavy duty on the wines that were shipped direct from the Portuguese Wine Islands to the colonies. The same wines shipped through England, through Joseph Tully's warehouses, were cheaper in the colonies. It was perfect, the culmination of a lifetime of work. So Joseph ordered son number three to move to Philadelphia and open trading station number three. Joseph and Sons were about to become rich—except for one thing . . . well, two things."

"And one of them was family quarreling."

"Yes. How did you know?"

"You said family dissension—"

"Right. Right. I did. Well, Henry's the real culprit. He became a colonial. He married a colonial lady. He took the colonists' viewpoint against England's trade acts . . ."

"And he fired a musket at Concord at British troops."

"Yes. And you can imagine the reaction of the father in England to that. Well, the whole thing was to blow galley west anyway. The colonists went into revolution. The wine trade went to absolute hell, and the four sons found themselves cut off from England and home, and destitute. They knew only the wine-importing business. They had no money—the war had wiped them out. And they had to dig with their bare hands to grow food and cut wood to keep their families from starvation. Henry, of course, was a member of the Continental Army.

"When the war ended, the whole grand scheme had died a wretched mess. The family was destroyed. Henry never again had any contact with any of them. Roger returned to England after his family burned to death— practically feebleminded. Algernon seems to have gotten lost here in the wilds of New Jersey trading with the fur trappers."

"And the fourth son—what's his name? Thomas."

"Ask me in a few days. I have to go to Brooklyn to find his history."

Judge Cooper fixed his eyes on Willow. "Tell me, why are you doing this? Are you a descendant of the family?"

"No."

"Ummm. Are you representing a legacy?"

"No."

"Hmmmm. Everytime I get near that question, your

eyes slide sideways. Willow, you look guilty enough to hang without a trial."

Willow looked sideways out at the frozen lake and the reed-bending wind.

"Willow. I have a feeling that I'm talking to a bright young man with a very promising future who's about to take a wrong turning in the road. I think you'd better think things out again."

Willow looked at the lake and felt as separated from the rest of the human race as a crystal of snow blowing away in the bitter-cold darkness.

10

The pages were typewritten, thermofacsimile copies of an original manuscript and in a linen-covered binding. The volume contained page after page of names, collated and alphabetized from every known church record in two counties.

"There were two of them," said Judge Cooper, pointing to the names. "Eric Lermonx, date of birth unknown, who died in 1792. Clearly the wrong man. He was dead long before Algernon Tully was. And this Eric Lermonx. Born 1779. Died 1809. Age thirty. He sounds like our man. The other Eric may be his father or an uncle. Both of them are buried in Mt. Ephraim, which is just on the other side of White Horse Pike. I think we ought to check probate records first and see where that leads us."

Judge Cooper roused his fire with a poker and looked out at the hemlock which was bobbing and swaying in the stiff breeze. A branch rubbed forlornly on a windowpane. "Hardest freeze I can ever remember," he said.

"Well, I'm going to have a glass of wine and get some sleep. You're welcome to sit here as late as you want. The shelves on this side contain lawbooks, collector's items mainly. A lot of them go back to the Elizabethan era, but your Latin had better not be rusty. This bank of shelves contains old history books, mostly local, mostly counties in New Jersey and Pennsylvania. And that bank over there contains American biography. Mostly legal and political. There's enough reading to occupy you through ten lifetimes, but I'd suggest that you get up-stairs to sleep so we can roll out first thing. Courthouse in Woodbury opens at nine."

"Judge, I still think I'm imposing on you."

Judge Cooper looked at him with candid eyes. "You're not. If I didn't want to do this, I wouldn't. I must admit to you, Willow, that my motives aren't all altruistic. I can't take walks in this kind of weather. Can't garden. I've been a widower for over ten years so I ought to be used to the quiet around here, but to tell the truth, I'm delighted to have a finger in your genealogical pie. It's as stimulating as a detective story to me. Confidentially, if I were starting out all over again, I'd chuck law and spe-cialize in historical research and genealogy. The most fascinating life I've ever run into."

11

Judge Cooper used a paper tissue to polish his glasses with care. Then he fitted them deliberately at the ears and bridge of nose. Next, he addressed himself to the Index of Wills and Testaments. "L L L. Hmmmm. Le Ler. Here we are. Ler." He opened the heavy volume and riffled a few pages. "Okay. Ler. E for Eric, 1809.

Here he is. Waiting for us all this while." He turned to the volume indicated in the index and tapped its spine with a pointing finger.

Willow reached up and pulled it down. He laid it on the metal work surface and let Judge Cooper open it. Practiced fingers leafed the corners of the pages. "Now, let's see. Hmmmm. Petition. I was afraid of this. He died intestate. Maybe that'll be a help. We'll get a lot of information about him we wouldn't have gotten from a last will and testament." Judge Cooper fell to reading the documents, skipping the standard legal phrasing and picking out the names of the persons involved in disposing of the property of Eric Lermonx.

"Kiln maker?" asked Willow, reading over the judge's shoulder.

Judge Cooper nodded. "Jersey sand. Some of the best sand in the world for glass making. All these towns around here were called glass towns. Glass making, bottle making was a major cottage industry. And this man Lermonx apparently built kilns for glass making. Interesting." He turned the page and read on, slowly trailing a forefinger down the crabbed lines of handwriting. He grunted and nodded periodically. His reading slowed down and he leaned closer to the book when he got to the inventory of Lermonx's possessions. "Well now, that's very interesting. He owned the Weeks House in Mt. Ephraim. The Weeks family, after generations of living there, recently deeded it to the County Historical Society. Beautiful colonial building. Now what would Lermonx be doing with that house? He was a bachelor. See, right here. Bachelor. What would a kiln-making bachelor with a modest income be doing with the Weeks House? Interesting."

Judge Cooper skimmed the rest of the documents and stood up. "My curiosity has gotten the better of me. Why don't you continue conning these documents and arrange to have copies made? I'm going to look into the Index of Deeds and find out where he got that house from."

With that, he left the chamber.

12

Matthew Willow was putting copies of the Lermonx will into his attaché case when the judge returned. He nodded at Willow and shook a finger at him. Wordlessly, he went to the Index of Wills and Testaments and opened it. He found the volume he sought on the shelves and lifted it down. A moment later he had it open and was reading it. He turned at last and looked at Willow, frowning. Then he beckoned.

"Your Eric Lermonx inherited the house from the first Eric Lermonx."

"Oh." Willow was losing interest in the Eric Lermonxes and the Weeks House.

Then he saw the judge's finger tapping on the page. He leaned down and looked.

". . . to my nephew, Eric Tully alias Lermonx."

"Tully!" said Willow. "What's that mean—alias Lermonx?"

The judge raised his head and looked him in the eyes. "Bastardy," he said.

13

Judge Cooper led Willow quickly through three dif-

ferent offices of the building. First he took him to a
docket of court cases. He searched the bastardy cases for
the approximate year of Lermonx's birth. When he
found the name, he looked at Willow, holding his finger
on it.

"Margaret Tully," read Willow. "Eric Lermonx was
her illegitimate son?"

Judge Cooper shrugged and went down to the archives. A short time later he had the court summary of
the case. In 1779 Margaret Tully was brought before
court on charges of having given birth to a child out of
wedlock. She named as the father Eric Lermonx, glass
maker.

Willow sat himself slowly down, frowning. "Any issue
from Eric Lermonx would be bona fide descendants of
Joseph Tully of London."

The judge nodded. "But. Well, Willow, I guess I
moved too fast. The uncle gave Eric that house because
of the young man's incurable shyness around women.
He hoped the house would make the nephew a worthy
catch for the young ladies of the community. It didn't
work, Willow. Lermonx died a girl-shy bachelor."

14

"There are," said Aunt Eta, "very few things worth
lying awake nights worrying about. And insanity isn't
one of them. At least not for you, Peter." She lifted the
cherry from her Manhattan by its stem and put it in her
mouth.

Richardson looked at her. "I just may be mad as the
March wind, Aunt Eta."

"Peter. Peter." She dropped the stem in the ashtray.

"There are only us two chickens left of our immediate Richardson branch, so—to mix two metaphors—it's difficult for me to prove it to you, but there were no nuts in our family tree. Damn, I made a bad pun. Charlie would have killed me. Howsomever, my advice to you, dear Peter, is multiply. Find a healthy country girl with broad hips and beget. Skip these gaunt thin-boned New York tarts, Peter. That's what was wrong with that Bonny. She was so busy dashing around in her costumes to show off her starving bones, how could you have ever gotten her pregnant even if she wanted to? Your trouble is you have nothing to worry about except yourself. If you don't do something soon, you're going to come down with a whole range of psychosomatic diseases. When your Uncle Charlie died, for two years the loneliness nearly drove me crazy. I used to wake up at night, sure I was having a heart attack. I thought I was suffocating, you see? Well, soon enough, I 'got wise,' to use Charlie's favorite expression, and got busy." Aunt Eta shook a finger at him. "Loneliness is a killer. It's a disease with a million disguises."

She pulled a large sagging handbag onto her lap and groped a hand into it. She extracted a small jar of maraschino cherries and removed the cap. She pulled out three cherries by the stems and lowered them into the Manhattan.

Richardson watched disinterestedly.

"Any brain tumors?"

She smirked at him. "My God, Peter, you're like a hypochondriac on a shopping spree. Insanity. Brain tumors. Look. I can go back at least three, possibly four generations of Richardsons. There were some accidental deaths. There were two who died in childbirth. Infections and fevers killed some others . . . but the bulk of them just plain wore out and died. In their eighties and nineties. No brain tumors and no one in the nut house." She lifted one of the cherries from her drink and ate it. She cocked an eye at him while she chewed, then reached out and touched his arm. "Saturday's child," she said. "Lift up your head and be cheerful. Get out of that building you're in and that neighborhood. Get away from the memories and the unhappiness and you'll be miraculously cured. Take it from dear old Aunt Eta. I've been around a lot longer than you. There's no such thing as ghosts and hauntings and that nonsense."

He shrugged unhappily.

"Tell you what, Peter. Why don't you move in with me for a few weeks? We'll scout out an apartment for you, move your junk in, then we'll take off for the leaky roof racetrack circuit. My God, I haven't had a good junket since Charlie died—I can talk you deaf, dumb and blind about horses for a few weeks. Such stories. I ought to write a book about it. *I Remember.* That's the title. And I do remember. I remember that fantastic year when Citation took the triple crown—1948. I can shut my eyes and see him running. Breathtaking animal. I can tell you what jockey was up. I can tell you Citation's time in all three, the Derby, the Preakness and the Belmont. I can tell you every horse in the field for the three races." She nodded her head. "Sad days too. I remember when Tim Tam broke his leg at Belmont a half mile from the finish and ran on three legs. And finished second! I cried for him for days. When we get back home, you'll be stone deaf. Won't hear any more funny noises. Okay?"

"How about my mother's side of the family?"

"Oh, the Daweses? Good stock. Yankee. Vermonters and upstate New Yorkers. Lots of lawyers in that family —and farmers. There was a horse breeder too. Not thoroughbreds. But fine cavalry horses—roughneck animals, tough as old shoes. But no tumors. Let's see. How many Daweses did I know? Your mother, her brothers and sisters; come to think of it, there's a lot of them still around. I knew your grandparents and a bunch of their relatives. People drop out of sight. That's what getting old is really all about. People disappear left and right and one day you can't find anybody who knew you when you were young." She poked the third cherry into her mouth almost angrily. "Damn it, don't get me started on that old-age stuff. Let's see— Oh, Peter, this is silly! The Daweses were a long-lived lot, too. No mental disorders, no mysterious illnesses. Oh, this is silly. Why don't you ask Billy Dawes? He's still up in Poughkeepsie, I'm sure. He was always big on that genealogy stuff. He probably can trace the Daweses back to Europe in 1066 or something. Oh, Peter, kick it—the whole thing. Let's take off for Florida and forget the damned Daweses and Richardsons. They're all dead and buried anyway."

See-saw, Marjorie Dawes.

15

The wrecker's ball described a classic parabola as the swaying boom led it to the point of contact on the wall. The ball hit and thundered in air. The wall bowed in and the bricks shot apart as the ball carried through the wall. The wall was staggered, weakened; then in a slow tilt it fell in on itself, and a cloud of mortar and brick-dust ascended, roiling above the building.

Behind the wrecker, another tractor crane was at work with a giant clamshell, picking up tons of debris and dropping them into dump trucks. It seemed to be eating the shattered buildings.

The wrecker's foreman strolled down the abandoned street to the next block. He was thickly padded in clothing, mittens, hood and yellow hard hat. His practiced eye estimated the work in hours and quarter hours. He looked at his clipboard that showed the diagrams of water mains, gas mains, sewer lines and electric cable ways.

The corner building contained a grocery store. Waite's. He walked into the shop, looked around, peered into the old storage room in the rear and walked back out on the street.

Number 1028 stood next to the grocery, a three-story brownstone with double doors and large windows. It was the classic Brooklyn row house. The foreman ascended the steps and pushed both of the glass doors. They slowly swung inward. He strolled through the rooms of the first floor, following a common row house floor plan he could draw in his sleep. He went to the cellar, scanned the water meter, gas meter and electric control box, then ascended the cellar steps, walked along the hallway to the front hallway. He turned at the newel post and climbed the chestnut staircase to the second floor. At the landing he turned and walked toward the front of the building, peering into the bedrooms and the bath as he went. At the turning of the stairs to the third floor, the condition of the walls struck him, and he started up the stairs, paused and swallowed. Weird. He slipped his crowbar from a loop in his leather tool belt, pressed his hard hat down further and climbed the stairs, stamping his feet loudly.

At the landing at the top of the stairs, the foreman stopped in awe, gazing at the walls in the fast fading light of the winter day.

It was perfectly still inside the building. The sound of the tumbling walls and the tractor engines was remote. The building seemed suspended, frozen in a permanent moment of time. In the middle of the room stood a pressure-type white-gasoline lamp with mantles. It was out.

With his foot, the foreman pushed the door open fully. Near the closet, he saw a shadowed form in the semidusk of the floor. He stepped closer. Then he backed a step, turned, and strode out of the room. He reached the landing and hurried down the stairs. He ran along the hallway of the second floor and took the next flight of stairs down two at a time. He ran through the front doors and down the brownstone steps and turned.

"Goddamnedest thing I ever saw in my whole life," he said aloud, and scurried directly across the quadrangle, a distance of more than four blocks. He hurried in a shuffling trot, holding his clipboard in one hand and the crowbar in the other. His shoes squeaked in the frozen snow.

At the other side of the quadrangle was an old saloon and he hurried up to it. He pushed open the door and stepped in. Warm air touched his face and he smelled the familiar saloon odor of stale beer. His heart was pounding and he had to take several deep breaths before he could talk. The men at the bar stood wordlessly looking at him and at the open door behind him. Bitter cold air was pouring into the saloon. Someone stepped over to it and shoved it shut with his foot.

No one said a word. No one smoked. No one drank. They waited, suspended, all eyes on the foreman's face.

"Goddamnedest thing," he said at last. "Never saw anything like it before." He doubled himself over the bar, puffing heavily and trying to dislodge the stitch in his side. "Listen," he said to the bartender-owner. "Better call the police. There's a stiff in one of the empty houses."

The bartender stared at him solemnly. "Dead?"

"Dead? He's frozen stiff."

"Did you check him?"

"Huh? Check him? What do you mean, check him? He's frozen hard as this goddamn crowbar. Blue lips. And the skin on his face is frozen and covered with frost. Give me a double hooker of whiskey."

The bartender poured the double into a glass almost as a reflex action. "That doesn't mean he's dead. I was on the North Atlantic run for more winters than I want to count and I saw them in gun tubs, with them screaming Atlantic rollers going and the wind right off the North Pole. You'd have bet your life they were dead in there, frozen, but they got up and walked to breakfast nice as you please."

He got a dime from the till and handed it to a regular. "Here, John. Give a call to the cops. What's the number of the building?"

The foreman consulted his clipboard. "Right next to Waite's," he said. "Ten twenty-eight."

"Tell them to bring an ambulance," said the owner. He snatched a bottle of brandy from the bar and stepped into his living room just off the bar. After several moments he returned with his overcoat and hat and several blankets. His wife appeared right behind him.

"Button that damned coat, now," she said to him. "No sense catching your death, too." She went behind the bar, and her measuring eye scanned the level of liquids in the glasses of the patrons.

The owner left. He shut the door behind him and began the long walk across the quadrangle. The foreman downed the drink and started for the door.

"Hey," called a patron. "What did you see?"

"You'll never believe it in all your born days." The foreman stepped through the saloon door and hurried after the owner.

In the great expanse of flatness, the two men walked together toward 1028.

The owner shifted the life-giving bottle of brandy to a pocket of his overcoat and shifted the blankets to his other arm.

They walked in silence, hurrying, their twin breaths pluming rhythmically in the frosty air.

It was nearly dark.

16

The sound of the siren carried clear and thin when the owner and the foreman reached the front doors of 1028. "Damnedest thing you ever saw," mumbled the foreman.

"Third floor you say?" asked the owner.

"Yeah. Third floor."

The owner hurried up the steps. Behind him strayed the foreman, carrying the crowbar before him.

Last light was touching the ceilings of the building.

The owner reached the top of the first flight and turned, moving quickly along the gritty-floored hallway. He turned to ascend the second flight and paused involuntarily, one foot in the air, arrested. He gazed at the wall of the staircase and at the wall at the head of the stairs.

Then he shut his mouth purposefully and stamped up the steps. The room was nearly dark when he entered it. The gasoline lantern just showed its green cap, looking in the darkness like a merry gnome. The owner stepped past the lamp and fumbled at his coat pocket. He struggled with it for several moments. "Hot damn it," he cried at his pocket. "Let go of it."

The flashlight came free with an abrupt fling of his arm. Through his gloved fingers, he worked at the sliding switch of the flashlight. It snapped up and he quickly aimed it at the form on the floor. He studied it for a moment, then leaned still closer.

Down in the street, the siren shrilled.

The owner pulled off a glove and laid the back of his hand on the throat of the man. He shook his head. "Dear God in heaven, have mercy on our souls," he muttered. "The man is frozen like a stone."

The corpse lay on its side, legs drawn up, hands thrust between the thighs, hugely like a giant baby. The face was a mask of white frost. The clothes consisted of an old zippered jacket, a shirt and a pair of trousers. The feet were in a pair of paint-splattered work shoes.

Coarse shoes scraped and thumped on the stairwell below. Voices intruded on the frozen silence of the house. Two policemen called up the staircase. "Where is it?"

"It's up here," said the foreman.

Other shoes and other voices now bumped and

scraped up the stairs. The truck drivers and the operator of the cranes hurried up the stairs. All of them, policemen and construction workers, paused in silence and stared at the walls, then at the corpse. One of the policemen knelt beside the corpse and placed a warm pink hand on the corpse's throat. "Wheeee. He's been here for a few days. It's going to take a long time to thaw him out. Anyone know who he is?"

"Dear God," said the owner, "I've poured many a beer down that throat, and I've knelt beside him at mass on Sunday more than once."

The policeman turned and looked at him. "What's his name?"

"Goulart. Ozzie Goulart."

17

Richardson watched Bobby Pew prepare to go home. Pew pulled on his salt-caked rubbers, took off his jacket, put on a sweater, put his jacket back on, wrapped his scarf around his throat, and struggled into a pile-lined quilted parka. He drew the hook up over his head and pulled the zipper shut along the crown of his head.

He watched Richardson watching him. He smiled. "This is part of my war against that bus to Flushing. I used to wait for it in conventional clothes. And when the bus finally came, the driver would get out, tilt me over like a frozen codfish and lean me in the corner of the bus." He strolled over to Richardson's office, smirking. "The only bad part about it is getting downstairs. By the time the elevator gets me to the first floor, it's a raging inferno inside this parka. But I don't care." He saluted Richardson casually and walked to the front office door, bearing his attaché case. "One thing, I'll never freeze to death."

Richardson was alone. He leaned back in his chair and looked at his coat. No reason to stay. No reason to go. He got up and put on his overcoat, then turned and looked at his attaché case, packed, ready to go for its nightly subway ride, lumpishly lying on his desk. He reached for it. Then the phone rang.

He looked at it speculatively, guessing. He let it ring again. He hesitated. It rang again. He brushed a hand in air at it and pulled the case off the desk. He turned and walked purposefully through the main office room. The phone rang again. He reached the front door and opened it. The phone rang again.

Richardson sighed. He put down the case on the floor and walked back reluctantly to his office. Maybe it would stop ringing before he got to it.

He entered his office, leaned over the desk and picked it up.

"Hello."

He listened. And frowned. And sagged. And struggled around the edge of his desk and sat down. He bowed his head, still listening.

"Oh my God," he said.

18

The cars down in the street went on as before. The pedestrians walked stiffly, shivering, to the subway entrances. As before. The shop windows threw out their rectangles of light on the snow-streaked sidewalks as before. And lights all over the borough in strings and clusters winked warmly in the winter night. As before.

Everything went on as before, flatly indifferent. Even the telephone on his desk remained perversely unchanged. Richardson stood at his window, still in his overcoat, remembering the night he'd stood in the middle of those empty lots looking at the Waite's Groceries sign. He should have followed his instinct and gone over to the row of buildings. He could have. But the cold put him off. Something to haunt him for the rest of his life.

He felt alone. Abandoned. Menaced. All was being taken from him. Carson had said it: "Lost wife, lost friend, lost neighborhood, lost childhood, lost identity." Disease: modern life.

He walked out of the office and down the hall to the elevator. A life half-done, only just begun. Ozzie missed the pungent part. The game gets in earnest. The loves grow stronger: the hates more consuming; the fears greater; the number of daily battles and skirmishes lost increases. The paws slow; the teeth wear; the prey grows faster, more elusive. The hell with it.

Maybe Ozzie escaped. Beat the rap. Skimmed over the wall. He's drunk the top off the wine barrel and fled. No dregs for Ozzie. Got away on a glassy sea before the dirty weather hit. Maybe he'd had the best and knew it. Maybe dying was smart.

The elevator door opened and Richardson got on.

He wished fervently that he were dead.

19

The lights were right.

Ozzie Goulart was a creature of lighting. And his apartment was a victory of strategic lighting. One switch put them on—low lights behind plants, on tables, over the drawing table. No glare. No overhead lights to flash out all line and tone and character shadows.

Richardson shambled across the room to Ozzie's drawing table and sat down at it. He stared at the large square of blank white paper. He touched it. He took up a brush and held it, then slowly drew a dry invisible line on the paper. Nevermore.

He heard someone behind him and turned to see Clabber pushing the apartment door open with a finger. Clabber stood looking silently at him.

"I see you've heard the news," he said finally.

Richardson turned his back to Clabber, nodding. "Yeah."

There was a long pause. "Did you hear about the walls of the house?"

Richardson reluctantly turned away from the white pad like a man interrupted from an intense labor. He looked at Clabber. "Walls? What do you mean?"

Clabber studied his face for another long moment. "I think you'd better come with me over to that house. There's something there you ought to see."

20

Their feet crunched in the dry snow, smooth and untracked under the full moon that soared amidst traveling clouds.

Clabber carried a pressure-type gasoline lantern, unlit. He kept his head down from the cold as he walked.

Richardson looked ahead fearfully. He saw the grocery sign in the moonlight. Beside it, the crane's boom rose at a steep angle into the night sky, menacing the helpless buildings around it. A fox in the chicken coop.

They crossed the expanse of white in moonlight at a rapid pace set by Clabber. Richardson glanced at Clabber's face and realized that Clabber was excited.

The cold got in at Richardson's ankles and wrists, burned his face and tortured his earlobes. He was shivering, apprehensive, and filled with a terrible sense of loneliness. He felt as remote from Clabber as a patient alone with a masked surgeon.

When they reached the intersection, they walked into the midst of many tracks. In front of 1028 the snow was trampled.

Richardson followed Clabber up the steps and stopped as Clabber knelt in the vestibule. He expertly pumped pressure into the fuel chamber in the darkness.

A moment later a small ball of match light illuminated his cupped hands and the profile of his face. He reached the small flame to the mantles. The lamp emitted a sighing sound as bright light filled the vestibule—a harsh light that flattened every plane and washed away all shadows.

Clabber stood up and lifted the lamp by the wire bail. Carrying it at his side, he mounted the stairs. Richardson reluctantly followed. Clabber was to have his dramatic moment.

Their booted feet rang loud on the wooden steps. Clabber reached the turning and stepped along the hallway. The spindles of the hall banister loomed monstrously, then fell away as the glaring lamp passed them. Richardson followed the turning, passing semidark rooms, empty, abandoned. He dared to think of the *whooshing* noise in his apartment. The thought of spending a night alone in this empty building in darkness filled him with panic.

At the foot of the second flight of stairs, Clabber paused long enough to look back at Richardson. Then he began to mount, slowly, one slow step, then two, then three. He looked again at Richardson.

At first Richardson thought it was the weird effect of the lantern. Then he saw it.

The wall going up the stairs and the wall facing him at the top were covered with figures. White plaster walls, virginal in their whiteness. Someone had peeled off the old paper and drawn on the walls.

Clabber halted, watching Richardson's reaction. Richardson stepped up several more steps and peered at the drawings.

"Madness," he said involuntarily.

21

The figures in the foreground were gigantic—over seven feet high—and gowned about in monks' cassocks. Menacing, thick figures they were, with their faces hidden by their cowls, phalanxed in a row up the wall like chess pieces. Solid overpowering masses of monks' brown.

Between them, below them, above them in stunning contrast were phantasms in violent furious colors. Flagella, toadstools, bottle-shaped figures with twisting follicles, all limp as though melting and ready to ooze down the wall and onto the steps. They were done in heavy black outline and filled in with chrome yellows, deep reds, blues, sickening bilious greens.

There was a third layer of figures. These smaller and seeming distant, well into the background, very dark in blues, grays, greens. They had large staring eyes—

mad, frightening eyes, panic-stricken, beyond soothing, beyond reply. Amorphous, terrified and terrifying.

Every line was distorted. Everything was frightening.

Richardson looked with wonder at it. Then he shook his head at it all in disbelief. Clabber began to mount the stairs, and as he moved, the lantern illuminated the figure on the wall at the top of the stairs.

This was another monk, larger than the others. The peak of his cowl reached up the wall to the ceiling. The monk in the roadway at the bottom of the iron fence? His face was shadowed dark but partly visible, and the eyes were burning, remorseless, insane. One hand rested limply on the handle of a great battle sword that was planted in the foreground in front of the monk. He expressed the towering rage of divinity.

The other hand—the left hand—pointed directly down the stairwell at Richardson.

Richardson hesitated, staring at it, intimidated by it.

"Come on. There's more," said Clabber. He climbed to the top of the stairs and turned, waiting. Richardson had had enough. He wanted to leave.

Clabber beckoned with a finger. "The best is up in this room."

Richardson mounted the stairs slowly. The risers of the stairs seemed imposingly high and he felt small and powerless, passing each menacing, malevolent, enormously high figure. Eyes everywhere, multitudinous eyes peered out from behind the monks, stared at him with awe and dread—the most infinite transgressor in the universe.

When he reached the top of the stairs he felt almost impelled to kneel before the pointing, accusing, silent monk.

Clabber waited patiently in the doorway of the room, watching Richardson's eyes study the figure. At last Richardson looked at him. Richardson didn't want to go into that room.

Slowly, Clabber's arm raised the lantern. As it passed his face, his frosty breath was illuminated. He turned with the raised lantern and entered the room. Richardson stepped to the doorway and looked in.

Human figures, smaller than life, half size, formed a writhing, upward-struggling pyramid of bodies, nude in pasty grays, unhealthy figures with sagging thews and soft, bloated bodies panic-stricken; seeking to escape upward, they attempted to climb the wall, to climb each other, standing on other fallen figures, figures struggling to rise with the weight of others on them. Many were supine and motionless, trampled to lifelessness. All the climbing writhing figures were partly turned so that all of them stared in frozen motion in silent sound from that wall directly at Richardson.

What they sought to escape from was him. Richardson. Panic beyond control.

Adjacent to them was an oversize human head. A large pair of tinsnips had cut open a portion of the skull. A horde of hideous demons poured out of the incision. Above them stood an ethereal cherubic angel in a white robe. He held a flaming sword.

These figures filled the entire windowless wall except for the middle. There was a huge head from floor to ceiling in a black derby. An extraordinary portrait: a man with dark hair, dark eyebrows, clean-shaven, about thirty, with a tan complexion and a thin-lipped determined mouth. The eyes were enigmatic, ambivalent.

Purposefulness on the face, however, was dominant, almost overpowering, utterly implacable.

Richardson stared at the colossal face. A face he'd never seen before, a face he'd never mistake, not ever, if ever he were to see it.

The wall adjacent at right angles to it was incomplete.

It was a hand-lettered statement. In ponderous, unadorned letters of enormous strength but irregular as though almost clapped onto the wall in desperate haste, a final warning. It said:

"Richardson! Run for your life!"

22

Richardson blundered along beside Clabber, with bowed head and shivering dog's body, feeling his shoes crunching through the snow.

He was guilty. Guilty of a vast unspeakable crime. The loneliness, the separateness from all other human life, seeped up through his wet shoes into his soul. He glanced once at Clabber and felt he was being led by a keeper. The cold, the endless bitter cold was no longer a part of the environment; it was a presence, a spirit, a tormentor bent on destroying all the fight in him.

He was struck with how fragile human life is.

"It's the time-honored thing to do for shock," said Clabber. "Actually, alcohol is a depressant, but maybe it will help." He poured three fingers of brandy into a small glass.

Richardson looked at it, then looked around at Clabber's kitchen. He was seated in the same chair again, in his overcoat again and sensing again that he should get up and walk out. Instead he picked up the brandy and took a mouthful of it. He swallowed it and felt the warmth like a ball sink slowly to his stomach.

Clabber sat down cross-armed and watched him. "Well, at least there are three people who believe that someone is trying to kill you."

Richardson scowled at him. "Three?"

"Well, there *were* three."

Richardson frowned at him.

"You, and me and Goulart."

"You knew about that, Clabber?" Richardson waggled a thumb in the direction of the empty house.

"Ah, no, not that. I knew that Goulart was convinced he had psychic powers—"

"And I can guess who convinced him."

Clabber shrugged indifferently. "I let him read my books. And I talked to him. Beyond that he went by himself."

"What do you mean 'beyond that'?"

"Drugs is what I mean. Goulart started with certain meditation exercises that are described in one of my books. And he had flashes and insights, so he drew them. Fragmentary pictures they were—one of a Roman centurion, I remember. Goulart had an artist's mind, so everything was visual. He might have been sketching things he'd seen years ago. That's not a psychic experience or insight. I warned him not to be too impressed. But he was convinced he was on to something. About a month ago, he told me he was experiencing strong psychic shocks. He sensed that you were in trouble. Something was going to happen to you. I think he was already using hallucinogens. And as far as I'm concerned, that destroys the validity of the experience. And I told him so. He said he was convinced that he could see who was going to hurt you, see his face, if only he could have a strong enough psychic manifestation. Well, you see the result."

Richardson looked doubtfully at him. "That stuff made sense to you?"

"Oh, some. Look, Richardson, you can see artwork like that in any insane asylum. Most of it is typical of the dangerously paranoid mind."

"Paranoid! Goulart was insane?"

Clabber waggled a hand doubtfully. "That's an iffy thing. He may have had an authentic experience—"

"Explain that artwork to me."

Clabber poured more brandy into Richardson's glass. "No. I'm not equipped for that. But I think he painted the whole thing for you. That artwork isn't complete unless you personally are standing within it. All those figures are focusing on you, looking at you. Some express menace—directed at you. And the others are clearly terrified of you."

"Me? What the hell are you talking about?"

"I don't know. But all those paintings in the back room focus at a point in the middle of the room. If you stand there in the exact center of that room, then all eyes focus on you. Everything, including that enormous face with the derby. There's only one way to find out what Goulart was trying to say." He looked at Richardson and waited.

"What am I—the straight man? Okay. I'll bite. What way?"

"A séance."

Richardson slapped a hand on the table in disgust and turned his face away. "Clabber, you're just too many.

You're—you're as persistent as a guy selling hot watches from a dark doorway. I have no intention of going to a séance. Goulart killed his mind with drugs and I've lost my best friend. Beyond that it's all pure bullshit."

Clabber rubbed his fingers on his chin and regarded Richardson. "Then explain how he heard it, too?"

"Heard what?"

"That *whooshing* sound."

CHAPTER VII

C arson knocked on Richardson's door. When it was
opened, Carson looked sourly at Richardson.
"What's a working stiff like you doing home during office
hours?"

"Oh, I had to give testimony at the inquest this afternoon."

"Okay. Now, ask me what I'm doing home."

"Okay. What are you doing home?"

"I'm watching them load a moving van, that's what
I'm doing home. No matter where I stand, they tell me
I'm in the way. We're going to be out of here with all our
goods and chattels in a few minutes, so I wanted to give
you your last-minute sailing orders. Okay? Invite me
into your leafy bower."

He stepped into Richardson's apartment and sat slowly down on the arm of a chair.

"You look kind of frazzled, Christopher. What's the matter?"

"That's my line to you," said Carson. "You look kind of frazzled. But if I look frazzled, too, well then that proves that life is sometimes a kick in the head for everybody. It is not so?"

Richardson nodded.

"Okay, then heed the words of old Perfesser Possum here. You get your can in gear and move the hell out of here. Away from that creeping Jesus down there in his monk's cave, away from mysterious noises, away from psychedelic wall paintings. If you hang around here much longer they're going to certify you to Creedmoor and you'll end up making raffia picture frames for the rest of your life."

Richardson stared at him solemnly.

"Okay," said Carson. "Some days you can't get a laugh for trying. But you know what I'm talking about. It's all over. The whole damn thing. End of Act I. It's a perfect time to make a clean break and start fresh somewhere else. Forget the noises in the dark and Goulart's tragedy. The whole thing adds up to zero. *Nada.* Goose egg. And worst of all is creeping Jesus down there. Pete, he's a number one crackpot and you should stay the hell away from him. He's the one that got Ozzie started. He's a bad influence. Listen, can you get a few weeks off, say ten days?"

"Yeah. I suppose. Why?"

"Haul your butt over to Kennedy and flap down to Florida for a couple weeks. First move your crap out of here into a new place, far away from here, then get down to some sunshine, girls, night spots."

2

"Okay. I'll do it. I'm okay. I'm making it."

"I know, I know. Don't worry about you. Is that it?"

"Well, sure."

"Bullshit. That woman I'm married to has been making my ear bleed. Abby has been calling me ten times every night. Griselda feels so bad she's threatening to burn her whole dammed deck. And you tell me not to worry. No. I'm here with a simple message. Stay away from that flaming fanatic, find an apartment and go have fun in Florida." He stood up. "Yeah?"

"Yeah. Okay."

Carson stepped to the door. "Now when Carol comes up, tell her we talked and everything's going to be okay; okay?"

"Yep, yep. I'll do it."

Carson left.

Richardson stared at the shut door for a time. Then he nodded his head. "Okay." He opened the newspaper to the Apartments For Rent columns.

3

Carol Carson looked tired. She stood in his doorway holding out a hand, and he took it and held it, feeling it soft and small in his palm.

"Well, we'll keep in touch, Pete."

"Yes, we will."

"And you're going to move out of here? On the double? And that's a promise?"

"Yep. On the double."

"Houses can go bad just like people, Pete, and this house is 'going bad.' "

"What does that mean?"

"It means that this house is a bad place now and you should move out."

"Woman's intuition?"

"No. More. I've felt it the last few days. So. Out. Yes?"

"Okay, Carol."

"And take a vacation."

She studied his face, then put her arms around his waist and hugged him. He put his arms around her and patted her shoulder. "It's going to be okay. Don't worry." He smelled the scent of her hair and remembered another scent, another head.

"Good," she said. "Good." She stepped back. "Please get out of here and get back to living. And keep in touch with me. I may need a shoulder to cry on." She turned and hurried down the staircase.

"Hey," he called after her. She stopped and turned. "Smile," he said.

She smiled grimly at him. "In my next reincarnation, I'm coming back as a nightclub blonde."

4

Sunshine had melted much of the snow in the roadway.

The Carson moving van left two tire tracks in the slush of the roadway.

Now Clabber and Richardson were the only tenants in the building.

5

At dusk, Willow stood by his apartment window and looked out at the harbor. His mind went over the Algernon Tully line. Reviewed all the documents. No slips? No little bastard carrying on the line and populating whole counties? Line extinct? Line extinct.

He turned away from the ever-busy harbor and got a chair. He placed it before his wall chart and stood on it. With care, he reached up and drew a line in red ink through Henry Tully's name.

He wrote: "Line extinct."

Then he drew a red line through Roger Tully's name and wrote in red ink: "Line extinct."

Lastly, he put a line in red through Algernon's name. "Line extinct."

One left. Right here in Brooklyn. The brother, Thomas.

He made himself a scotch on ice and saluted the air with it. "*Bona fortuna,*" he said. "May your mission fail."

Tomorrow morning: Thomas. The last one.

6

The Reverend Dr. Aspinall was quite precise in his manner. "Yes, Mr. Willow," he said. "He was most emphatically a sexton in our church. The records are quite clear. From February 1764 when he first appears on our rolls to September 1773. As you can see." He pointed at the church register open before Willow. "The facsimile copy of the original register is rather easy to read. His wife, Alice Barton Tully, and his only child, Joseph, aged thirteen, died of black fever September 14 and 15, 1773. They are buried right outside in the church-yard where I showed you. From what you've told me, I would suppose that Thomas Tully emigrated here from Boston in that year, 1764, registered his family as mem-bers of the congregation and also became sexton. It sounds as though he arrived with the highest recom-mendations from Boston."

Willow stood up and looked at the Reverend Aspinall. "You've been most helpful."

"Alas, I haven't, Mr. Willow. The Thomas Tully line of the Tully family ends in our churchyard, I'm afraid."

"Yes. Well. Thank you." He walked on thick, richly woven carpeting toward the hand-carved door. Through the floor faintly, he felt the vibrations of the heavy trac-tor trucks rolling by the church on the road to the Brooklyn-Battery Tunnel.

He stepped out into the sidewalk. He strode quickly along the slushy streets, a soft glop that would freeze at sundown. He walked the narrow Brooklyn streets, passed wrought-iron fences, stone stoops, and naked buttonwood trees under pale winter sunlight.

At a corner, he turned toward the harbor and saw a neighborhood taproom he'd noted earlier. He trod through the slush to it and entered.

"Scotch," he said to the bartender. "With a side of water."

As he poured the scotch, the bartender resumed his conversation with two men.

Willow turned away, intent on his own thoughts. He

looked at the harbor at the end of the street. The evidence was explicit. The search was over. None of the four Tully sons had left an heir. All four lines had become extinct. Extinct. Four lines extinct. He was free. He could go home.

Willow writhed with suppressed joy and stared at his scotch. He could walk back to his apartment. He could call BOAC and catch the next jet back to London. On the weekend he'd be down at the boatyard in a sun-warm shed out of the Channel wind. He'd strip the finish from his mast, back to the bare wood, and add a new finish. He'd take some of the brightwork home with him and wait out winter in his flat polishing brightwork—wait for spring, wait for that first regatta, the first crack of sail filled with wind.

He smiled tightly and took a drop of the whiskey. No slip-ups. Each line definitely ended and extinct and documented. Henry: "Denied the natural issue of my body." Algernon: bastardized grandson lives out his days a recluse bachelor with a morbid fear of women. Roger: family destroyed by fire. Thomas: wife and only child— a son—dead of black fever.

He writhed again, the insistent image of his boat, his flat, his friends, his London haunts, his law practice all rising in his memory. Freed. Released.

He counted the bodies. Henry and wife are buried in Goshen. Algernon, wife and daughter are buried in Camden; illegitimate issueless grandson buried in Mt. Ephraim. Roger is buried in England; wife and children in Connecticut. Thomas—wife and son buried in a Brooklyn cemetery a few blocks distant. He paused. Thomas is buried where?

Willow took a mouthful of whiskey. Where's Thomas?

Old Thomas. Heartbroken Thomas. His wife and son dead and buried, he relinquishes his post as Sunday sexton and goes—where? To his wine warehouse at the foot of the Heights, on the harbor quayside, near the piers. Yes, that's what he did. The year?—1773 of course. Bad year for trade. All the 1770s were bad years. The quarrels with England. The resolutions passed by the colonial assemblies. The strident voices. The balled fists, hammering the tavern tables. The stamp taxes and others. And smuggling. And finally, the dumping of tea.

And Thomas is in trouble. Sitting in his warehouse, a lonely old widower. How old? Born 1729. Widowed in 1773. Age forty-four. Not old enough, his loins still capable of conceiving children. Where's Thomas after 1773, and his viable loins? A lonely widower or suitor for the hand of a second wife?

Willow hurried out of the barroom and through the streets. He reached the steps of his apartment, unlocked the front door, hurried past the large old clock up the softly carpeted stairs, unlocked his inner door and entered his apartment. He seized the telephone book and quickly thumbed the pages, then ran his finger down the column of type. He found the number and dialed it, then waited as it rang.

"Oh. There you are, Reverend Aspinall. I've committed a most glaring error. I've not got any information at all on where, when and how Thomas Tully died." He listened attentively and slowly sat down, slowly nodding.

"And that's the end of it, 1773? No further record of him at all? But if he removed himself from the church rolls, wouldn't there be a record of his new affiliation? None? Hmmmm." Willow pondered that for a moment.

"Well, thank you again, Dr. Aspinall. Your patience is greatly appreciated. Yes. Goodbye."

He put the phone in its cradle and sat in deep thought. Was is possible that one of the brothers got away from him? 1773. No wife, no son. Soon, no wine trade. What did he do, that Thomas Tully? Where did he go? Willow had a sudden vision of himself wandering the libraries and churches and churchyards of the eastern seaboard of the United States, seeking Thomas Tully's grave. Suppose he was buried right here in Brooklyn. A recluse, a bankrupt, a widower with no church affiliation after his family dies. And then he dies alone somewhere—possibly in a fever carried by one of the waves of epidemics that seemed to come every winter and spring. One of many carted off to a common grave and buried. No record. Willow felt panic. He stood up and quickly walked up and down the room, staring at a stoneless plot of ground —a common grave unmarked and long forgotten in a backyard or garden in Brooklyn, beyond finding, unrecorded, unmarked forever.

Did Thomas Tully leave any issue? Willow knew he had to know or spend the rest of his life wandering, seeking, tormented until the day he died.

He poured himself a few fingers of scotch and pulled himself up. Probate records next. Tully never died in potter's field. There would be real estate records, Revolution or no Revolution. But suppose he abandoned it all during the Revolution and returned to England.

Easy. Easy. One step at a time. Organize, control. He glanced at his watch. Tomorrow morning. Probate and Register of Deeds. No more panic. Calm down. How about dinner with Alice Polsley? The Lady of the Legs.

The phone rang.

Willow put the glass down. The panic returned. A man who leaves his church leaves his community. Willow knew that Thomas Tully must have left Brooklyn in 1773. And only God knew where he went.

The phone rang again. And again.

Unhappily, Willow picked it up, feeling weary, awed by the vision of the years of searching labor ahead of him.

"Mr. Willow?"

"Yes."

"This is Dr. Aspinall calling. Maybe this is a straw that drowning men cling to, but I have a small clue that might help you. I have just reviewed the volume on the history of our church which was published in 1820. There is a list of all the sextons who served in the church up to that time, and I find Thomas Tully's name listed as expected—but in the margin in faded pencil is the word Winelandia. Does that help you?"

7

The first ray of light came at eight o'clock that night from Kenneth Smith. It was a sixty-four-page brochure found in the vertical file of the public library titled *A History of American Wine Grapes.*

Willow pushed away the several piles of volumes he'd conned during the afternoon and evening and sat back with Mr. Smith's chatty history in his lap. . . .

America had always been a legendary land of fabulous wine grapes. Leif Ericson named the part of North America he visited Wineland because of the abundance of delicious wild grapes. Authorities do not agree where

Wineland is. Some say it's all fable. Some place it in Providence, Rhode Island. Others at the mouth of the Hudson River.

When the first colonists arrived, they brought grape slips with them from European vines. Spanish missionaries brought Spanish slips. None survived. Blights and fungi not known in Europe attacked the grapes, while the New World plant louse *Phylloxera* attacked and destroyed the roots.

Colonists then turned to native grapes growing in the wild. These grapes were immune to *Phylloxera* and fairly resistant to fungi and molds. Under cultivation, they created new varieties. Most of these experiments were attempts to find a New World wine grape. Soon there was an active two-way traffic between America and Europe as varieties were swapped and studied on both sides of the Atlantic. The inevitable happened—in 1863 *Phylloxera* got into Europe, and in an incredibly short time millions of acres of Europe's best vineyards were destroyed.

Just in time, the roots of American vines were shipped to Europe, and on those American roots traditional European vines were grafted. The European grape in all its celebrated varieties was saved. Today, almost all European grape arbors are growing on American roots.

A curious sidelight to this story of the American grape took place at about the time of the American Revolution. Because of the various acts of the English Parliament, the colonist found that his wine, like his tea, was a political and fiscal toy. A group of men decided to make a concerted effort to develop and grow an untaxable American grape that would provide a good-tasting ordinary table wine. A number of sites were selected for experimentation. Favorite targets were the mountain slopes of northern New Jersey, southern New York, and Pennsylvania.

Lack of experience, coupled with an inadequate knowledge of the environmental needs of the grape, plagued the developers. The outbreak of the Revolution spurred on their efforts, however, when the inflow of wine ceased entirely.

The winters were too severe for the then-known grape species, the summers much too humid and wet; the excessive rain in poorly selected sites encouraged the growth of fungi and molds, and at first the whole adventure suffered defeat. Brave new communities like Winelandia disappeared.

Winelandia where? Where, oh where, Mr. Smith? Willow flipped the remaining pages of the brochure— the spread of cultivated grape growing, the new varieties of grapes, the era of Prohibition and the virtual disappearance of American wine-grape cultivation. But no further reference to Winelandia. No index. No bibliography. No footnotes.

Willow slumped in his chair and frowned thoughtfully. Winelandia is a place. Or it was. It was a domestic place, reachable by American colonists and protectable from English taxes. Winters were too severe—so that wiped out the southern states. Smith specifically mentions New York, New Jersey, and Pennsylvania.

Willow's weary reddened eyes roved over the banks of library books. Thomas lost his wife and son and probably his wine-importing business.

Then, as now, people start anew by wiping the slate— finding a new location, a new activity. Thomas chose Winelandia. Winelandia where?

In the reference section, he found the atlases and gazetteers.

He sat down with New Jersey and went through Windsor, Winfield, and Winslow Township. No Winelandia. New York had no Winelandia, nor did Pennsylvania. Smith had stated that Winelandia had disappeared, and it had.

Because New York State was a major grape-growing area, Willow got down a pile of books on New York's history: histories of countries, chronicles of agricultural development, the building of the Erie Canal, the Spirit Way west, transplanted New Englanders, a history of the immigrants. No Winelandia. He turned to New Jersey.

He found a history of the Pine Barrens; a history of the secret building of warships in Lake Alloway during the Revolution; Indian tribes of the seacoast; history of glass manufacturing; a four-volume study of Trenton's history; New Jersey biographies; mining, fishing, industry; and then—a curious volume. *Old Jersey Towns: Lost, Strayed or Annexed.* The contents included Towns That Died, Towns That Changed Their Names, Towns That Were Absorbed, Ghost Towns. In the index he found it. Winelandia, page 208.

The author substantiated Smith's account. Winelandia survived for sixteen years. It was such a small settlement it hardly qualified as an independent community. It died in 1794 when promising developments in grape culture in New York State lured most of the residents up into Sullivan County. A few years later, Winelandia was a ghost town up in the old mountains of northwest New Jersey.

Willow sighed. Another car ride.

8

"It was," said the curator, "an unbelievably hard life."
His quick hands put the key in the lock and opened it. He
lifted the hasp on the door. It opened slowly. "Now, as
I explained to you, Mr. Willow, this is really a replica
of the typical frontier cabin in what were the wilds of
New Jersey in colonial days." He led Willow inside.

"Those people who came up here were not city types—
Tully notwithstanding. The first thing they did when
they settled on the frontier was build a cabin just like
this. After a few years of unremitting exhausting labor,
they'd build a new and more elaborate house, like the
one next door, which I'll show you in a moment. But
this is the key structure. In order to get into the relative
opulence of that house next door, you had to go through
this. Now this cabin and the hard times that went with
it soon found out the weaklings and—simply, it killed
them. Well, you can see. It's a one-story hut, all logs
with two rooms—a kitchen and a sleeping room. It
usually faced south and was built near a spring or a
creek. A stone chimney and fireplace was imperative.
Life could not have survived without it. For windows,
they sawed through the logs. They covered the window
with paper that was weatherproofed with lard. Let in
light, kept out the cold—some of it, at least. That fireplace gave off some heat, but a bucket of water three
feet from it would freeze solid. The floor was dirt, packed
down with many feet, the roof a clapboard affair. The
wind blew through the cracks in the winter, and in
summer, life was a screaming hell of insects and sweat-
soaked bedding. In fact, it got so cold in here in winter
that a man went to bed simply by taking off his shoes.
In he got, wearing his home-knitted socks and shirt, his

leather pants and fur-lined coat and knitted hat. If he was lucky, he'd have a few comforters—big thick things stuffed with duck down. Nobody washed above the wrist or below the collar until spring came."

He led Willow outside. "I slept in that cabin one night with a roaring fire in the fireplace. Temperature was down around twelve degrees. I had a modern camper's sleeping bag with me, and I tell you it was cold. Now down here next to the house was the root cellar, and this decided whether he and his family would make it through the winter or starve to death." Willow ducked his head as he entered it.

"In late autumn, the head of the family would come down here with his wife, and they'd take stock and count mouths. To make it through the winter, he had to have this place stuffed to the walls with all kinds of food. Flour, lots of it. Smoked hams, bacon, cheese, eggs, pickles, sauerkraut in barrels, piles and piles of potatoes, butter, a small mountain of turnips and parsnips, vinegar, rum and ale and cider, barrels of them. If he figured correctly—and if weather didn't delay spring planting, if the rats and other burrowing animals didn't get in, if the family remained healthy through the winter—well, then the following summer he got the chance to try to grow enough to last through another winter. Maybe.

"Or if he guessed wrong, the snows soon came and buried him and his family until spring. If the food ran out, they just starved to death waiting for things to melt.

"Keep in mind that while the whole family was involved in this scratching with bare hands to get enough to eat, and cutting enough wood to keep from freezing to death and to cook the food, and praying to the Lord that the fire didn't go out during the night—worrying about the horse getting sick or the cow drying up or the chickens dying with a pox . . . during all that, these people were trying to establish a grape-growing industry, a subject about which they knew precious little."

The curator looked with an ironic smile at Willow. "It was, as I said, an indescribably lousy life."

Willow looked with awe at the crude cabin and the root cellar. "How did a man who'd led the life of a comfortable gentleman ever adjust to this?"

"Many a so-called gentleman did—trying to recoup his fortune lost in the world market. Oh, this was the great leveler. You either coped and conquered or you died, no matter how elegant your previous life was."

"It must have been doubly hard on a bachelor."

"Bachelor! Mr. Willow, no bachelors lived here. The three most important animals a man had were a horse, a cow, and a wife—a fertile wife at that."

Willow turned and surveyed the terrain that surrounded the cabin. "Not a trace of written records, you say?"

"You see what's here. That's it. Six or eight foundations for cabins, one or two remnants of fireplaces and chimneys, and a general scattering of buried artifacts. I understand that there are some historical accounts of the place down in the archives in the state capital."

"Where's that?"

"Trenton."

"Wasn't there a church or a newspaper—a school?"

"Mr. Willow, there was nothing. I doubt if there was a quill pen among the lot of them. Most of them were illiterate. Newspapers were unheard of, and the church —there was none—not for miles around. This was an out-and-out wilderness, and the people who lived here just barely managed to be a little better than animals in burrows. Try Trenton. You might find something there."

9

The Kittatinny Mountains descended in tucks and folds to the Piedmont Plateau under a snow cover. Route 519 was a wet black ribbon that twisted down and away into the distance.

The winter landscape under a dead gray sky was a weariness to Willow. Leafless trees stood out against the whiteness of the snow. A flight of crows rose, slowly flapping, above the trees, turned and dropped into a frozen field. At the foot of the field, a stream broke through its cover of ice and snow, tumbled through a rock-filled bed for a few feet and disappeared again under the whiteness.

The wind whistled at the metal beading along the edge of his car roof, reminding him that the arctic air was still in firm control of the land.

"If they figured right," the curator had said, "they'd make it through the winter. If not, they'd starve and freeze to death. It happened all the time."

Willow looked out at the terrain again, feeling the warmth from the car heater around his ankles. He was acquiring a considerable admiration for Thomas Tully. Of the four brothers, Thomas was the boldest. A hell of a man, in fact. A study in opposites and extreme contrasts, Thomas and Roger. Roger, losing his family, pined away, defeated and transfixed with horror. Thomas immediately responded to a greater challenge, choosing to live still closer to personal catastrophe.

Which to admire—the meek, loving man or the bold, unflinching one?

10

Trenton, ambling along the curling edges of the Delaware River, looked like a city being rebuilt from its own ruins. New buildings, many of them state government structures, rose up in the midst of the old red brick buildings trimmed in white marble. Interspersed were tracts and flat lots of cleared land waiting for new buildings.

Everywhere the sooty, sick-gray remnants of the snowfall added a depressing decoration to the city.

Willow gazed at the buildings of the city as he drove through. Somewhere here was there information on Thomas?

11

The librarian shook his head. "Sorry," he said.

Willow stood in the Archives and History Division of the New Jersey State Library, State Department of Education, State House Annex, and watched the slowly wagging head.

"No."

"No," said the librarian. "There have been several attempts to reconstruct the history of Winelandia. Several scholars from Princeton got a grant to compile a bibliography and inventory of research resources not too long ago, but the results were disappointing. It's a nettlesome piece of history. It's quite probable that at least two commercially valuable strains of grapes were developed by those people, but there are practically no

written records. Maybe you can locate some information right at the site. I understand there's a recon-
structed cabin and small frontier house on the original
ground."

"Been there," said Willow. "This morning, in fact.
Nothing."

The librarian watched him silently, sorrowfully.

"Well," said Willow, "thank you. I'll have to regroup
and find some other avenue of approach."

"Yes. Sorry. Good luck. Oh, if you turn up anything,
I'd like very much to hear about it."

"It's not very likely, is it?"

"No, I'm afraid not."

Willow turned and walked toward the exit. A wave of
panic swept him again. For months he'd been living with
the prospect of an implacable dead end, but it hadn't
been real until he'd started on Thomas. The first real
scare was the church in Brooklyn. By all genealogical
odds, he should have lost the trail there, except for a
chance word on the margin of an old church history.

If Thomas had remarried in Winelandia, begotten
children and died with no records, then his descendants
could be walking about with no known way to connect
them back to Thomas. Appalling thought: Willow would
wander forever in a kind of genealogical limbo.

He shrugged. Like Mr. Micawber, he hoped something
would turn up.

But he didn't believe it.

12
If anything, the day had gotten grayer. The snow,
dirtier. And Trenton, more depressing.

Willow pushed open the glass door and felt the rush of cold air pounce on him.

"Excuse me," called a voice behind him. "Excuse me."

Willow turned and looked back through the glass door. The librarian was walking rapidly down the corridor. Willow pulled the glass door open and stepped back inside.

"You didn't see the circuit rider's collection, did you?"

"Circuit rider?" murmured Willow.

"Stupid of me. They're the only source books we have. After you left, I realized that—well, I assumed while we were talking that you'd already gone through them. Do you know anything about them?"

"No. Nothing."

"Well, I don't want to raise false hopes. The information is pretty skimpy, but you really should go through them." The librarian started back and Willow walked at his side.

"You see, it was a wilderness up there. There were few settlements. Most of the people up there were trappers and the like. So the colonial sects and churches created circuit-riding preachers and ministers. And they went by horseback all through the frontier."

Willow followed him to the stacks and watched him search a shelf. "Ah. Poe." The librarian pulled down a volume. He tapped it lightly with his fingertips, holding it forth to Willow. "Volume I. This is the daybook and diary of Aristotle Poe. He was an ordained minister and he covered a great deal of territory in those mountains. He went into Pennsylvania, New York, and New Jersey, and he kept fairly complete records. There are twelve volumes. And one of them just might have some references to your man. I know that he visited Winelandia regularly over a period of years. There are several other saddlebag ministers' diaries here, but I think Poe's your best bet." The librarian left him holding the volume.

Willow sat down at a library table. Another volume, another search. "Good luck," he murmured to himself as he opened the cover.

13

Aristotle Poe gave Willow a clear picture of life on the frontier. He apparently rode several thousand miles a year, preaching as often as twice a day and three or more times on Sundays. He spoke from tree stumps, from boulders, and even from the back of his horse. In bad weather he preached inside log huts and crude houses, in barns and often in tents.

The people walked for miles to see him—to hear him preach and to have him marry and baptize and shrive.

Cold, dirt, vermin, hunger and disease were the enemies. During the winter months, Poe's diary was constantly referring to warm fires. "Preached at the Martin farm. Farmer Martin provided a good fire as it was fearful cold abroad. After, we had hot cider. Slept in good comfort in the hayloft over the cow in an abundance of warm hay with God's grace. During the night a tree burst with frost."

And: "Preached at Jedediah Downes's farm. A goodly crowd, but firewood was low and we sat shivering until the press of people warmed the kitchen. Three Downes children died last month during a local outbreak of fever."

He baptized children everywhere, some two years after their birth, some in their teens. His marriage activities soared in the spring. He spiked the activities of long winter nights with terse good humor: "Married this day Noah Veryman and Margaret Goodsteeple with the fervent blessings of both families. The marriage is none-too-soon for they have already well-begun their family. The weather being fair, a large gathering assembled from around the county for a celebration." He noted stoically when he was plagued with fleas or infested with ticks, chiggers and body lice. In March he would look forward longingly to a bright warm spring day when he could wash his tormented, bitten body in a stream and drown the vermin in his clothes and bedroll.

His teeth went bad along with all others' in his territory. It was an obliging farmer who would grip the rotting stump with a blacksmith's tool and rip it from the gum.

Willow was absorbed in the life and trials of this infinitely patient, faithful minister, and the first reference to Winelandia caught him unawares. Aristotle Poe reported factually that he had visited Winelandia, a new settlement with fourteen families—a large gathering for that time and place. Willow sat up and continued reading with attention. He began now to skim impatiently. It was 1774. Six months elapsed before he visited it again. Between the two visits, eight children died. He lists them, names and ages and place of burial. Two adults, also dead, are duly recorded. And two marriages. Willow stopped reading and stared:

"Married this day one Thomas Joseph Tully, late of Brooklyn, aged 46, bachelor and widower by his own account, grape grower and farmer, and Anna Schipstadt, 17, daughter of Herman and Helga Schipstadt, farmers."

Willow lowered his head to his hands. Seventeen. She'd have children—years of abundant childbearing ahead of her.

Willow walked to the librarian's desk. "Is there an index of names and families for Poe's diaries?"

The librarian shook his head. "I'm sorry. If you'd like the job, I'm sure I can get you a grant for it." He smiled. "It's long overdue."

"Thanks," said Willow. He walked back to the diaries. He had to find a way to abbreviate his search.

He quickly leafed through the remainder of the first volume. Three visits to Winelandia in one year. Willow pulled down the second volume. He paged it quickly, seeking references to Winelandia. As he went, he noted the dates of the visits. Poe was a meticulous man. His progressions were orderly, although his winter travel was apt to be interrupted for several weeks at a time.

Willow projected Poe's preaching circuit and reached down the third volume. If he ran true to his schedule, Poe would visit Winelandia in March of 1777. Willow flipped to that month. March 18, Poe arrived. July would be next. Poe arrived July 23. November? Yes, last November. He arrived during a snowstorm and stayed with the Tullys. Willow stopped his projections abruptly. Listed under baptisms was Joseph Thomas Tully, aged two months. Willow took a deep breath and settled down again at the library table.

Aristotle Poe recorded his steady round of ministrations, recording the birth, growth, flowering, mating, and aging of a whole territory. Willow used Poe's meticulous habits to track him through the diaries for just the visits to Winelandia.

After a few years of diary entries, Willow became quite familiar with the families of Winelandia. Poe recorded all vital statistics, crop news, weather, new road construction, bridges and natural calamities, fires and barn burnings, cattle diseases, epidemics and floods.

Anna Schipstadt gave birth to a daughter in 1778. Margaret. None in 1779. None in 1780. None in 1781. Then another daughter in 1782. Elizabeth. Then silence. No news from the Tully family. Other families added children every other year. Willow continued to skim through years of colonial history, tracking Aristotle Poe's visits to Winelandia. Families moved away. Then more families. The grapes weren't good and the land wasn't suited to much farming. Life was too hard, with no prospect of improvement. Bottomland in Orange County lured some. Others packed up and went looking for the Shenandoah Valley. Several migrated toward the vast prairies of the West. Winelandia was dying.

In December 1789, Anna Schipstadt went into difficult labor. It exhausted her and killed the infant. A week later, Anna Schipstadt died in a fever. She was thirty-one. Two years later almost to the day, Thomas Tully died. Aged sixty-one.

The three Tully children moved in with the Schipstadt family. More families left Winelandia. Poe's visits diminished to two a year. In 1795 in the late spring, Aristotle Poe retired from circuit riding and became a minister in a small church near Princeton. In the last month of his circuit riding, he performed nine marriages.

One of them was that of Margaret Tully. Age sixteen. And with her brother and younger sister, she went to live with her new husband in a civilized town in Vermont.

Her husband's name was Edward Dawes.

15

Cassiopeia westered. In the evening sky, she lay in the northern quadrant, following Andromeda to the western horizon. A stiff breeze cleared the night sky.

Richardson walked from the subway with a bag of groceries and his attaché case, weary of the case, weary of the cold and of winter. There were lights in windows and figures moving to and fro and warmth inside and the business of living. He was a stray stealing past the orbs of warmth, a vagrant, a wandering star.

Brevoort House lay against the night sky like a tombstone. A single light showed from the building, probably Clabber's window. Richardson felt the sudden urge to get out of that building, to find a new place, a clean slate with new faces.

He paused in the midst of the sidewalk, looking at the building and telling himself not to go in, to turn and walk away. He felt the need to be shut of all the baggage and impedimenta of his life.

There was also something about the house that gave him a strong sense of danger.

16

The chilly night air entered the hallway eagerly with him. Like an alert and curious dog, it spun through the vestibule seeming to sniff and seek. There was no light in the vestibule.

Richardson shut the door. He felt along a wall and found the light switch. The vestibule filled with light. He wondered which of the tenants it had been who used to put the vestibule lights on at dusk. He opened his mailbox. It was empty.

Near the foot of the stairs was Abernathy's door. It stood ajar. Richardson peered into the apartment. It stood empty and dark. He shouldered the door open and stepped into the apartment.

It was completely silent. Was there someone standing in the bedroom, holding his breath and listening? Richardson groped for a wall switch and moved it. A garish overhead light went on. The living room was empty. He crossed and looked into the kitchen and the bath and the bedroom and the small den.

"Is there anyone here?" he said aloud.

He turned back to the door and snapped off the light. He walked across the vestibule to the Carsons' apartment door. It was shut. He turned the knob and the door opened. He pushed and watched it slowly swing inward —arcing into the darkness. He stepped into the darkness. A faint odor of old cigar smoke assailed his nostrils.

He tried the switch to the living room ceiling light. It didn't go on. He stepped across the bare floor, hearing his footsteps ringing on the wooden floor. He tried the kitchen light. It went on.

Richardson strolled around the apartment dully, poking into each room, peering into closets. He saw Carol Carson's face and her hair catching the light. He saw the wistful look when someone mentioned children, the unhappy glance at Ruth Abernathy's frank eagerness to be pregnant.

The Carsons were gone; the unhappiness, unaccountably, had remained like the odor of old cigars. And he was an intruder, sniffing into other people's privacy. He snapped off the kitchen light and walked out of the apartment.

At the foot of the stairs, he looked up. No hall lights

on any floor. He tried the bank of switches at the base of the stairwell. The second floor landing lit up, then the third, then the passageways.

He mounted the steps. He wished he didn't have to go up to his apartment. At the landing on the second floor, he stood face to face with Griselda Vandermeer's apartment door. Down the hall from it was Goulart's door, and between them, Clabber's door, with a slit of light at the foot.

Richardson tried Griselda's door. It was unlocked and he pushed it open. Several keys lay on the floor in front of his shoes. He smiled. Keys to locks that would never lock again. He sniffed—a phantasm of her scent, a perfume. Again he had the feeling of someone, arrested, frozen in movement, waiting behind a closed door, listening to his footfall, expectant, with bated breath.

He shrugged and walked away, leaving the door wide open. He stepped past Clabber's door to Goulart's. He tried the knob. It was locked. He reached into his pocket and withdrew a key and inserted it into the lock and opened the door.

Many dark shadows and lumps here. He reached into the room and turned a light switch. For a moment he was shocked. Half the plants were gone; all the art supplies were gone; cardboard cartons stood on the floor and the tables. Richardson stepped in. The closet was empty. The bedclothes gone and the mattress awry. Other cartons waited to be filled. The paintings and illustrations and the leather portfolios were gone. The taboret and drawing board were naked, exuding a disturbing neatness.

Richardson pictured Patty packing her brother's possessions. How many times did she stop to weep? he wondered. Folding a familiar shirt. Seeing anew a years-old painting. Touching his art-school paintbox.

Richardson felt his eyes burning and angrily snapped off the lights. Who are you griping for—Ozzie or yourself?

He backed out of the apartment and mounted the steps. At the landing he found Abby Withers's door open—wide open. He listened for the trill of a ghostly canary, half expected the terrier sinuously to crowd around his legs, snorting gleefully. He pulled the door shut.

He struggled a hand into his pocket and pulled out his key case. He pushed the key into the lock and opened his apartment door. It too was in darkness, and he snapped on the overhead light. Then he dropped the attaché case and the grocery bag on the couch and went about putting on lamps. He toured his apartment, finally lighting the oven. He hung up his overcoat and suit jacket, yanked off his tie and rolled up his shirtsleeves. Then he pulled from the bag a frozen dinner packed in a foil tray and tossed it indifferently into the oven. He couldn't remember what he'd bought—the chicken dinner or the pork. No matter; they all tasted alike.

He walked into the bedroom and found *Tom Jones*. He carried it into the kitchen and propped it up against the table lamp. Getting more like Clabber every day. Maybe they could get an apartment together and eat their evening meals alone together separately—each with his own book propped up. The thought of living in Clabber's barracks amused him and he chuckled.

"Just the two of us left, dearie," he said aloud.

He went to his attaché case and checked through the papers. He estimated an hour or two of work. He stood by the couch looking through the newspaper. When the food was heated, he discarded the paper and went into the kitchen. He withdrew the tray and peeled the foil back. Chicken? Pork maybe. Who knows? Horse or hog, maybe rat, or even people.

He sat down with it and began to idly eat, reading *Tom Jones*. For a while he entered another world, following Tom to London. Then he got up and carried the book into the living room. He sat in a comfortable chair and continued reading. At elbow was a glass of port wine.

17

The cat. Ozzie's cat. He'd forgotten about her.

Richardson stood up. Walking to the kitchen, he opened the refrigerator to pull out an opened can of cat food. He carried it to the apartment door and went into the hallway. Someone had put out the hall lights again. He snapped them on as he descended. There was still a slit of light under Clabber's door as he passed. Griselda's door was shut. He paused. Hadn't he left it open?

He descended the staircase. Both the Abernathys' and the Carsons' apartment doors were shut. He opened the cellar door, then turned on the lights.

Slowly he descended the steps, looking at the cat's feeding dish and bowl of water. Yesterday's food was untouched.

"*Psssst, psssst,*" went Richardson. "Here, kitty. Here, kitty. Come on, you slope-headed cat. You'll die if you don't eat." He listened and looked. The cellar was silent. The glowing eyes of the sulking cat were not visible. Where'd she get to? His eyes searched the empty bins, the shadows and the slats of light. "*Psssst. Psssst.*"

Silence. Again, he had that feeling of hushed, hidden, expectant waiting in the shadows. Who?

"*Psssst. Psssst.*" Richardson thought of Patty. Maybe she'd gotten the cat. He put the can of cat food on the lower step and walked tentatively down the main corridor between the bins. All the bins were empty except his. Even Clabber's and Goulart's. Had Clabber moved? Maybe that light was shining in an empty apartment. His eyes rested on the door to the storage room. He walked down to it. His feet crunched in the silence. Could the cat be shut in there by mistake? He opened it and looked in. It was solidly dark in there, like a room-sized block of coal.

"*Psssst.* Kitty."

No cat.

There was a light switch on the wall outside the door jamb. He flipped it and a small light went on inside the room. He stepped in and looked about. The outside exit door on the right was shut and bolted. For the first time, he noticed a door on the far wall: a metal door with large old-fashioned hinges. The door was not quite shut.

Richardson crossed the empty room and stood at the metal door. A light. There was a light somewhere beyond the door. And a sound. He pulled the door open. Metal grated on metal with a soft squeal. He peered in. It was a corridor. There was a doorway off it to one side, glowing with light. Richardson heard a shuffling sound. He entered the corridor and walked softly toward the doorway. Softly, softly, a slow step, then another slow step.

He reached the edge of the doorway and extended his head. He looked into the room.

A man was sitting there in a wooden chair at a plain

wooden table, with his back to the door. He was wearing a derby.

On the desk was a tape recorder connected to several electric wires that rose to the ceiling. Richardson's heart was throbbing in his ears. Yet he heard the click of the tape recorder as the man pushed a button. The two reels began to turn in unison. The first sound astonished him.

The tape recorder went *Whoosh!* and *Whoosh!* again.

Richardson stood immobile. Then his peripheral vision pulled his eyes to a drawing on the opposite wall. A cowled figure, outlined in heavy black, high and wide, a looming bulky figure.

The cowled head moved. Richardson nearly panicked. He turned to walk rapidly toward the doorway. Abruptly a light filled the corridor, a strange light. Richardson turned. The cowled figure was now moving toward him, holding a rod or a tube or a shaft of light—seemingly a neon or fluorescent strip of light. A sword?

He hurried to the door and stepped through. The lights ahead of him were out. The cellar was dark. He was now terrified. He stumbled and shuffled through the dark room, through the other doorway, finding his way by memory, down the corridor. He groped his way up the stairs.

He heard Goulart's cat cry.

The lights in the vestibule were out. He mounted the hallway stairs, turning on the lights as he went, running two steps at a time. When he reached his door, he thrust it open and slammed it, then slid the bolt home.

When he turned, the noise in the middle of his living room greeted him.

Whoosh!

The copy of *Tom Jones* lay sprawled on the floor. Richardson's heart was thumping rapidly and he was covered with perspiration. He looked around the room, looked at the book and realized that he was sitting on the edge of his chair.

How had that happened? He hadn't seated himself.

He stepped to the door and listened, listened for the sound of a mounting footfall. It was silent outside his doorway.

He stood there for a moment, frowning.

Then he walked to his desk and lifted a phone book out of a drawer. Clabber. No. Not in the phone book. No phone. Damn.

He went into the kitchen and found his broom. He got a ball of twine from his desk and a carving knife from a kitchen drawer. With the string, he fixed the knife on the end of the broomstick, bayonet-wise. Then he went to the doorway and opened it. The hall lights were on. He went to the landing and looked down.

The stairs were empty. The vestibule in the area of the stairwell was empty. Richardson descended the first flight, then scanned the vestibule again. Griselda Vandermeer's door was now wide open.

He descended the flight of steps to the vestibule. No cowled figure. He looked into the cellar. The lights were on. He stepped onto the landing and crouched, looking into the cellar and its bins. He saw Goulart's cat skulking away. He descended and stood at the foot of the steps.

Silence. Oppressive silence. Waiting, expectant silence. He walked toward the end of the corridor. He was trembling and the broomstick shook. He was ready to thrust at anything that moved.

He walked the length of the corridor, feeling his soles crackling on the cement. He reached the door to the empty room and paused. It was firmly shut. He stood regarding it. Then he turned and looked about the cellar, his eyes searching the bins, examining the shadows and the strips of light.

He turned his attention to the doorknob. He looked at it unhappily. Then he reached out with one hand and turned it. It moved. He pushed the door. It opened several inches. Richardson took the broom in his two hands like a rifle, ready to thrust, then shoved the door open with his foot. The door swung inward. He stood looking into the dark room, waiting until his eyes were used to the darkness. Nothing.

He pushed the light switch. A small light went on. He looked across the empty room to the opposite wall.

There was no doorway there.

CHAPTER VIII

The glass of whiskey sat on the kitchen table, quietly reflecting the overhead light, patiently waiting. Richardson rested his head on his arm, his arm on the table before the glass of whiskey. He stared at the floor, feeling a slow anger fill him. He was sick to death of his fears and sweats and his elusive adversary. He raised his head and slammed a fist on the table. He reached out and lifted the glass. He had the whiskey down in two gulps. With the back of his hand, he wiped away the pendulous drop from his lip and stood up. The first thing he was going to do was find that sound.

From the closet by the bathroom, he pulled out a small tape recorder. He checked it, threaded the tape, put the plug in a wall socket and started it. He set it on the coffee table.

He made a circuit of the living room. Four speakers, one in each corner, could be synchronized to broadcast a sound that would meet in the middle of the room. Speakers smaller than a thumbnail. His eyes searched the walls of his living room, slowly, section by section. Next he got on his knees and crawled around the perimeter of the baseboard, groping behind furniture, pulling back the rug.

He stood up. "I'll find you," he said to the room. "You're in here somewhere. You're real. Real. Goulart heard you, too. I'll find you!" He hammered the heel of his fist on the wall. "I will!"

He took a deep breath and tried to think. Someone was planning to kill him. Why? Why?

Who? The Carsons? The Abernathys? Abby Withers? He smiled at that. Griselda Vandermeer? Clabber?

Clabber?

Richardson went to the living room closet and opened the door. He pulled out the driver from his golf bag and looked at it. Clabber, eh?

He looked up at the ceiling and made a tentative swing. Ceiling too low. He stepped to the center of the room and swung the club like a baseball bat.

Whoosh! He swung again. *Whoosh!*

But that wasn't quite it. He swung again. Close but no cigar. There couldn't be any mistake: he'd never forget that noise as long as he lived.

He addressed the head of the club to a tuft in the carpet. Clabber. Clabber. Clabber.

Clabber could do it. He could put a speaker in the living room and another in Goulart's room. He had had Goulart's attention; he could have insinuated anything into Ozzie's thinking. He could have built up that whole fantasy world of Goulart's—walls and walls of forbidding figures, terrifying scenes. Monks with faces hidden in cowls. Monks pointing, indicating guilt. That would fit a warped ecclesiastical mind. He could have planted that face in a derby hat. Maybe Griselda was his helper—with nightclub magic.

Abel Navarre? Explain Abel Navarre, a police detective dead twenty-two years. Richardson sat down, frustrated. Explain Navarre. The hell with it. Somehow it's tied up with Navarre and that Renaissance fanatic. What's his name? Bruno of Nola.

Richardson went to his desk and picked up his key ring. Then he walked to the door and stopped, looking at the bolt. It reminded him of the cellar. He'd forgotten about the cellar. Carefully, he opened the door and peered out. He stepped out on the landing and looked down. He listened.

He descended the steps to the second floor and stopped in front of Clabber's door. He listened. He put his ear to Clabber's door and listened again. No noise. Maybe reading in the kitchen. He stepped to Goulart's door and put the key to the lock. He pushed the door open and snapped on the lights. Everything as it was. Cartons of books and furnishings ready to be carried off.

Richardson squatted and opened the flaps of several cartons. He studied their contents, then lifted the flaps on several others. He reached down and lifted a book.

Renaissance Philosopher. He arose and left the apartment, locking the door behind him.

He mounted the stairs two at a time. Some of the answers were in the book. He was sure.

Nola is sixteen miles east of Naples.

There Filippo Bruno was born in 1548—thirty-one years after Martin Luther had nailed his ninety-five theses to the door of the church at Wittenberg to sunder the Holy Roman Catholic and Apostolic churches.

Bruno of Nola was a mystic, a seer, a soaring romantic, a poetic spirit, a polemicist, an indefatigable writer and a permanent embarrassment to the Catholic Inquisition in Italy.

At seventeen he changed his name from Filippo to Giordano and entered the Dominican monastery in Naples. There he discovered God, pantheism, Latin, theology, logic and the pagan classics. While his brain absorbed the harsh, humorless, dehumanized narrow Catholic theology of the Counter Reformation, his imagination drank from the other books: Democritus and Epicurus and Lucretius, the Moslems Avicenna and Averroës, the Jewish philosopher Avicebron. The mixture did terrible violence to his Latin mind and imagination.

He became a priest, but his brain became a cauldron of conflicting beliefs, contradictions, of visions and mystic dreams. He was difficult to manage. He found the frigid boxes of logic packaged by Thomas Aquinas shackling. He raised questions; he challenged conclusions and ancient church authority; he dipped too deeply into pagan books. The Trinity bothered him: how could there be three persons in one? Twice he was chastised by his superiors. Aristotle's pages of logic-chopping—major premise, minor premise, conclusion—syllogism after syllogism infuriated him. God wasn't a problem in logic. Logic couldn't embrace life, emotion, love, the great brotherhood of the universe. It was all too much.

He fled.

It was 1576. The Inquisition was a fury let loose upon the land, a fanatical homicidal effort to restore the Church to its ancient authority. It was a perilous time to raise any questions. Bruno left the monastery with little more than the cassock that flapped at his heels.

He dropped his monk's habit, and he moved steadily northward, a wanderer: Rome, Genoa, Savona, Turin, Venice, Padua, Brescia, Bergamo, Chambery, Lyon, Geneva. There in Switzerland, he collided with Calvinist authority: he was summoned in doctrine and fled again, now at home with neither side in their tedious doctrinal quarrels.

Back to Lyon he went. Then to Toulouse. He became a lecturer on that sententious Aristotle, barely masking his scorn, but he stuck at it for eighteen months. Then he moved again. To Paris. He became a teacher to the King of France, Henry III, to whom he taught ancient secrets for developing a good memory. Henry made him a full professor of the Collège de France. He stayed for two years, then wrote a comedy, *The Torchbearer*. It combined humor with a moralistic fury that descended on the sconces of monks and professors, pedants and rogues, lovers of gold, misers and cutpurses, virile women and effeminate men. It was time to move again.

He went to England and joined the household of the French ambassador to London, Michel de Castelnau, a practical man who wasted no time on silly metaphysical quarrels. Bruno stayed his usual course—two years. He met all the intellectuals of Elizabethan England, including the Queen, whom he praised, much to the fury of the watching Italian Inquisition. At Oxford he taught the astronomical discovery of Copernicus, heretical matter to the Inquisition.

He returned to Paris, to the Sorbonne, to teach and attack Aristotle. Thence to German universities, even at Luther's university at Wittenberg—the usual two years. Then to Frankfurt and Zürich and back to Frankfurt. Two years of labor to publish his works in Latin— and thereby hand the Inquisition enough material to burn a thousand—ten thousand—Brunos. Volume after volume appeared. He was yearning for Italy.

He went to Venice—a city notorious for its protection of heretics sought by the Inquisition. He stayed a short time, then planned to return to Frankfurt. His host, one Mocenigo, appalled at his thundering heresies, denounced him to the Inquisition. Before he could cross the canals to the mainland, he was a prisoner. After sixteen years, the irrepressible, questioning, wandering Neapolitan bird was finally caged.

It was May 23, 1592.

He remained caged for eight years. He was periodically questioned, occasionally tortured, poorly fed, and as difficult to handle as ever. Statements taken from his books were shown to him, clear evidence of his heresy. Principal heresy was his earliest nemesis: the Trinity. For eight years he fought an army of scribes and researchers— fought with rebuttals, sharp exchanges, expressions of fidelity and devotion to the Pope. He lost.

On February 19, 1600, he was led, naked, to the Piazza Campo de' Fiori in Rome. There, his tongue was tied and his body bound to an iron stake on a pyre. Denied the merciful and customary release of strangling prior to burning, he was exposed to the flames alive. His body was consumed to a white ash, and the ashes were scattered to prevent future martyrdom.

More a mystic than a systematic philosopher, he contradicted himself many times in his various volumes. He expressed opinions—usually unorthodox, often heretical—on every possible subject, from the Trinity to incarnation, virgin birth to Hebrew history, and the dimensions of infinity. He was particularly interested in the transmigration of souls.

Reincarnation.

3

Richardson shut the book and pushed it onto the table in disgust. Only a rag-and-bone-shop brain like Clabber's could root through the many volumes of a sixteenth-century Dominican to locate fine, long-dead, doctrinal quarrels and espouse them four centuries later. Incarnation.

It's too many for me, said Huck Finn.

The memory of that black cobbled road leading over a sere brown countryside returned, and Richardson considered it. White buildings, orange-tiled roofs. Where was that place?

Whoosh!

He leaped from the chair.

He was awake. He'd heard it. Right in the middle of the room. Every light in the apartment was on. The living room was in full view before his eyes. No mistake. He knelt quickly before the tape recorder. It was still running.

He spun it back a few feet, then put it on speaker.

It turned slowly, broadcasting the silence of the room.

There was a slight bump—when he'd put the book on the coffee table. Then silence and the rhythmical turning of the two reels. Then—

Whoosh!

His tape recorder had captured the sound.

4

There was the speaker in his living room, a hidden speaker. Had to be. The only rational explanation. Had he really seen a man in a derby in the cellar working on a tape recorder—or had he dreamed it?

That would explain it all—a secret room in the cellar of the building with a tape deck wired to his living room.

How real it had been. He mentally retraced his steps. He'd gotten a can of cat food from the refrigerator and carried it to the cellar, placing it on the cellar steps. Then he'd discovered that strange room. . . .

That was it. The cat food. If that trip to the cellar had been real, the cat food would still be on the cellar steps —not in the refrigerator. He paused, uttering a fervent wish. Then he pulled the door open.

The photograph of a Persian cat smiled at him from the label of the can.

5

A door slammed.

Inside the building, a door had slammed. Richardson stood up from his chair and walked to his door. He listened. Someone was walking across the vestibule. He heard steps on the staircase, steadily rising, firm, purposeful. The footsteps sounded on the second-floor landing, scraped along the passageway, then sounded on the staircase, rising steadily toward Richardson's door.

Richardson backed away. No one had a key to that front door anymore except himself and Clabber.

The footsteps reached the landing and stepped along the passageway. They stopped just outside his door.

The silence was awesome. No sound. No knock. Then abruptly, after a long silence, a fist thumped on the door panel. Richardson hesitated. He considered the fire escape. He stood immobile in the midst of his living room. Waiting.

There was a second knock, firmer, louder, longer.

Richardson stepped softly to the door. "Who's there?"

"It's me. Clabber."

Richardson opened the door. The piercing eyes of Albert Clabber greeted him from the tied hood of his fur-lined parka.

Richardson nodded at him wordlessly.

"I just came by to pick up my mail and give you my new address."

"Address?" said Richardson.

"Yeah. Sure. I told you. I moved this morning."

Richardson's mouth gaped. "Moved? There's a light—"

"Yeah, I saw it when I walked up the street just now. Must have been left on this morning. Eerie, isn't it, a light burning in an empty apartment."

"Moved," said Richardson again.

"Yep. You're the last of the Mohicans, Richardson." Clabber looked at the tape recorder. "Homework?"

"Oh. No. Ah. Yes." Richardson stepped away from the doorway and let Clabber walk into the apartment. Clabber pushed the door shut behind him. He was visibly shivering.

"Find an apartment yet?"

"I have to go look at two tomorrow morning after the funeral."

"Oh yes, the funeral. Ten o'clock. You'll be well out of this place, Richardson. There are too many skeletons in the closets around here."

"What's that mean?"

"You know perfectly well what I mean. You lived here with your wife—your ex-wife. Your best friend was right downstairs—dead best friend. How long a list do you want?"

Richardson brushed a disinterested hand at him. "Okay, okay."

"I think you're a bit disoriented, Richardson."

"Yeah, sure."

"Okay. I'll shut up. I'll see you at the funeral tomorrow morning, and when you're ready to move, call me. I'll help."

"Why? I didn't help you."

"You're too suspicious, Richardson."

"No, I'm not. You're after something and I can sense it."

Clabber sat down on the edge of the couch, hunched forward, hands between his thighs. His nose was still red from the cold, his hands were thickly gloved, and his wavy-soled brushed-leather shoes looked entirely inadequate for their job.

"Got a pencil?"

Richardson opened a desk drawer and picked out a pencil. He found a torn envelope and handed the pencil and envelope to Clabber. He watched Clabber write on the envelope, his hands still gloved. Clabber tossed the pencil on the coffee table. "Here. The phone number's the same. Are you recording this conversation for a reason?"

"No." Richardson poked a button and the machine stopped.

Clabber lay back on the couch and slouched down, his arms limp at either side. "What's new?"

Richardson smiled and shook his head. "Jesus, Clabber, the role of the casual conversationalist doesn't fit you. If you're going to play at it, at least take the goddamned gloves off and open your coat."

Clabber didn't move. "Richardson, I'm half frozen to death. When I warm up, I'll take these things off. In fact—for God's sake, can you spare a lousy tea bag and a cup of hot water? I don't even care about the sugar or the milk."

6

Clabber held the scalding hot cup in both palms, drawing in the heat and sipping at the steaming tea.

Richardson sat across the table from him, staring at the floor.

"I saw Anna Quist last night," said Clabber.

"Good."

Clabber watched him for a moment. "She asked me to bring you over sometime."

Richardson raised his head. "Grand. An evening with Anna Quist's glass bowling ball. Just what I need."

"That's right."

"No more," said Richardson, sitting up. "No more. I don't want to go to Anna Quist's. Okay?"

"I think you should."

"You nearly finished your tea?"

Clabber looked at his cup, then stood up. He poured another cupful of steaming water from the kettle, then lowered the dangling tea bag back into the cup by the string. "The greatest things on earth are still the simplest. Like this. A cup of tea, Richardson, right now is an unforgettable pleasure."

"Good. Enjoy it and you can think about the pleasure of it all the way home."

"I got the hint the first time."

"Nothing personal, Clabber."

"I understand. It's just that I interrupted your recording sessions with that whooshing sound."

Richardson stared silently at Clabber.

"I thought that would rouse you, Richardson."

"What—how—"

"Goulart, Richardson—Goulart did the same thing. He hallucinated trips to the newspaper store. He was hallucinating whole symphonies. And they were so real he tried to record them."

"What did he get?"

"Silence. That's all he got. Silence and a funeral tomorrow morning." Clabber watched and waited. "There's only one way you're going to get that information, Richardson."

"What information?"

"The source of that sound."

"I know the source of that sound, Clabber. It's a speaker hidden in my living room somewhere."

"Is it?"

"Isn't it?"

"I don't know. But there's one way to find out."

"Hoy. Games. If you have something to say, why in God's name don't you say it? That's why you walked all the way over here, isn't it?"

"You have to ask Goulart."

"Goulart! Are you—oh, I get it. The spirit world again, hey? Mrs. Quist. I get it." Richardson sighed. "Are you finished with your tea yet?"

"Look, Richardson, I can't believe that you're as pig-headed as you make yourself out to be. If you have a sitting with Anna Quist, one of two things can happen: nothing or something. If nothing happens, then you're not hurt and you can blab all over New York that spiritualism is a fake. Okay? And if something happens, then it'll help you—might even solve a big problem for you. You'll be ahead of the game. Now why don't you pry open that closed mind of yours and come see for yourself? Anna Quist is a sincere, intelligent woman. Very kindly. Very gentle. Wouldn't harm a soul. She took a genuine liking to you, and she's sure she can be helpful. Why don't you let her try?"

Richardson slumped back in his chair and idly steered a spoon in a circle inside his teacup. Finally he put the spoon down. "Look, Clabber. Maybe you're a sincere guy and maybe you really want to help. My opinion is you're just selfish and you think maybe there's something going on here that you can put in a book or use to further some of your pseudo-scientific theories. In any case, I have to tell you, Clabber, I'm just one good kick away from the funny farm. I think if you yelled boo at me loud enough, I'd just stand up right here and flake away in big pieces like one of those brick buildings out there that get smashed every day. Frankly, Clabber, I'm not too tightly wrapped these days. There are moments when I really think I've gone around the bend and should be certified to the laughing ward. Okay? If you get me into Anna Quist's apartment and anything happens, it's going to take sixteen weight-lifters to catch me and cage me."

Clabber stood up. "Tomorrow night. I'll pick you up here and we'll drive over in your car. Eight o'clock here. I'm going to help you and you're going to help me." He took a last sip from his cup and walked to the front door of the apartment.

Richardson followed him.

Clabber nodded curtly. "See you at the funeral tomorrow morning." He went down the first flight, turned, walked along the passageway to the turning and clumped down the next flight. Richardson saw him cross the vestibule at the bottom of the stairwell. A moment later, the front door slammed.

Richardson stood at the stairhead for some minutes, listening attentively. He was alone with the silence of the Brevoort House.

7
It was a dull thud that woke him. A familiar, painful, distant thud.

Richardson opened his eyes. He was in his wingback chair in a blanket. He glanced at the tape recorder. The take-up reel had completely wound up the spool and now turned slowly, trailing a stuttering strip of tape.

Richardson jabbed a button with his fingertip and the machine stopped.

Richardson stood up and stretched, balled the blanket up and dropped it on the chair, then looked around at the electric clock in the kitchen. Eight ten. Sunlight lay in a broad band across the living room.

The dull thudding drew him to the window. Across the quadrangle the wrecker's ball was at work. It had, at last, reached Waite's grocery and had battered a large piece of the corner of the building to rubble. Waite's looked like a statue with its nose broken off.

On the ground partly covered with bricks was the sign: Waite's Groceries. The boom drew back, then swung in an arc like a bat or a club. The willing ball and its cable followed and slammed against the brick wall.

How many times had he gone in there? How many loaves of bread? An ocean of milk. The soda case had stood by the front door. He could visualize every detail of the lid and handle. He remembered the interior darkness, the rounded pieces of partially melted ice, the six inches of cold water that the soda bottles stood in, the fizzing sound of the caps yanked off by the opener. Soft summer tar in the roadway, drying sweat, broomstick bats and rubber balls, and cold soda under Waite's awning. With Ozzie, who could hit a ball two manhole covers.

Another shot by the wrecker and more brick tumbled into the gutted building. A smaller shower landed in the street and on the sign. Waite's.

Richardson dressed for the funeral as he drank coffee and watched the wrecker's ball pound Waite's Groceries into the past.

Next was the building with Ozzie's wall drawings.

By the time he was ready to leave, most of Waite's was down. He stood sipping steaming coffee by a window and watched the building die in the beautiful winter sunlight.

8

Abby's hat and veil undulated in the sharp breeze as Richardson walked with her across the parking lot to the church. The draft swept into the church vestibule when he pulled the heavy wooden door open.

The coffin was in position at the head of the center aisle before the altar. A number of people were already there.

Abby seemed quite serene now, all her crying done. "It's February 14, Saint Valentine's Day," she said. "Quite appropriate." She sat in the pew looking at the people around her. Each time the front doors opened, cold air swept around their ankles and fluttered the flames of the red-cupped vigil candles.

Richardson saw Ozzie's sister and her family along with several other relatives. Around them were a number of people from the neighborhood, including many who'd moved away. The saloonkeeper and his wife sat behind Ozzie's sister. Occasionally, old people murmured to each other *sotto voce* and twisted their rosaries around aging fingers. There were people from the art world, the college, advertising and publishing. Richardson was impressed with the number who'd come.

There was a very strong odor of roses in the church.

More people arrived. Each time Abby felt a draft on

her ankles she half-turned her head to look at the door. At one point she gave Richardson a slight tap with her elbow.

Clabber had arrived. Mrs. Quist was with him. He untied his parka hood and stuffed his gloves into his deep side pockets, strolling with Mrs. Quist toward the altar, his rumpled hair standing up from the back of his head.

They reached the head of the aisle and looked briefly at the plain oak coffin, then turned their attention to the small collection of roses. They inclined toward each other and whispered.

"They noticed it, too," said Abby in a whisper.

"What? They noticed what?"

"The roses."

"What about the roses?"

"The smell."

"What do you mean, Abby?"

"Don't you smell the roses?"

"So?"

"The odor is very strong. Those few roses at the altar could never make that much odor."

"So?"

Abby turned her face to him. "Some people believe that the strong smell of roses means there's the spirit of a dead person nearby."

Richardson frowned and looked at Clabber and Mrs. Quist. Their eyes went everywhere in the church, watchful and expectant. They were more like investigators than mourners and seemed to be waiting for something to happen. They strolled slowly back down the aisle and stepped into a vacant pew near the back of the church. Clabber took a small tape recorder from his pocket and set it running beside him. Mrs. Quist studied it severely for a moment, watching to see its mechanism work, then looked forward at the altar.

Clabber began to pray. He prayed in an authoritative murmur. Entwined around his clasped fingers was a string of rosary beads.

"Pater noster, qui es in caelis, sanctificetur nomen tuum. Adveniat regnum tuum. Fiat voluntas...."

"Maybe he's trying to reach you," said Abby.

"Who?"

"Ozzie. Maybe he's trying to reach you."

Richardson sat back and stared at her. "Ozzie?"

"Maybe that's what the odor of roses means."

"... sed libera nos a malo. Amen."

9

Father Duranty with a palsied hand and a tired stoop helped with the mass and gave the sermon in a surprisingly strong voice. He compared Ozzie Goulart's career as an artist with the Prime Artist of the Universe, praised him for his exemplary, gentle life, mourned his passing, asserted his belief in the afterlife and blessed the assembled mourners. Through his sermon, winter coughs sounded like pistol shots in the high groined roof.

The casket was wheeled out of the pale light that fell from the cupola and was guided down the aisle to the doors. A strong rush of wind filled the church as the mourners followed the casket to the street and the auto caravan.

At the curb Mrs. Quist nodded at Richardson and Abby, then got into her car with Clabber. Clabber saluted Richardson with a wave of a finger.

Richardson seated Abby and got behind the wheel of his car. He watched the people from the neighborhood, noted the age that had reached each one and shook his head.

"It's a mass funeral, Abby. For everyone. For Ozzie and the whole neighborhood. They rubbled Waite's this morning and now we're all going to the cemetery to be buried today."

The caravan went north on the Brooklyn-Queens Expressway to the Long Island Expressway to the cemetery. A numbing breeze flowed continuously through the open fields of tombstones. Shivering, the funeral director hastened the ceremony. Father Duranty pulled his old black fedora from his head and contritely intoned a last benediction. Ozzie's sister stood straight and wept. A cross of salt was poured on the casket, and each mourner dropped a single rose on it, then filed away.

Back at the car, Richardson helped Abby into her seat. "When we get back, I'm going to make us a hot cup of tea," said Abby.

Richardson nodded absently. He was watching Clabber and Mrs. Quist progressing to her car against the bitter wind.

"Happy goddamn Valentine's Day," he said.

The unmistakable, excessively strong odor of roses was carried on the wind.

10

The delivery boy carried the white box under one arm. He kept both hands pocketed and walked across the wind with his face averted. It was a cold Valentine's Day.

He saw a typewriter bolted to a stand outside a business-machines store. He paused and read the notations on the flapping paper typed by passersby.

"TINSTAAFL T. I. N.S.T.A.A.F. L. There is no such thing as a free lunch. Mad dog god dam mad dog."

"Ping pong spelled backwards is gnip gnop."

"Now is the time for all good men to kill the quick brown fox."

"The lazy dog bit the fox."

"The lazy dog got rabies."

The boy pulled his gloved hands out of the pockets. His leather-covered fingertips pecked out a message.

"I will not talk in class one hundred times." He punched a series of x's: xxxxxxx, Happy Valentine's Day. I LOVE MARION WAKEFIELD.

Patiently, he forced his gloved hands back into his coat pockets and resumed his walk. At the corner a rush of wind pressed down on the white box under his arm, and he crossed the intersection walking sidewise with his back to the wind.

He walked along the next street, pausing to look through the steamy windows of the delicatessen. He studied the dangling meats and the trays of slaw and salads. Inside, the clerks in short white shirts and pink arms cut the meats and packaged them in white paper. It looked warm inside.

He passed the old colonial Dutch Reformed Church next and walked past the wrought-iron fence of the cemetery. The wind caught him again and he put his head down and away from the wind.

Hic Jacet. The words caught his eye and he stopped in the wind.

Hic Jacet Johannes Niewkirk. Anno Aetatis Suae 1714.

There were many other stones, but the wind drove him onward. At the corner he turned into the wind; he walked half a block and turned again, into a cobbled alley with townhouses on either side. He walked to the middle of the block, found his number and rang the bell.

A buzzer unlocked a grated garden door and he paused.

"Come to the back, please," said a speaker.

He pushed the grated door open and walked a brick walk along the alley to the back of the house. A garden in winter wraps opened up—small leafless trees, shrubs packed in tarpaper, and a bright green lawn. A man stood inside a doorway, peering out from a large white door.

"Yes."

"Ummm." He struggled his hand out of a pocket, pulling a receipt book with it. "Ummmm. Miss Alice Polsley."

"Come in."

The boy stepped over the threshold onto a thick blue carpet. The man shut the door. "Wait here," he said.

The house air felt hot on his cheeks. The boy's eyes wandered over the white woodwork, the gold stars on the curved ceiling of the entryway and the fierce-looking carved eagle on the wall of the circular stairwell.

The blue carpet marched away in every direction to closed white doors and paraded up the circular stairs.

"This way."

He walked into the room. More blue rug and desks. The lady looked at him with large green eyes. He eagerly surrendered the white box to her and held out the receipt book.

Quickly, with accustomed efficiency, she thumbed the pages until she found her name and office address. She signed her name and handed it back to the boy. "Wait," she said.

She left the room and returned. She held out two quarters. He pushed them down into one of his gloved hands. The coins were warm.

"Thank you," said the boy. "Happy Valentine's Day." He followed the butler back to the door and stepped out into the freezing breeze again.

"Pull that gate shut after you," said the butler.

The boy did.

11

She pushed the office door shut and sat down at her desk. She looked at the box, then pulled it onto her lap and looked again. White box, white crepe string. She opened a desk drawer and withdrew a pair of scissors. She snipped the crepe string. Then she lifted the cover. Green tissue paper filled the inside.

She pulled it back.

It was a rose. A single red rose.

Alice Polsley sat looking down at the boxed rose in her lap for a long time.

Next to it was a white card.

"Farewell."

CHAPTER IX

Richardson sat in his apartment, at war.

He'd played the tape recorder with idiot reiteration. Now he sat with the recorder in his lap slowly turning, waiting to record any sound. As he sat, his eyes studied the ceiling, millimeter by millimeter, seeking a hole, a pinhole, a telltale bulge.

He heard a door slam. The front door down in the vestibule. He listened alertly. A footfall in the hallway. He drew a deep breath and waited. The sound slowly rose up the staircase, stumped along the passageway and rose up the next flight. The steps crossed the hallway to his door and paused. A knock sounded.

Richardson rose and walked to the door. "Who's there?"

"Me. Clabber."

Richardson opened the door.

"It's colder than ever out there," said Clabber. "I hope your car has a heater."

"Gets cold out there every winter, Clabber."

"Not like tonight. Tonight we have a special treat from the weather service. It seems that the clouds have blown away and there's nothing up there to hold any heat in. We have also had a windy cold front going through all day with air direct from the Arctic. Neat? It's going to be the coldest night in fifteen years."

"Why don't you stay home, reading a good book by your radiator and drinking nice hot tea?"

"Don't think I didn't consider it, Richardson. Are you ready?"

"I don't know if I'm ready or not."

Clabber's face flushed. "Richardson, I'm through playing games with you. I went to some trouble to set this up with Anna Quist. She's been exhausting herself with sittings lately, and that goddamn Brother Brendan is mouthing off about the English and Sir Robert Peel endlessly."

"What are you talking about?"

"Nothing. Nothing. Just get your coat and let's go. This may be the most important night in your life." His prodding hand nagged Richardson toward his closet.

"What did you expect at that funeral today, Clabber? You and Anna Quist were all eyes."

"Maybe something did happen today, Richardson. Come on. Get your coat."

"What does that mean?"

"It means get your coat."

Richardson stood at his closet door, then turned to Clabber. "So help me, Clabber, if anything happens tonight, I'm going to run you through a pencil sharpener."

Clabber sighed, then looked angrily at the ceiling. "Thousands of people sit down every night all over the world to conduct séances. Thousands and thousands of people. Sometimes they reach the spirits of dead people they are trying to reach and sometimes they don't. I'm telling you again: there's nothing to be afraid of. No harm will come to you. And we can stop it anytime you say. So relax and let's see what happens. Okay?"

"I think I need to have my head examined." Richardson reached into the closet for his coat.

"Wear five scarves and two extra sweaters," said Clabber.

2

Richardson drove south on Flatbush Avenue along Prospect Park to Ocean Avenue. Clabber rode in silence, huddled before the rush of warmth from the humming car heater.

The wind was gusting, rocking the car and whistling at the car windows. An occasional pedestrian ran along the sidewalks under swaying store signs, frozen face bunched, head down, hunched against the breathtaking cold. Near Parkside Avenue, a traffic policeman directed traffic in and out of a funeral home while trying to keep his back to the wind. As the car passed him, Richardson saw water running from his reddened eyes.

The traffic was light on Ocean Avenue. The wind, skimming down the faces of the two solid rows of apartment buildings, cuffed the car alternately from two angles.

"Oh boy," murmured Clabber.

"What's the matter?"

"Parking. I don't see any place to park. We're going to have to walk blocks."

"Where is it?"

"Right there. That's her apartment building."

Richardson turned off Ocean Avenue and cruised through the streets, circling a block at a time. He found a place three blocks from the apartment. Clabber got out reluctantly.

"I'll bet the wind-chill factor is at least fifteen below."

"Walk fast," answered Richardson.

Clabber adopted a shuffling sidewise trot, trying to turn away from the wind. He was heavily muffled in the fur-lined parka, leather mittens and scarves. He drew a flap from the hood across his face and snapped it in place. Only his eyes showed.

Richardson pulled a scarf from his neck and put it around his head, tying it under his chin, then he fitted his felt hat over it, holding it by the brim against the wind. His hand began to freeze.

They hurried along the street and turned the corner. By now, Clabber was doing a crabwise jog and Richardson was stepping fast behind him. They went two blocks wincing with pain before turning the corner to Ocean Avenue. The last half block to the apartment house they did in a sprint.

Inside the lobby, Clabber sat down on an old red-velvet-covered chair, gasping.

"My lungs are frozen," he said.

"Get out. They could run you up the North Pole in that outfit and let you blow in the breeze for a month and you'd come down nice and toasty warm, Clabber."

"I tell you I'm frozen."

"Then get your money back on the coat and hood." Richardson peeled the scarf from his head, feeling the deep pain in his skull from the wind. "You know, this is silly. Really silly. Here we are about to communicate with the spirits of the dead. We're going to rattle the gates of heaven itself, and there you are—an invincible colossus bestriding the earth above matters of the flesh —complaining about the cold like any mortal. It does your image great damage, Clabber."

Clabber stood up and angrily pushed the elevator button. "A hairshirt I could stand. You understand? Temperatures in the desert—I could stand them too. Gruel three times a day. Penance on my knees on a marble floor for hours, days! I can even stand the cold. I sleep with my windows open. And if I had to, I could stand out there right now all night. But I will tell you, Richardson, of all the various pains and aches in the universe, cold is the one that bothers me most. And I don't need any remarks about it. I notice you were running right behind me."

Richardson opened his mouth to speak, then stopped. "Okay," he said.

The elevator was an antique. After they entered the car Clabber banged the metal door shut, then pulled the reticulated inner gate shut. He pushed a button and from below issued an electric motor whine. The car gnawed its way up the shaft, lurching arthritically.

Richardson stared at Clabber, who scowled back at him. Richardson's earlobes were now hot and were burning.

"I still feel that this whole thing is ridiculous."

"Wait and see what happens. Judge for yourself."

The car stopped with a shudder. Clabber pulled the folding gate aside and opened the metal door. They stepped into an old hallway and walked on a marble floor—along corridors lined with murals and old plaster scrollwork. The wall lights wore metal shades of an outmoded design.

They passed apartment doors silently, hearing television programs, bumps, bangs and muffled voices.

Clabber led him to a door and stopped. He glanced at Richardson's clothing, then lifted his chin and worked his neck inside its turtleneck sweater. Then he pushed the bell.

"Shrimp," said Clabber.

"Huh?"

"Someone is cooking shrimp."

Richardson considered that for a moment. He shrugged concessively. "What else would you do on the coldest night in fifteen years?"

The door opened.

Anna Quist looked at Clabber, then at Richardson. She was dressed in a pale blue floor-length gown and wore an ankh symbol on a chain around her neck. She nodded gravely. "Mr. Richardson. Good of you to come." She stepped back from the doorway to permit them to enter. She looked tired. Her eyes seemed dull and there was something withdrawn, preoccupied in her manner.

"Albert told me that you were very reluctant about all this. I'm glad you finally decided to come. We may be able to help you."

Richardson murmured, "Thank you," and took off his overcoat and hat. Anna Quist hung them in a closet and then waited patiently for Clabber to undo his hood, unbutton and unzip his parka, remove the several scarves, pack the heavy leather mittens in the parka pockets.

"I know Albert will have tea. Will you join him, Mr. Richardson?"

Richardson nodded. "Sure." His earlobes and cheeks were burning now, hot to touch, but the pain in his skull was subsiding.

Anna Quist seemed elfin as she padded away in her gown. A faint odor of cooked food hung in the air. Clabber inclined his head toward the living room.

Richardson followed Clabber past the kitchen door. He saw a small grease-stained bag of garbage standing on a table by the dumbwaiter door. At the stove Anna Quist was heating water for the tea.

The apartment was heavily draped and thickly carpeted. Several small oriental-type rugs lay on the wall-to-wall carpeting. The only lighting came from several small lamps in the living room and the dining area next to it. The general effect was a muffled twilight.

It reminded Richardson of the inside of a coffin.

"Sit, sit," said Clabber.

Richardson sat down on a couch next to a portable television set. He watched Clabber kneading his thin hands and twiglike fingers together. Then he gazed about the living room and dining area.

There were dozens of places they could conceal a speaker. They could have *whooshes* coming from left and right. He looked at the dining room table. They could have that thing dancing in air from nearly invisible piano wire.

He noticed a portrait in full color on the dining room wall—a painting of Jesus. The right hand was raised, showing the stigmata in the middle of the palm. The left hand indicated the glowing red heart at his breast. Jesus was smiling.

"First time I've ever seen a portrait of Christ smiling," said Richardson.

Clabber raised his chin from his fists and turned his preoccupied eyes to the portrait. "Anna," he murmured.

"Family pictures?" asked Richardson.

"Huh?"

"The other pictures on the wall. Photographs of people."

"Oh. They're . . ." He paused. "They're pictures of famous clairvoyants. There's a picture of Houdini there somewhere." He put his chin back on his fists and stared at the rug. He was shivering.

Richardson began to feel hot. The apartment was warm—very warm, and dry. He glanced at Clabber. The two of them, Clabber and Anna Quist—thin as threads each—probably reveled in heat. Richardson stood up.

"What's the matter? Sit down."

"It's okay, Clabber. I'm going to take off this jacket and the sweater too. Okay?"

Clabber nodded and rubbed knuckles against a palm vigorously. "Now that I've got you here, I think we ought to explain a few things to you, but I'm going to let Anna do the talking. I hope that that flannel-mouth Brother Brendan stays off the sauce."

"How many more are coming?"

"More? No more. Just the three of us."

"What about Brother what's-his-name?"

"Oh. Yes. Well. More about him in a moment. Let me get some hot tea down first."

Anna Quist approached softly, bearing two cups brimming with hot water. She set them down on a long coffee table. They rattled slightly in their saucers. "Milk and sugar," she said, walking back to the kitchen.

She returned with a small silver tray holding a milk pitcher and a bowl of sugar. In her other hand she carried a third cup of tea. "I suppose I shouldn't drink this at this hour, but it's so cold out. I felt it flowing off your clothing when you came in."

Clabber dunked his tea bag eagerly, spooned two servings of sugar into the cup, squeezed the bag and stirred. Then he picked up the cup and held it in both palms, sipping rapidly.

"I didn't have much opportunity to speak to you at the funeral, Mr. Richardson," said Anna Quist. "I wanted to tell you how sorry I was that you lost your friend. He was an exceptional person and truly your friend."

"Friend!" exclaimed Clabber. "He died for him!"

"No, no, Albert. That's overstating it completely. Ozzie went too far with those pills he was taking. He needn't have frozen to death—and he certainly didn't believe that freezing to death would help Mr. Richardson here. No, no. His death was completely unpremeditated and unintended. That's what makes it all the more lamentable." She turned to Richardson. "I must tell you that I was very fond of Ozzie Goulart. He was here on a number of occasions and we talked the night away. He had unusual powers, and I'm convinced he had an extraordinary career ahead of him as a clairvoyant. I talked at great length to him the last time he was here— and that was shortly before you had your party. I told him again and again not to use those drugs. They made everything he did invalid. He was obsessed with the idea that someone intended to harm you and that if he could foresee the event—if he could at least see the face of your enemy—he might help save you."

"How come he didn't foresee his own death?" asked Richardson.

"I'm afraid he did."

3

Clabber helped Anna Quist set up a small hexagonal table with a carved beading around the edge. Mrs. Quist put a small vigil candle in the center of the table, then sat down on the couch next to Richardson.

"I feel, before we get started, that I ought to explain a few things to you. You are emitting strong psychic disturbances."

Richardson pointed a finger at himself. "Me?"

"Yes. As you sit there. Ordinarily, I will not sit under such circumstances. It takes all my strength of concentration to communicate with the other world, and I have found in the past that if there is just one person in the room who is not wholeheartedly with us, then it causes unbearable strain for me and I'm out of sorts for days after. You see?"

Richardson nodded and started to rise. "Yes, I see. Maybe another time."

"No no," said Clabber. He looked at Anna Quist and she looked silently back at him.

He turned to Richardson. "Look. What Anna is saying is that she feels more than skepticism coming from you. It's hostility. Anger. You understand? You're a skeptic and that's bad enough, but also you're scorning the whole thing. Now, unless you put aside the violent mental

225

emissions, we won't be able to get—get—get this thing off the ground. Understand?"

Richardson sat back irritably. "Look, Clabber, you set this up. Not me."

"I know. I know. I know. It's very important. Very important. Maybe—well—" He turned to Anna Quist. "How's Brother Brendan behaving?"

Anna Quist shrugged. "Ecclesiastes."

"The whole thing?"

She nodded and studied a finger ring unhappily.

Clabber sighed. "Okay. Well. Let's get back to Richardson here. Look, Richardson. This is what we do. We sit at that table and we clear our minds. I'm convinced that Ozzie Goulart had more information he wanted to give you. So all you have to do is sit at that table with your mind cleared of everything. Just think about Ozzie. Or if that disturbs you, forget it. Just clear your mind entirely. Okay?" He looked at Anna Quist. "Okay?"

She sat with her hands in her lap. "I'm not—ah. Well."

"No tricks," said Richardson.

Clabber's shoulders sagged. "Come on. I didn't come out on a night like this for fraternity-house tricks. Why don't you take a look around here—no trapdoors or magic-lantern shows. No spooky noises."

"Maybe," said Anna Quist, "nothing will happen."

"Let's sit over," said Clabber.

4

Anna Quist sat down in a small straight-backed upholstered chair with her back to the drapes that covered her windows. She watched Clabber put out the several lamps. Then Clabber and Richardson sat down in straight-backed wooden chairs from the dining room.

Anna Quist put both hands on the table. She extended her left hand to Albert Clabber and he took it. Their clasped hands rested on the table. She extended her right hand to Richardson. He hastily took it, then saw Clabber's left hand being extended to him. He grasped it. Now all six hands were clasped and resting on the table. The room was in darkness save for the small candle in the red vigil cup at the center of the table.

Albert Clabber's hand was cold to the touch. It felt hard and dry. It gripped Richardson's hand almost too firmly. Clabber was intent on the sitting. His face was white and faint, with both eyes shut. His lips were firmly shut.

Anna Quist's hand was so small it was like a child's—or like a small paw. The fingers were cold and her grip was pliant and trusting. Richardson realized he felt great sympathy for her, a deep sorrow. Her vulnerability was frightening.

He felt her fingers stir in his palm. "That's better," she said. "Much better." Her face was pale and featureless and her eyes were shut, calmly, patiently, as though in sleep.

Richardson looked from one face to the other. Nothing happened. He tried to clear his mind. He felt, instead, a sadness. He sighed. The sadness was deeper and he shut both eyes. He felt Anna Quist's fingers stirring in his palm again. They had become warmed from the heat of his hand. It was all so very sad. The sense of depression was frightening and he opened his eyes. Neither Anna Quist nor Albert Clabber was aware. Enough, thought

Richardson. Too much sadness, an overwhelming depression unlike anything he'd ever felt before. He opened his mouth to speak.

Anna Quist's hand stopped him. It slowly closed around his four fingers. More. More. Extraordinary strength now. He was astonished by the grip. He began to pull his hand away from the terrible strength, the shooting pain. Then, it ceased. The hand grip relaxed.

Richardson looked at her. Anna Quist had slumped in her chair, her head turned downward and inclined toward one shoulder. It rested on the upholstered chair back. There was a deep crease between her eyes—a deep furious frown.

Richardson looked at Clabber. Both of Clabber's eyes were open and staring at him. He made a shushing shape with his lips and reshut his eyes.

Richardson waited. It was as before, except for Anna Quist's resting head. The depression he felt continued. He sighed. Anna Quist's small, harmless, defenseless hand was overwhelmingly depressing.

Clabber's hand stirred, then rested—a light firm grip.

Richardson shut his eyes and sighed again.

Anna Quist's hand moved again. The grip became firmer, now more aggressive. Emphatic. The whole character of the hand and the grip had changed. The hand now emanated authority.

She turned her head upward, still resting it on the chair back. The mouth had become a pronounced, implacable downward crescent. She grunted a deep baritone grunt.

"Ohhh, a dreadful thing," she said. Her voice was deep; the accent was Corkian Irish. "Dear God in heaven, the man is stark raving mad. The food relief that they all babble about is a pittance. The blight covers everything. There's not a whole potato from one side of the country to the other. The people have nought to put in their mouths. Starving they are—in the roadways, by the thousands. And him listening only to the Orangemen, worried about the cost of feeding the starving. Billy Peel. Orange Peel is his right name."

Richardson watched her face with fascination. It hardly looked like her. The voice was strong and masculine, commanding . . . with a heavy slurring, typically rising, Cork accent.

Richardson glanced at Clabber. Clabber's eyes were open. His face was angry and he was looking at Anna Quist's face. "Brother Brendan," he whispered.

"Now. Now. Just the first stanza," said Anna Quist.

"*Omnia tempus habent,*" crooned Anna Quist, "*et suis spatiis transeunt universa sub caelo. Tempus nascendi et tempus moriendi*—and a time to save the Irish from starvation."

Clabber sighed and gazed heavenward.

"Ah, Clabber, Clabber, Clabber," came Mrs. Quist's brogue. "It's always the same questions with you, over and over. Even when you get the answer, you ask the question again. There's one here who knew you. Says to watch your datives and ablatives or you'll never make it to the seminary. Carthy. Maeve. Greenwood Lake. An easy door to step through. Defeated again. *Omnia tempus habent.* A grown man living on a potato diet will consume more than twenty pounds a day. Can't you just picture a man starving to death in his earthen home with his family and along comes the constabulary with a piece of paper and drags the starving bodies out on the roadway and leaves them there for nonpayment of land rent. By order of the landowner snug somewhere in England.

229

Now when you multiply that by the millions—Clabber, can you draw?"

Clabber's head snapped up. His eyes were open and alert and he studied Anna Quist's sagging face. She was breathing adenoidally and slowly turning her head as if in pain. Clabber flicked a glance at Richardson, then looked back to Anna Quist. She strengthened her grip on Richardson's hand and banged it thrice on the table, restlessly. "Draw. Draw. Miss Mocksun is going to give you a D in Art."

Clabber lowered his gaze, waited, listening expectantly, like a man with his ear to a radio. Anna Quist's hand relaxed, as though in sleep.

"Maeve. Greenwood Lake. You are in grave danger."

Anna Quist's hand became increasingly restless. It rolled from side to side and her expression became pained. "No more," she said. "No more." She raised her hand, and with it, Richardson's, and pounded them on the table angrily. He felt again that supernatural grip and cried out. Her grip relaxed.

A moment later Anna Quist opened her eyes.

5

The first part of the ride back home was agony for Albert Clabber. After the three painful blocks of jogging, during which the incessant wind drove a mortal chill into his thin body, he had to ride in a frozen car waiting for the car's engine to warm up enough to operate the hot-air heater.

Richardson felt the seat shaking from Clabber's shivers. He aimed the car back down Ocean Avenue and was caught by a red light. He sat watching the temperature gauge on his dashboard. It rose slowly—still far from the operation zone. Clabber made no conversation. He concentrated on the cold, feeling it, intimidated by it, menaced by the wind that howled at his window. He was shuddering violently.

At last Richardson pushed the heater button, and a flood of hot air rushed into the automobile. Clabber yanked off his gloves and washed his skinny hands in the jet of warmth. After a few miles, he pulled off his army boots and held each one in the path of the flowing hot air. He was still washing himself in warmth when Richardson pulled up at his front door.

"It's just twenty feet to your front door," said Richardson.

"I'll call you," said Clabber. "I want to talk to you." He quickly laced up his boots, thrust his hands into his gloves and held his front door key at the ready. "See you."

He jumped out of the car and into his apartment house.

6

When Richardson arrived home, he opened the door to his apartment, snapped on the overhead light and walked directly to the wall next to his fireplace. His eyes scanned the half dozen framed photographs that hung there. He found the picture of his mother and aunt.

He wondered if Anna Quist had studied the picture when she'd come to the cocktail party.

In white ink down in the corner, his aunt had written: "Maeve and me. Lake Greenwood, 1931."

You are all in grave danger.

7

The tapping sound captured his attention.

Richardson walked curiously to a window and looked out. The quadrangle was lit with moonlight. Pinto patches of snow glowed in an ethereal silver. In the midst of the quadrangle stood the tractor, not fifty yards from Brevoort House. It seemed to be crouching like a sphinx and contemplating the house. The boom was raised and aimed like a great club. The ball sat on the ground.

A long cable with a length of chain tapped against the boom. Tapped. On the frozen metal, shaken by the bitter wind. *Tap. Tap. Tap.* The sound was so cold under that pale moonlight. So alone and godforsaken cold. It made him ache inside.

Richardson went to the cabinet and poured himself two inches of brandy. He sat down in his chair and sipped it, feeling the warmth thaw the chill inside him.

It was all a fraud. Somehow, someone was getting to him. Thimble-rigged *trompe l'oeil,* a shell-game. Tape recorders—something.

But it always came down to the same questions: Why? Who would want to kill him or bend his mind? Old ground. Tiresome old ground: what he owned no one would invest great time and effort into stealing.

A legacy? A secret fortune from an unknown relative? Richardson sighed and drank some more brandy. The chill was leaving him.

He had to think about moving. He had to find an apartment.

He sat with the glass of brandy, thinking about moving and hearing the *tap-tap-tapping* of the frozen chain on the metal boom. Homeless and alone.

8

The fence was so real.

It was drawn iron picket fencing. Black and frozen with cold. His hands were in gloves. Mittens. Black leather mittens that belonged to Clabber. The mittens kept the flesh of his hands from sticking to the frozen metal.

He was cold. So cold he was shivering. The shivering was so violent it vibrated on the fence. He had to get down—get to some warmth, or he'd freeze. Safety down at the ground.

Richardson felt drowsy in the chair, and he knew, as always, he had to climb down the fence to sleep. How could an idea become so obsessive that he couldn't not think about it—had to comply even though he knew he was imagining the fence, imagining the cold, imagining the gloves and the shivering.

Only, it was so real. He was truly freezing to death on that fence in that wintry blast of wind.

He began to clamber down. Familiarly with practice.

He was so tired. So spent. So cold. Emotionally drained. He thought of his mother. Anna Quist had slipped a fake message to him. But that didn't fit the innocence and sincerity of her child-hand. Nothing added up.

He hurried his feet, climbing down faster now. Slid the shoe arch down along the drawn iron bar until it reached a crosspiece. Stood on it and slid the other shoe down along the drawn iron bar until it reached the crosspiece. Down. Down. Down. Crosspiece after crosspiece. The cold and wind were numbing him. He had to move faster. His hands would slip soon. He passed between other fences, descended below their rows of waiting malevolent spikes.

He was nearing the bottom. He was sure. He looked down. There was that strange road. Black cobbles. A humpbacked road. Rutted. In darkness, it paraded away to invisibility. There was a moon, a cold moon. And shapes. Trees? Too dark to see. He was coming down faster now. Where was warmth? Was there a building?

He looked down. He saw—he saw a figure. A man: a friar. A babbling friar mumbling Ecclesiastes. *Omnia tempus habent.* Brother Brendan. And now he saw another figure: the man in the derby. A long face. Aquiline. Sour eyes under a craggy brow. Sullen, sunken cheeks under high cheekbones. Thin, pursed lips. And the derby. A racetrack tout? English, possibly? There were now other figures there. Lumpish, dark brown and shadowed. Cowled.

The man in the derby stood next to a wicker trunk. He reached down to open the lid.

Richardson knew what was in that basket. Only he couldn't remember. He began to moan and scrabble back up the fencing. Leaden feet, not fast enough.

The man in the derby had the basket hasp open. He lifted the lid. A brown cassock rose as though swelling with pumped air. It rose straight out of the basket and strode quickly across the black cobblestone roadway to the fence and began to climb. It climbed with incredible speed right after him.

The cowl was lifted up and looking at him, closing fast. Richardson cried out when he saw the inside of the cowl. A glowing skeletal face. It screamed a high piercing scream at him.

And he screamed back. It had reached him.

9

He found himself standing in the middle of the living room. He was bent at the waist and swinging his arms, ape-fashion, crying terrified grunts like an ape. Every time he swung his fending arm, it emitted a familiar sound.

Whoosh!

He was standing in the middle of his living room, gasping, struggling for breath. He was near exhaustion and he stood trembling. He let himself sink slowly to the floor to sit cross-legged. He lay back finally and stretched fully on the rug.

Enough. Enough. He could stand no more.

He was wet. Soaked. And he was terribly thirsty. He went to the kitchen and turned on the taps. He bathed his face in his cupped hands, then drank from them, deeply.

He found a dish towel and wiped his face and neck with it. Then he went back to the living room and got his sweater and jacket and overcoat and scarves and gloves.

He carried them in his arms to the doorway and opened it. He stepped into the hallway. Dark. Completely dark. He listened. Then he groped along the wall and found the light switch. He pushed it.

Lights went on down the two staircases and he stepped quickly down, hurrying, still wet, still panting, frightened and spent.

In the vestibule, he crossed quickly to the front door. Goulart's cat cried from the cellar. Pale eyes in the dark cellar. He descended the outside steps to his car and threw the clothes on the front seat. He felt the freezing wind congealing the sweat on his skin.

The wind rapped the tractor chain. *Tap, tap, tap.* Cold. Cold. So cold.

10

As he drove, he dressed. His body temperature dropped rapidly. The frozen steering wheel drew all the heat from his hands. He fought two arms into the sweater, then stuffed his head through the neck opening. He got the two scarves around his neck, forced the sweatered arm through the sleeve of his suit jacket. The car was drifting dangerously. He straightened it and found the other sleeve opening of the jacket. He forced his arm through it, then began to work on his overcoat.

"Stop stop stop!" he shouted at himself. He pulled over to the curb. Now, with deliberate slowness, he adjusted the sweater, pulling it down in the back where it had rolled. Then he drew the sweater sleeves down from his forearms where they'd bunched, adjusted his jacket and put his heavy overcoat on, smoothed it and buttoned it.

When he got back into the car, he was shivering again. He felt tormented beyond endurance. And he realized that he was being irrational.

His apartment door had been left standing wide open.

11

Clabber's apartment lights were on.

Richardson parked the car and strode up the steps. He opened the outer door and studied a row of mailboxes with doorbells.

He found the name: Clabber, A. He pushed the button.

He heard himself breathing heavily through his open mouth. He shut it. Then he looked down at his clothing, absently fumbling for his necktie. He was still out of breath.

The door opened. Clabber's expression was a mixture of surprise and irritation.

"Ah," said Richardson. He lurched through the partly opened hallway door and into the inner vestibule. "Just the guy I want to see."

"Wait. Wait," said Clabber. He groped an ineffectual hand after Richardson. The inner door banged shut and Clabber hastened after Richardson.

"Waitwaitwait!"

"Wait my royal Irish ass, Clabber. I want to talk to you." He strode down the hallway toward an opened apartment door. The light within looked like sanctuary to him.

Clabber got a hand on his arm just as he reached the doorway. "Now wait, Richardson."

Richardson stopped. There was a man in Clabber's apartment. Sitting in a chair in the kitchen. A huge man. Very familiar. Where?

Richardson touched his lips doubtfully. Then he had it.

Abel Navarre. The dead detective.

Richardson began to back away. He vaguely brushed Clabber's hands away, backing down the hall. Abel Navarre stood up.

"It's okay!" cried Clabber. "Okay, okay. Calm down. Calm down. It's okay. Get ahold of yourself, Richardson."

Richardson looked wonderingly into Clabber's eyes. "Who? Where? I don't—"

"It's all right. All right. It's all easily explained." He got a firm grip on Richardson's arm.

Richardson stepped reluctantly into his apartment. Abel Navarre attempted a weak smile, his huge arms dangling limply, awkwardly at his sides.

"Here," commanded Clabber. "Sit down here."

Richardson sagged down. "I'm going crazy. I'm cracking up. I'm so thirsty. So thirsty."

"Okay, okay, okay. You're not cracking up. Just relax and hold tight. I'll get you some water." Clabber scurried to his kitchen and turned on the spigot. In a moment he was back with a dripping glass of water. Richardson drank it eagerly.

"More. More."

Clabber hurried back to the kitchen and returned with another tumblerful of water. Navarre sat slowly down. Richardson had begun to study him.

"Here. Now. Wait." Clabber stumbled around a sprawl of cardboard cartons. Richardson noticed the bookshelves. Long, long bookshelves. Clabber had already shelved many of his volumes. He bent over a carton and scrabbled at the contents, then prized out a bottle wrapped in newsprint. He held it up and squinted at the label. He stepped over and around cartons back to Richardson. "Here. Hold that glass up."

Richardson watched him pour.

"Easy, easy," he said to Clabber.

"You get that down. Then I want to hear what happened. I can explain everything to you. Slowly now. Slowly. Take some of that."

Richardson took a swallow of brandy and felt it fill him with long fingers of warmth. He was so tired. He would have gladly lain down there on the floor and slept.

He filled his lungs and sat up attentively. Then he fixed his eyes on Abel Navarre.

"Just tell me first, Clabber. Who is that sitting there?"

"Abel Navarre."

12

"Real," said Clabber. "Very real. Flesh and blood and thirty pounds overweight." He clapped a hand on Abel Navarre's shoulder. "I'm sorry, Richardson. I must have damn near scared you to death." He turned and pointed. "Abel Navarre is my oldest and best friend. We were unfrocked together."

"Together?"

Clabber nodded. "That's right. Abel was a man of the cloth, as they say—just like me. The church thinks it renounced us—well, it didn't. We renounced it."

"I don't understand," mumbled Richardson. "How can he be a dead detective and an unfrocked whatever?"

"He's just an unfrocked whatever," said Clabber. "His father was the detective."

"Oh."

"After you and I went through Goulart's stuff," said Navarre, "what did you do? Call the precinct?"

"Yeah."

"And they told you that Navarre was killed years ago?"

"Yeah."

Navarre shook his head in disgust. "That was something we didn't plan on." He looked with embarrassment at Clabber.

"What did you plan on?" asked Richardson.

Navarre looked at him, then looked at Clabber for an answer.

Clabber hesitated. "More brandy?"

"Clabber. All you ever do is soak me in brandy. Now what was the bit you put on with what's-his-name here?"

Clabber sat down on a carton. "Information. That's all. I wanted some information. I thought you were holding out something that Goulart might have told you. I thought you'd talk to a detective. That's all it was."

Richardson leaned over and carefully set the glass on the wooden floor. Then he stood up. "You know, Clabber, I think I'm going to kick the shit out of you. Right here. Right now." He stepped toward Clabber and shook a finger at him. "Do you have any idea what kind of nightmares you've put me through? Do you know that I was actually believing that my mind was unhinged? I was ready to commit myself to Creedmoor as a raving lunatic. Do you have any idea what it feels like to think you're going insane? Really insane? Ha! You meddling, nosy bastard, come here while I kill you."

Clabber had risen and stepped away. "Hey. Easy. Don't start anything you can't finish, Richardson. Neither one of us needs this."

Navarre stood. He placed a hand on Richardson's chest. "Sit down. Sit down. Sit down."

Richardson stood with the hand on his chest. He stared at Clabber. "It's all your fault, Clabber. You and these cuckoo books on ghosts and spirits and all that cockamamie bullshit. I think you put Goulart around the bend. I think if he hadn't met you and that screwed-up mind of yours, he'd still be alive."

"Believe what you want," said Clabber. "I didn't kill Goulart. Neither did these books. They didn't hurt a hair on his head. That cold out there killed him, and he brought that on himself bad-tripping with hallucinogens. And he did that without my blessing. You heard Anna Quist tonight. We both told him to stop crapping around with drugs. Now you can say what you want—think what you want. I know the truth, and the truth is, Goulart killed himself with his own excesses. Period."

Richardson stood listening. He remained silent for a moment. "Tomorrow, Clabber, tomorrow. I'm too tired to tear your arms out of their sockets and stuff them in your ears. But tomorrow. Tomorrow, I'm going to do you in."

"Oh, nonsense."

Clabber and Navarre watched Richardson sit down.

"What happened?" asked Clabber.

"What?" answered Richardson.

"What happened?"

"Where?"

"Just now. Just before you came in here. What happened?"

The brandy and the warmth of the room were getting to him. He stood up and removed his overcoat. "Goddamnit, Clabber. This isn't an apartment, it's an oven." He took off his suit coat and pulled off the sweater. He sat down again and found Clabber and Navarre silently watching him.

"I had a dilly of a nightmare, that's what happened. I fell asleep in my chair and had one dilly of a nightmare."

Clabber looked at Navarre. "See. There's a bad manifestation in that building. It's always been there." He turned his head back to Richardson. "Describe the nightmare."

Richardson scowled at him. "Oh, come on—"

"It's all right, Richardson. Navarre has shared this case with me from the very first day."

"Case! I'm not a 'case.' I'm me. Pete Richardson."

"No no. You're not a case. But this whole thing is a case. It's a major outcropping of psychic phenomena."

Richardson turned his face away with disgust. "Oh, stuff it."

"Richardson," said Clabber, "why did you come here?"

Richardson considered his question. "I came to talk to you about a picture of my mother and my aunt."

Clabber shook his head slowly. "No."

"No, what? What do you mean, no?"

Clabber shook his head. "No. That's not why you came here. You came here for help. You think I can help you. And you're right."

"Oh, God, here we go again." Richardson lowered his arms to his knees and laid his head on them.

"It's true. You know from that sitting tonight that we're the only ones who can help you. You know very well that someone or something is after you. You're in danger. Much as you try to pretend that it's just your imagination, you know it's real. If you don't get help, you're a dead man."

Richardson raised his head. "What? Dead man? What are you talking about? What do you know?"

Clabber shrugged. "Do you need an inventory sheet of psychic phenomena that have occurred in your life recently—and in Goulart's, just to name two?"

"Ah." Richardson brushed a hand at him and stood up. "I'm going to get out of here." He picked up his sweater.

"You know, Richardson, there's one thing you've not mentioned lately. When we first talked, you were obsessed with trying to remember something. Some vital fact or situation. You were always on the verge of remembering."

"Yeah," said Richardson, nodding. "That's right. It must be like amnesia."

"I think you ought to work on that angle."

Richardson shoved his arms into the sleeves of the sweater and butted his head through it. "God, I'm muscle-bound from this sweater. On and off all night."

"I don't think you heard me."

Richardson turned. "Clabber. I heard you. And I know what you're leading up to. Hypnosis."

Clabber slapped his hands on his thighs. "I can tell from the tone of your voice—"

"Yes. I don't ever want to talk about it. After that thing tonight, you can have your parlor games, hand-holding—the whole nine yards. What I need is a group from the police crime lab to go over my apartment. Then I need some good locks and an old-fashioned horse pistol to shoot the sonofabitch when he climbs through my window. That's what I need, Clabber."

Abel Navarre cleared his throat. "What you need is hypnosis."

Richardson put on his jacket in silence.

"There's a part of your mind that's been blocked off. One vital piece of information." Navarre paused. "I have one overwhelming reason why you ought to be hypnotized."

Richardson stopped and looked at him. "Name it."

"It might save your life."

He got the car started and sat in it, parked at the curb with the engine running, watching his breath vapor condense on the windshield.

He was shivering again. Indifferently shivering now, cold and fatigue being part of his permanent state, something beyond protesting.

He wasn't going to go back to the apartment. He needed a rest from that building. He'd sleep elsewhere. Even the car with no heat was preferable to the torment of that place. He looked at his watch. Eleven-twenty. Incredible. He'd been to a séance, fallen asleep, had an incredible nightmare, fled across the city, been given a violent shock by Navarre, had a conversation with Clabber about hypnosis, and now sat in his car. And it was only eleven-twenty.

He decided. He'd go to Abby's.

14

The terrier's claws scraped forlornly on the kitchen linoleum as he paced up and down, panting unhappily. Occasionally he'd sit and watch the two at the table. Then his eyes would begin to glaze and his head to drift to one side. The pacing would begin anew.

"You go lie down," Abby Withers said to him. "Go on."

He skulked like an alligator mournfully from the kitchen and to his bed. He settled down with a sigh and groan, composing his mouth with a yawn.

"You'd think he'd have settled in by now," said Abby Withers. "He's terribly restless. I suppose he thinks he's going to go back to the old apartment after a while. He'll learn. My heaven, isn't it cold tonight? I put on every stitch I had to take him for a walk but we only managed a block or so. He pulled me all the way home, shivering and sighing. Oh, what an act it was! That cold went right through me. Tell me, did you get an apartment yet?"

"Ah . . . no. No apartment," said Richardson. "I have an appointment to see two tomorrow. That crane is right under the window, licking its chops and all set to pulverize Brevoort House."

"Oh, don't tell me. I don't want to hear it." She waved her hands at him. "Oh, it's so sad. Tell me about the two apartments."

"Nothing to tell. I haven't seen either one yet."

Abby poured more coffee into his cup and nudged the dish of cookies closer. She eyed him thoughtfully, grasping the dressing gown at her throat. "Peter. You look so tired. You have circles under your eyes, and your face is drawn. You walk like you're a hundred years old."

He nodded unhappily, with his eyes shut. "I'll be okay. I didn't tell you about the séance yet."

"Séance? What séance?"

"Oh. Clabber took me to— Was the funeral actually this morning? It seems like years ago. It was this morning, wasn't it?"

Abby watched him askance. "Yes. This morning. Don't you remember?"

"Yes. It's just that so many things happened today."

"What about the séance?"

"Oh. Nothing. It was a washout. Clabber took me."

"To Anna Quist's?"

"Yes. A washout. If I didn't feel so tired, I'd tell you the whole story."

"Tell me in the morning. I'd like to hear all about it."

"Clabber says I need hypnosis."

Abby Withers pressed a small fist to her lips and sat back.

He frowned at her. "What's the matter?"

"Nothing. Nothing."

"Do you know something I don't know?"

"It's late. You're exhausted."

"Tell me."

"It's nothing. Let's go to bed."

"I want to know, Abby."

She shook her head at him. "I—nothing. I know nothing. We can talk more about it in the morning." She waved a hand at him. "That's enough now. Bed. Sleep is what you need. God's best medicine."

15

Trucks whined distantly. Scurrying through the frozen dark city through the tunnels to Jersey and turnpikes west. Warm in the cab and heading west. Coffee and talk with the driver and drowsiness. No mysterious noises, no nightmares. He wondered what to do, what was happening to him. He lay under blankets on Abby's couch, smelling the camphor under the cushions, hearing the trucks whine and the ticking of Abby's wall clock.

Outside the cold waited. So tired.

16

Long columns of slanted sunlight. Coffee: the smell of fresh coffee. And a cigar? The sound of claws pacing again on the kitchen linoleum. And voices. Murmuring voices. In the kitchen. Yes. A cigar.

Richardson looked at his watch. Eight-fifteen. He looked at it alarmed. Late. He'd slept as though drugged. Now, he had to get back to his own apartment, shave, shower, dress and get downtown to the office. He sat up and cast back the bed covers. Voices again. He tried to place them. One was Abby's. The other was familiar. Soft. Low. A man's?

Richardson kicked on his trousers, then put on his shoes and socks. He walked toward the kitchen, stuffing his shirttails into his pants. It was a man talking. Christopher Carson, with cigar.

"Well, like Aphrodite rising from the sea. You've arisen."

Richardson nodded. "Yes. And I'm late."

Abby stood up and went to the stove. She poured a cup of coffee. "Sit," she said. "Sit here, Peter." She placed the cup at a vacant place.

Richardson sat. He put some sugar in his coffee and stirred it. He saw them watching him stir.

"How have you been?" asked Carson.

"Fine. Missed you at the funeral yesterday."

"Well, I got back just in time not to go. Still suffering from jet lag."

Richardson nodded. "You always have breakfast here?"

Carson puffed at the ceiling. "No, as a matter of fact, I don't. Do you?"

"I called him, Peter," said Abby. "I asked him to come over."

"Okay. It's your home, Abby, not mine."

"She called me because she was worried about you."

"Me? What's to worry about?"

"Nothing. At least nothing yet. Abby says that Clabber's trying to get you under hypnosis."

"Oh. That's it, huh?"

"Pete. Let me tell you something about hypnosis. It's very very very very very—is that six verys?—dangerous. There are very few men who are qualified to do it. Not everyone can be hypnotized. Not everyone should be hypnotized. In some cases it can be harmful even under the control of a true professional. And you know how I feel about that old crock Clabber. I wouldn't let him hypnotize a chicken. He has to have the very worst credentials in the world. He can get you into something and not get you out again. He can create such psychic disturbances that you'll end up in a mental institution for months or years or forever. Your mental state is not good now and—"

"Enough."

"What?"

"I said enough."

"Right," said Carson. "Enough." He puffed his cigar. "Beautiful day," he said to Abby. "It's still very cold out . . . no warmer than yesterday. But beautiful sunshine. Air is clear as a bell."

"Please don't go," said Abby Withers.

Richardson frowned. "What?"

"Don't go. Don't let him hypnotize you."

Richardson sighed. The conspiratorial atmosphere between Abby and Carson was still evident. What had they been talking about when he woke up? "It's okay, Abby."

"If you like," said Carson slowly, "I can recommend several first-rate men. People I trust implicitly."

They were treating him as though he were sick. He was in bed in a hospital and they were visiting him, messengers from the world of the healthy and free, come to stare down at him and, in their eyes, reveal how bad he looked, how shockingly sick he was.

A terminal case.

He watched Carson write on a piece of paper. "Here. Here are five names. And I can get more. Pick any name and I can set things up. But if you'll listen to me, you'll skip the whole thing. No hypnosis. And whatever you do, stay away from Clabber."

For a moment, Richardson entertained the possibility of a conspiracy. Abby and Carson and who else? Hidden microphones. What else?

He nodded at Carson. "Okay. I'll take it easy."

"Good," said Carson.

Abby patted his arm gently.

Richardson saw a book on the table at Carson's elbow. *Genealogy for Americans.*

17

He was right. He'd left his apartment door wide open all night. Now, sunlight from his living room window flooded the apartment and angled partway down the flight of hall stairs. He entered and looked around.

Harmless. Bright and cheerful. Happy days. Marriage and laughter and parties and foreverness.

He shed his clothes and showered and shaved.

18

He saw one of the two apartments at eleven. Then

hurried back to the office, skimmed the telephone messages and ate a sandwich at his desk.

He made a list in his head. He'd done everything he could think of. Thrown food away, had a physical, gone to a séance, checked his aunt, searched for hidden wires. The hell with it. Moving would solve all. He'd simply move out and not tell them where he was moving to.

Conspirators. Abby and Carson and who else? Could they be in with Clabber? Maybe all the criticism of Clabber was fake. Maybe they were intent by reverse English on driving him to Clabber for hypnosis. Maybe he had walked in his sleep and had seen them freezing Goulart to death. He shook his head irritably and picked up a metal clipper holding a sheaf of galley proofs. That was the road to paranoia.

At two he examined the second apartment. Outside, it was grindingly, wearily, inescapably cold. But the apartment was empty and he could move in right now. Today. Call a moving company and move in anytime.

He stood at the window of the empty bedroom and looked out, thoughtfully. The landlord, a fat man with bad teeth, opened the door to the closet and said something lamely enthusiastic.

"Can I sign the lease now?" asked Richardson.

"Absolutely. Right now. Down in the office. You pay me the first month's rent in advance plus a security deposit equal to another month's rent. Matter of fact, I'll tell you what. I'll let you *move in* right now pending a reference check. Of course, if you flunk the reference test, you're out. How's your reference?"

"Great."

"Well, there you are. See? Sign and move in."

He stared down at the back of a house. Streaks of snow lay in the shadow of a roof where the sun never reached. The backyard looked so cold. So everlastingly cold.

He'd move in tonight. Sleeping bag and air mattress and all his backpack equipment. Clothes too—at least some of them. And he'd get the moving company to get the rest of the stuff as quickly as possible. And he'd never sleep in Brevoort House again.

He felt released suddenly. A great burden was lifted. A new apartment, a new start. His troubles were behind him.

19

Thames Street Building Supplies. The wooden sides of the truck flapped violently as the vehicle crawled over the uneven terrain behind Brevoort House. The name of the company was lettered on the wooden fencing of the truck sides that shuddered and flapped.

The driver, heavily bundled and wearing a hood with a leather face mask, stopped the truck and stepped down. He'd halted at the outside door to the cellar of the Brevoort House.

He unloaded the supplies. Cement. Tools: a bucket, a trowel, a small pan. A metal grating. Miscellaneous bags and supplies. Then with an electric chain hoist and clamps, he lowered a half load of brick to the ground. He pulled a heavy-gauge clear plastic sheet over the supplies, put a brick on each corner and regarded the arrangement for a moment.

Satisfied, he drove off. The chilly ground wind flapped the clear sheet lightly. Dusk was nigh.

20

The man arrived a half hour later. He studied the supplies, then went away. Shortly later, he opened the cellar door from within and stepped up to the supplies. Slowly he carried them into the cellar, trip after trip. He used a cardboard box to carry the stacked bricks.

When he had all the material inside, he shut the cellar door.

He set to work mixing the mortar.

CHAPTER X

February dusk. It was grainy and it seemed to fall like soot, putting the city into darkness a dot at a time. Sunset had been a violent flush of rose-colored smoke and cloud that had promised another freezing night.

Richardson rose from the subway and hurried toward Brevoort House. He could see the wrecker parked near the building, holding its slender boom up to the risen moon like a boastful gladiator.

Soon, he promised himself, he'd be away from toppling masonry, ground-shaking crashes, billowing clouds of brickdust.

He glanced at his car, parked at the curb. The back seat and the trunk would hold his clothes and sleeping gear, a large carton of miscellaneous junk. With that, he'd be able to make it until the movers dragged out the rest. All he needed was ten minutes to load up the car and he'd be gone—a new start that he should have made a long time ago. Ten minutes.

He unlocked the front door of the building, flipped on the stairwell lights and bounded up the steps. He put on all the lights in his apartment and quickly went to work. He packed a suitcase, packed an overnight bag, filled his three-suit garment bag and put them near the door. Then he pulled down his sleeping bag and air mattress. He carried them to the door.

His phone rang.

He looked at it, waiting, hesitant. It rang again. In the quietness of the empty building, the phone's bell was loud, peremptory.

Richardson rubbed his hands.

The phone rang a third time. And again. Richardson opened the hallway door and put the suitcase out on the landing. Another ring. He was close to bolting, wanting urgently to run down the stairs and away. He put the overnight bag out on the landing.

Again.

He surrendered. He couldn't run but he couldn't stand the bell. He answered it to silence it. "Hello."

"Richardson?"

"Yeah."

"This is Clabber."

"Jesus jumping Christ. You're as persistent as a tombstone salesman, Clabber. I can't talk to you now. I'll call you later."

"What's up?"

"Nothing's up."

"You're moving."

Richardson gave an involuntary "Hah."

"Where you moving to?"

"Around. Around. I'll let you know. I can't talk now. I'll call you. So long, Clabber." He hung up. He walked away from the phone, then turned and looked at it. He walked back to it. He picked up the receiver and left it on the table. It hummed a dial tone. He went back to his packing.

He needed a box. He went to the kitchen, found a chair and used it to pull down a large carton from a closet. Blankets she'd packed in camphor. Wool. Expensive. Wedding presents. He lifted one out of the box and looked at it. Soft. Thick. Why didn't she take— The hell with it. He dropped the blanket on the couch, lifted out the other one and shook the camphor flakes off it rudely.

He carried the box into the kitchen and packed some of his kitchen equipment. He overloaded it, but it was easier to carry it down to the car than to repack it. He opened the hall doorway, then returned to the kitchen, hefted the box and marched through the apartment to the hall. Heavy as hell. He descended quickly. At the second-floor turning he paused. He rested the box on the railing and listened.

There was a tapping coming from somewhere. *Tap tap tap*. He shook his head at it. Outside somewhere. He went down the stairs to the vestibule, pressed the box against a wall and pulled open the door. He staggered down the outside steps to the car trunk, rested the box on a fender and with one hand opened the trunk lock. The lid lifted and he pushed the box in. It just fit. The

255

cold had seized him in a few seconds. He slammed the trunk lid and hurried back into the house and up the stairs.

Toilet articles. He went to the bathroom and began to pack his shaving case. He heard something bang against the door. He hesitated. It banged again. Then Goulart's cat keened. Richardson's temper rose. Goulart or no Goulart, he was going to cream that cat. He quickly walked to the hallway and found the blackthorn cane. He heard the cat scream again. Quickly, he yanked the door open and raised the stick.

He saw no cat. His eyes searched the hallway, looked at Abby's doorway, down the stairs at Goulart's door. He walked to the stairwell and looked down. Pale light on each landing. Shadowed passageways. The silence of an empty house. No cat anywhere.

Richardson picked up the suitcase and the overnight bag and quickly descended with them, holding the blackthorn under one arm. He went all the way to the front door without seeing the cat. Weird. The door to the cellar was closed. He quickly put the two cases into the car and ran back inside. He paused.

He felt it, sensed it. Don't go back up. Leave now. Come back for the other stuff tomorrow. No overcoat. No shaving gear. Just get in the car and go. Now.

No, that was absurd. One more trip; just grab the stuff and be off. He had to have an overcoat in this weather. And he needed shaving gear. Up the stairs and back down before he could count one hundred.

He hurried up the steps, beating the air with the blackthorn, counting as he went.

He was up to thirty when he reached his door. He

kicked it shut, grabbed his jacket and coat, struggled into them. He was up to forty. He went into the bathroom, added a few more things, seized the shaving case and turned. When he reached the doorway he was at fifty.

The cat hit the door again, screaming. He grabbed the blackthorn and opened the door. The hallway was empty as before. The faint tapping had resumed.

He shut the door, stepped quickly into the kitchen, the bedroom, the bath. Okay. Go. Go. Go. Nothing more. He returned to the door and reached for the knob. He was up to seventy. And free. Just two flights of steps and gone!

The vestibule door slammed. The sound rose up the stairwell. He looked around. The fire escape. He waited a moment, cocking his head, listening. Footsteps. Richardson went into his bedroom and examined the window to the fire escape. Then he hurried back to the apartment door and put on the chain latch and double lock. The footsteps were moving along the second-floor hallway. They mounted the stairs to the third floor.

Richardson wrung his hands. Run, stupid, if you're so afraid. Down the fire escape.

The steps reached the third-floor landing. They crossed the landing to his door. A fist rapped on the door —so firmly he could see the door tremble slightly. A thin piece of wood between him and the knocker. The fist knocked again—three four five six times. Emphatically.

"Richardson."

That goddamn Clabber. Richardson looked around him. The fire escape was still there. No. He was going down his own stairs. He was going to carry that gear to his new apartment, then he was going to go to a restaurant and have a nice thick steak. Then he was going to sleep. Sleep.

He reached out and slipped the chain free. Then he undid the locks. Pulling the door open, he stepped out into the hallway, then pulled his apartment door shut and locked it. He turned around on the landing and looked at Clabber.

Clabber looked at the locked door, then at Richardson's overcoat and shaving kit. "That's emphatic enough."

"I'm up to eighty-five and I swore I'd be on my way away from here before I reached one hundred."

"Whatever that means."

"It means that I'm going to go right down those stairs, out the door and into my car, and never come back here again, is what it means, Clabber, old buddy. It means that in a few days when I become a human being again, maybe I'll be ready to talk to you. Meanwhile, gangway."

Clabber uncoiled an arm and pointed elaborately down the stairs. "Go. Help yourself."

Richardson stepped past him and started down the steps. He heard Clabber following him.

"Are you going to give me your new address and phone number?"

Richardson shook his head. "No no no." He stepped and turned to Clabber. "You know, I finally was able to put into words what bothered me about you. You make me feel like a specimen under glass."

"Sorry about that," said Clabber. He descended a few more steps behind Richardson. "Do you think," he asked tentatively in a low voice, "you'll escape that weird sound in your new apartment?"

Richardson paused, then halted. "Yeah. That's exactly what I expect. I expect to get a few nights' sleep too—without any hidden microphones. I expect to get away from whatever and whoever has been trying to turn me into a raving psychotic."

"Not I," said Clabber.

"Someone did, Clabber. Someone drove Goulart around the bend, drove him to some kind of frenzy that caused him to freeze to death. For all I know, they may have tied him up in that house until he did freeze to death."

Clabber's footsteps sounded behind him. "No," said Clabber. "You're wrong."

"No I'm not."

"Yes. You're panicked. You're running."

"You bet your blue booties I am, Clabber." Richardson stopped again. "I'm getting away from here, away from all the hidden props, the rigged atmosphere, away from a dead friendship, a ruined marriage—away from that wrecker's ball out there. Listen. You hear it. That *tap-tap-tapping*. That's the steel cable slapping against the boom of that tractor out there. I'm going to hear that sound for the rest of my life."

Clabber shook his head at him. "That sound is coming from someplace else."

"Yeah—well, wherever it's coming from, I'm not going to hear it anymore."

"You can't get away from yourself."

Richardson stopped. "I don't need to get away from me, Clabber. I need to get away from somebody else."

"You remembered, then; is that it?"

Richardson frowned at Clabber's shadowed face. "Remembered what?"

"What you couldn't remember. What you've been trying to remember for weeks."

"Ah, that's nothing."

"No. That's everything. The answer's right there." Clabber's gloved finger touched Richardson's temple. "Right there."

"Nah. Forget it, Clabber. What I need is a good steak, a night's sleep, and a good bowel movement. You can't help me with any of those, so good night. I'll be in touch." Richardson had reached the front door of the apartment house and opened it. The remorseless winter air hurried in around his ankles as the door opened. He glanced at his car, at the lumps of luggage on the back seat. Steak with mushrooms. Don't listen anymore.

"Who's Maeve?" asked Clabber.

Richardson stopped in the open doorway. He turned around and looked again at Clabber. "Maeve?"

"Yes. At the séance last night, she was the only one who sent a message. And you received it."

"Yeah? How do you know, Clabber?"

"I felt it in your hand. So did Anna Quist. Who's Maeve?"

"Clabber, you know damn right well who Maeve is."

"I'm sorry. I don't lie. I don't know who Maeve is." Richardson hesitated. "She's my mother."

"Mother!"

"Yeah. And with that, I bid you good night."

"Wait, wait, wait."

"No. No. No. No more waits. I'm leaving."

"Just a moment, Richardson. Please. Shut the door."

"Say it with the door open, Clabber. It'll make you briefer."

"Do you remember last night when you came to my

apartment? Do you remember that nightmare? You can't walk away from them. You'll have another tonight when you shut your eyes. And if not tonight, then tomorrow night. Those nightmares are from your unconscious mind. They're messages. And your unconscious is going to keep on making nightmares until you find out what it's trying to tell you. Now listen carefully. I can hypnotize you in less than a minute. In five minutes I can ask you several questions under hypnosis that will give you the answers you want. Ten minutes from now, you can be on your way with the information you've been trying to remember. Ten minutes." Clabber watched Richardson's face. "No more nightmares. No more funny sounds. Ten minutes and you'll know."

Richardson stood in the doorway, feeling the freezing air blow past him into the vestibule, watching Clabber shivering, feeling himself begin to shiver. He turned his head and looked at his car, so near. So far. He looked back at Clabber. "What makes you so sure?"

"Please, shut the door. We'll freeze like stone statues."

Richardson shifted from one foot to the other, regarding Clabber with great suspicion. Then he stepped back into the vestibule and pushed the door shut. The latch clicked.

"I've hypnotized hundreds of people, Richardson, and I've never had one mishap. I'm not going to stand here now and give you a list of credentials but I will later. I'll tell you case history after case history if you want to sit and listen to them. But right now, I can help you and— Tell you what." He reached into his pocket and pulled out a tape recorder. "I'll record every word of it and you can have the tape. It'll be your own words on tape. Ten minutes. Let's go." Clabber gripped Richardson's arm and pulled gently. Richardson took a step toward the stairs. "That's it," said Clabber. "Let's go."

Richardson started toward the stairs and Clabber followed him. "If this doesn't work, Clabber—"

"Don't worry. I know exactly what I'm doing. The sooner you get up there, the sooner we'll be done."

Richardson mounted the steps with Clabber behind him. Somewhere unplaceable, the tapping persisted. Then it stopped. Richardson stopped.

"What now?" demanded Clabber.

"That sound. It stopped."

Clabber shrugged. "Okay. It stopped. Most sounds eventually do. Let's go."

Richardson mounted the first flight of steps and turned to walk along the passageway past Griselda Vandermeer's apartment door, then Clabber's, then Goulart's.

He mounted the next flight to his apartment. He pawed at his key ring and unlocked his door. Clabber stepped into the apartment and Richardson followed him.

As he shut the door, the tapping sound resumed.

2

"Relax," said Clabber.

Richardson lay on his couch with his hands behind his head. He took a deep breath and waited with a skeptical expression.

"Now," said Clabber. "I want you to watch this little medal that I'm swinging from this chain. Don't take your eyes off it. All right. Now. Relax. Your whole body is relaxing. You feel very heavy. You need sleep. Sleep so desperately. When I count to three you'll be in a sleep.

Then when I say four, you'll open your eyes and you'll feel marvelously rested. Just relax. There's no need to resist. You'll feel wonderful. Better than you've felt in weeks. Just keep your eyes on the chain. Watch it sway back and forth, back and forth. Back and forth. I'm going to count now. I'm going to count to three, and when I do you'll fall into a deep sleep, and then when I say four, you'll wake up. All right. One. Watch the chain. Two. Your eyes are getting heavy. Three. That's it. Shut your eyes." Clabber watched Richardson's eyes close. He drew his chair a little closer to the couch and waited a few seconds.

"Four," he said softly.

Richardson's eyes opened.

"Now, you feel fine. Rest your eyes at the corner of the ceiling up there and answer a few questions for me. These are answers you want to hear, answers to questions you've had. First, what is your name?"

Richardson's eyes were fixed on the corner of the ceiling. His eyes blinked. His mouth turned down at the corners. His eyes squinted. He was extremely annoyed. He gave his name.

Clabber stood up almost involuntarily. The chair fell over as he stepped backward.

"Say your name again."

"Joseph Tully."

3
Clabber strode up and down Richardson's living room, wringing his hands, deep in writhing thought. He paused at his cast-off overcoat and groped in a deep pocket.

He extracted a small tape recorder.

He put it on the coffee table and started it. "What?" he demanded. "What do you say your name is?"

"I said my name is Joseph Tully." The voice was unmistakably British.

"Tully?" Clabber placed his hand on his mouth, hesitatingly. "Tully? Ah—what year is it?"

"It's 1779."

Clabber sat back in his chair and stared at Richardson's face. Gently he fanned his hand back and forth above Richardson's eyes.

"Stop that," said Joseph Tully.

4

Clabber returned quickly from Richardson's desk, grasping a pad of paper. He groped in his suit coat and found a mechanical pencil. "Tully, eh?" he said almost breathlessly. "1779. Tell me, what are you doing right now?"

"I was drinking a glass of port wine and reading my favorite book—*Tom Jones*."

Clabber tried to think of more questions. "Is there anything significant going on in your life right now?"

"I prefer not to discuss my business affairs."

"A—what? Ah-h—tell me about your family. Do you live with your family?"

"I have a family, yes. But now I live alone."

"Are you lonely?"

"Yes. I don't sleep well. I'm growing old."

"Why don't you sleep well?"

"I have bad dreams."

"What dreams?"

"I hear things. I dream of phantasms."

"What things?"

"I hear—I hear a sound I cannot identify."

"Do you hear it when you are awake?"

"Yes. Sometimes. How did you know?"

"A guess. Ah-h—just one moment, please." Clabber stood up and paced up and down the living room thoughtfully. Then he sat down. "Is this sound a *whooshing?*"

"Exactly. *Whoosh. Whoosh.*"

"Is there anything about it you can tell me? Anything at all?"

"No. I'm tormented with knowledge of something forgotten. Something just beyond recall, lurking out there—out there, in the darkness, beyond reaching."

Clabber reached over to the coffee table and picked up the chain with the medal. He considered it, then looked at Richardson's eyes. They were clear and alert, but there was something somnambulistic about them. Drugged.

Clabber put the chain down. Then he looked at Richardson again.

"How long have you been hearing this sound?"

"A few weeks. At least a fortnight. I must change my diet. I think it's some meat I've kept in the meat safe lately. Must tell the cook to cook it more. Pity. I love rare roast."

"Does the sound frighten you?"

"It—yes—actually, it disturbs me. I know what it is, but I can't quite recall it."

Clabber picked up the chain, hesitantly, doubtfully. He put it down again. Considered it. Picked it up. "I think we can identify that sound. Let us try an experiment. I'm going to hold this medal on this chain before your eyes. I'm going to swing it. You will feel very tired for a moment. Then I will count three and you will sleep. When I say four, you will awaken again. Are you ready?"

"Yes."

Clabber began to slowly sway the chain. "Concentrate," he said. "You now feel drowsy. One. Two. Three."

Richardson's eyes closed.

"Four," said Clabber.

Richardson opened his eyes.

Clabber studied Richardson's face carefully. The eyes looked directly ahead, staring at some distant fixed point.

"Can you hear me?"

"Of course."

"Tell me your name."

"Joseph Tully."

"What day is it?"

"It is my wedding day."

"Do you remember that strange *whooshing* sound?"

"I cannot identify it. It is something from my past."

"Go back in time—go back in time until you locate the source of that sound. You are now fifteen. Now ten. Nothing yet? You are five years old. Back more?" Clabber hesitated. "Have you identified the sound?"

Richardson was quiet.

"Where are you?" asked Clabber.

"I don't know." This was a different voice.

"Who are you? What is your name?"

"We have no names here."

"Where are you?"

"I stand on the ancient cobblestones of the Via Appia near the Catacombs. The stones shine in the moonlight. They are rutted from Roman chariots."

266

Clabber frowned and pondered the face before him. "Can you identify that *whooshing* sound?"

"Of course."

"What is it?"

"It is part of my current cycle."

"Cycle? What cycle?"

"I am atoning for a grievous sin. I am being pursued."

"What is your sin?"

"I caused the death of a man."

"Who? What man?"

"Matteo Villon. I also caused the death of his cousin."

"How?"

"I had them beheaded."

"Ahhhh." Clabber looked around the room, searching for questions. "Who is pursuing you?"

"Matteo Villon. He has vowed to behead me. He will pursue me through many lives if need be."

"How many lives has he pursued you?"

"Two since my death in Rome."

"Rome?"

"Yes. I had him beheaded in the Catacombs of San Sebastiano near the Via Appia. Since then I lived in Spain as a sculptor and in France as a groom."

"He didn't find you in either case."

"No. I died in Spain an old man before Villon was reborn. He missed me entirely. Before he found me in France, a horse kicked me to death in a stable."

"How does he know where to find you?"

"I am born into the same family. Always the same family."

"What family is that?"

"The name changes. Marriages alter the names and the geography."

"To find you, he must trace your family history?"

"Yes."

"Then what?"

"Then he will behead me."

"What is the sound?"

"It is the sound of a molten sword blade, swinging through the air. It increases the oxygen along the blade edge."

5

He turned the faucet on the bottle of oxygen, increasing the flow through the bed of charcoal. The color of the coals changed from deep red to an orange, from orange quickly to yellow, a pale white-yellow. He gripped the tang of the blade with a wooden socket and eased the blade from the deep bed of coals. It glowed almost translucently. He pushed it back into the coals and removed the handle.

He stepped back from the small furnace and looked at his anvil. He touched the peen-headed hammer patiently, then stepped back to the fire. The oxygen from the bottle hissed loudly in the coals. The charcoal was charring away too fast. He turned the faucet slowly and the flow of oxygen reduced.

He picked up the wooden handle, then leaned against the cellar wall. The room was filled with soft shadows cast by the fire and by a pair of candles that stood on the brick window ledge. The fire had heated the room and he was now stripped to the waist. On the gritty floor lay his shirt, his suit jacket and tie, his overcoat and gloves, a scarf and his bowler hat.

Matthew Willow stepped back to the fire and withdrew

the blade. He laid it on the anvil and, with the cross peen, struck a few blows along the upper shank. Sparks flew. *Tap. Tap. Tap.*

Soon.

6

"Come forward in time," said Clabber. "You have been born. What is your name?"

"Joseph Tully."

"What day is it?"

"My son's baptism day."

"Come forward more. Much further. Come to the moment we met. In 1779. You are alone. You are reading *Tom Jones*. You are drinking port. You are bothered by a strange sound and you are not sleeping well. Do you remember that moment?"

"Yes. Of course."

"What is the date?"

"It is 1779."

"Why is that date significant?"

"I do not know. I have been apprehensive the livelong day. I fear—I—"

"What do you fear?"

"I am old. I expect death, of course, but—"

"But what?"

"I feel someone wants to kill me."

"Who?"

"I do not know."

"Do you remember the sound?"

"Yes."

"Can you identify it?"

"I—sometimes. I— No, I can't for the life of me."

"It is an ominous sound."

"Yes, surely. I fear it most assuredly. The hour grows late. There is someone knocking on my door."

"Who can it be?"

"It is a bitter night tonight. A tiresome winter. Spring is far away. Decent burghers are not abroad on a night like this."

"Is there still a knocking?"

"Yes. A loud booming knock. None of my people are awake, I fear. I shall answer it."

7

The blade was ready. His arms and torso were running with sweat and the hairs on his forearms were singed. But the blade was ready. He withdrew it by its tang. And slowly he swung it.

Whoosh.

Willow turned with it, bearing it before him in both hands, and began a slow parade across the cellar to the stairs and the doorway. He mounted the steps toward the door. He paused and with one hand turned the handle of the door and thrust the door open.

He stepped along the tiles to the stairway and began to mount. The glow of the blade lit the stairs. He swung the blade out over the stairwell.

Whoosh.

8

"Where are you? What are you doing?"

"I am descending the stairs to my front door."

"Do you see anyone?"

"No. I see a glow—a mighty glow around the edges of my door. Someone is standing at my door with a glowing —a—what can it be? A lantern?"

"What are you doing now?"

There was no answer.

Clabber frowned. He put down his pad and pencil as he studied Richardson's face. "Mr. Tully? Mr. Tully?" The eyes continued to stare at the corner of the ceiling. They blinked once. Clabber fanned a hand over the eyes. "Are you there, Mr. Tully? What's happened?"

Hesitantly, Clabber took Richardson's left hand. He held it up and felt for the pulse. He let it fall and pressed his fingertips on Richardson's throat, below the jaw, just under the ear.

The pulse in the throat was strong and very rapid.

"Hey." He shook Richardson's face. He stood up. "Hey." He stepped back. "Dear God, help me. I can't rouse him." He stood looking at Richardson. The tape recorder turned soundlessly.

From the stairwell, Clabber heard the slow ascent of footsteps.